The BLUE BETWEEN SKY *and* WATER

SUSAN ABULHAWA

BLOOMSBURY CIRCUS

LONDON · OXFORD · NEW YORK · NEW DELHI · SYDNEY

Bloomsbury Paperbacks
An imprint of Bloomsbury Publishing Plc

50 Bedford Square   1385 Broadway
London   New York
WC1B 3DP   NY 10018
UK   USA

www.bloomsbury.com

BLOOMSBURY and the Diana logo are trademarks of Bloomsbury Publishing Plc

First published in Great Britain 2015
This paperback edition first published in 2016

British Library Cataloguing-in-Publication Data
A catalogue record for this book is available from the British Library.

ISBN: HB: 978-1-4088-6510-1
       TPB: 978-1-4088-6511-8
       PB: 978-1-4088-6512-5
       ePub: 978-1-4088-6513-2

2 4 6 8 10 9 7 5 3

Typeset by RefineCatch Limited, Bungay, Suffolk
Printed and bound in Great Britain by CPI Group (UK) Ltd, Croydon CR0 4YY

MIX
Paper from
responsible sources
FSC® C020471

To find out more about our authors and books visit www.bloomsbury.com.
Here you will find extracts, author interviews, details of forthcoming events and the
option to sign up for our newsletter.

For Natalie: my daughter, my friend, and my teacher

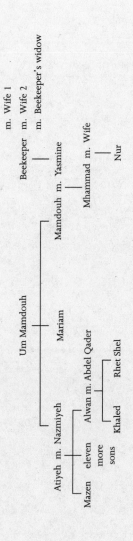

Um Mamdouh

Atiyeh m. Nazmiyeh   Mariam   Mamdouh m. Yasmine

Mazen   eleven   Alwan m. Abdel Qader   Mhammad m. Wife
     more
     sons   Khaled   Rhet Shel   Nur

Beekeeper m. Wife 1
          m. Wife 2
          m. Beekeeper's widow

IN THE LATE 1970S and '80s, Israel assisted in the rise of an Islamist movement in Palestine, which would come to be known as Hamas, as a counterweight to Yasser Arafat's Fateh party, a secular revolutionary resistance movement in the mold of similar guerrilla insurgencies around the world during the Cold War era. Following the Oslo Accords in 1993, signed between Israel and the Palestine Liberation Organization (PLO), an endless "Peace Process" was launched, and Hamas became the principal institution of Palestinian resistance to Israel's military occupation and ongoing repression of the native people's aspirations for autonomy. After two decades of failed negotiations that saw great expansion of exclusively Jewish colonies on confiscated Palestinian land and entrenchment of an apartheid system in the occupied territories, Palestinians launched an uprising and held elections for new leadership. In 2006, members of Hamas won majority seats in the Palestinian Authority in what were deemed to be fair and transparent elections. Israel and the United States, however, were displeased with the outcome of the elections and moved to subvert the new leadership. While Fateh continued to control the West Bank, Hamas gained control of Gaza. Unable to dislodge Hamas, Israel sealed off the tiny Mediterranean strip of land, turning it into what became known as the largest open-air prison in the world. Declassified documents, obtained years later, revealed the chilling precision with which Israel calculated the calorie intake of 1.8 million Palestinians in Gaza to make them go hungry, but not starve.

Khaled

"The idea is to put the Palestinians on a diet."

—Dov Weisglass

Of everything that disappeared, Kinder Eggs are what I missed most. When the walls closed in on Gaza and adult conversations became hotter and sadder, I measured the severity of our siege by the dwindling number of those delicate chocolate eggs, wrapped in thin colorful foil, with splendid toy surprises incubating inside the eggs on store shelves. When they finally disappeared, and the rusty metal of those shelves stared back naked, I realized that Kinder Eggs had brought color into the world. In their absence, our lives turned a metallic sepia, then faded to black-and-white, the way the world used to be in the old Egyptian movies, when my teta Nazmiyeh was the sassiest girl in Beit Daras.

Even after the tunnels were dug under the border between Gaza and Egypt to smuggle the things of living, Kinder Eggs were still hard to come by.

I lived in these times of the tunnels, a network of underground arteries and veins with systems of ropes, levers, and pulleys that pumped food, diapers, fuel, medicine, batteries, music tapes, Mama's menstrual napkins, Rhet Shel's crayons, and anything else you can think of that we managed to buy from the Egyptians twenty-four hours a day, seven days a week.

The tunnels undermined Israel's plans to put us on a diet. So, they bombed the tunnels and a lot of people were killed. We dug more that were bigger, deeper, and longer. Again they bombed us and even more people were killed. But the tunnels remained, like living vasculature.

Once, Israel convinced the United States and Egypt to install an impenetrable underground steel wall along the Rafah border to cut off the tunnels. People watched through binoculars from the sand dunes of Rafah, and they laughed for a month as the United States Army Corps of Engineers went to work. The Americans saw us, and though they left as uninterested as they had come, we were sure our laughter floating across the border had unnerved them. As soon as they were gone, our boys went to work inside the tunnels with blowtorches, cutting through the metal that was meant to cut off our sustenance. It was a gift, because the underground wall was made of high-grade steel that we recycled into other things.

We were used to being the losers. But this time we won. We outsmarted Israel, Egypt, and the great United States of America. Gaza was one giant party for a while. Our newspapers published cartoons that showed Mubarak, Bush, and Netanyahu scratching their heads and asses while we laughed from Rafah's sandy hills, holding what we had made from that excellent steel: car parts, play-ground equipment, building beams, and rockets.

My teta Nazmiyeh said, "Allah have mercy and protect us. All this joy and laughter in Gaza is bound to bring blood and heartache. Light always casts shadows." She must have been thinking of Mariam.

It wasn't long after that when I went into the quiet blue, that place without time, where I could soak up all the juices of life and let them run through me like a river.

Then Nur came, her mouth full of Arabic words that were sawed off and sanded at the edges with the curly accent of a foreigner. She came with all that American do-gooder enthusiasm that thinks it can fix broken people like me and heal wounded places like Gaza. But she was more shattered than any of us.

And every night, when Nur put my sister Rhet Shel to bed, Teta Nazmiyeh pulled the sky in place and Mama embroidered in it the stars and moon. And in the morning when Rhet Shel awoke, she hung the sun. That's how it was when Nur came back.

These were the women of my life, the songs of my soul. The men they loved were lost in one way or another, except me. I stayed as long as I could.

I

When our history lounged on the hills,
lolling in sylvan days, the River Suqreir flowed
through Beit Daras

My great-khalto Mariam collected colors and sorted them. Two generations later, I was named after her imaginary friend. But maybe it was not imagination. Maybe it was really me. Because we meet by the river now, and I teach her to write and read.

A VILLAGE OF VILLAGES SURROUNDED by gardens and olive groves and bordered to the north by a lake, in the thirteenth century Beit Daras was on the mail route from Cairo to Damascus. It boasted a caravanaserai, an ancient roadside inn for the steady stream of travelers who flowed across the trade routes of Asia, North Africa, and southeastern Europe. The Mamluks had built it in A.D. 1325, when they ruled over Palestine, and it remained for many centuries as el-Khan to the villagers. Overlooking Beit Daras were the remnants of a castle built by the Crusaders in the early 1100s, which in turn was perched on a citadel that had been built by Alexander the Great more than a millennium before that. Once a station for the powerful, history had broken it down into ruin, and what remained stood tenderly, holding all of time now, where children played and where young couples went to escape watchful eyes.

A river, brimming with God's assortment of fish and flora, ran through Beit Daras, bringing blessings and carrying away village waste, dreams, gossip, prayers, and stories, which it emptied into the Mediterranean just north of Gaza. The water flowing over rocks hummed secrets of the earth and time meandered to the rhythms of crawling, hopping, buzzing, and flying lives.

When Mariam was five years old, she stole her sister Nazmiyeh's eye kohl and used it to write a prayer on a leaf that she tossed into the river of Beit Daras. It was a prayer for a real pencil and permission to enter the building you go to when you have a pencil. What she wrote were scribbles, of course, despite the presence of an elementary school with two rooms and four teachers, paid for by monthly collections from the villagers. She would instead watch her brother and other schoolboys in their uniforms, each carrying a pencil in one hand—true status symbols—and satchels of books flung across their shoulders as they marched up the hill to that enchanted place with two rooms, four teachers, and many, many pencils.

As it turned out, Mariam didn't need the schoolhouse to learn, just pencil and paper. She created an imaginary friend named Khaled, who waited every day by the river of Beit Daras to teach Mariam to write and read.

The color of the river was an enigma to Mariam, who sat on its bank contemplating what seemed to be colorlessness, borrowing hues from everything around it. On bright days, it was a crisp light blue, like the sky. In the springtime, when the world was particularly green, so was the river. Other times, it was clear and sometimes cloudy or muddy. She questioned how the river could take on so many colors when the ocean was always blue-green, except at night, of course, when the purity of black dressed everything for sleep.

After much rumination, young Mariam concluded that only some things change colors. She also understood at an early age that her vision was like no one else's. People changed colors according to their moods, but her sister Nazmiyeh said only Mariam could see the changes. Imbuements of blue were the norm when people prayed, although not always. People's expressions did not necessarily match their colors. White auras felt malicious and some people had them even when they smiled. Yellow and blue were sincere and content. Black was the purest of all, the aura of babies, of utter kindness, and of great strength.

Flowers and fruit cycled through hues with the seasons. So did trees. So did the skin on Mariam's arms, from brown to very brown in the summer. But her hair was always black and her eyes were always the way they were: one green, one brown with hazel accents. The green left eye was her favorite, because everyone loved to look at it, but such curiosity made Nazmiyeh nervous that her little sister might become cursed with *hassad*, the misfortune of the evil eye that befalls one because of the jealousy of others.

TWO

My teta Nazmiyeh told me that she had been the prettiest girl in all of Beit Daras. She said she was the baddest, too, and I tried to imagine my teta in the glory of her youthful badness.

IT WAS UP TO Nazmiyeh to protect Mariam from the evils of hassad. Some people just had hot, greedy eyes that could easily lay the curse, even if they hadn't intended. So, Nazmiyeh insisted Mariam wear a blue amulet to ward off the envy people felt toward Mariam's unique eyes, and Nazmiyeh regularly read Quranic *suras* over her for more protection.

The subject of Mariam's eyes came up once among Nazmiyeh's friends as they washed clothes by the river. Most were recently married or expecting their first child, but some, like Nazmiyeh, were still unmarried. "How can she have only one green eye?" one asked.

Nazmiyeh flung off her headscarf, releasing a medusa's head of shiny henna-dyed coils, plopped her brother's white shirt in the wash bucket, and quipped, "Some Roman stud probably stuck his dick in our ancestral line a few hundred years ago and now it's poking out of my poor sister's eye."

In the private female freedom of those laundry mornings, they all laughed, their arms deep in wash buckets. Another young woman said, "Too bad it wasn't a double-headed snake so she could have two green eyes."

And another, "Mostly too bad for your ancestor, Nazmiyeh. How she might have liked a double-headed one!" Their laughter reached higher notes, liberated by the vulgar immodesty they dared. Such was Nazmiyeh's power to undress decorum, allowing those around her to acknowledge what lay unsorted in their hearts. She was crass in a way that both intrigued her friends and embarrassed them. Few dared reproach her, for though her tongue could be the charm to melt a heart, it could be a poisonous sting or path to appalling impropriety. People loved and hated her for that.

Nazmiyeh believed the odd coloring of her sister's eyes was related to her special ability to divine the unseen. Mariam was not a clairvoyant, but she could see people's shine.

"What do you mean *shine?*" Nazmiyeh once asked her.

"The *shine!*" Mariam traced her hand in the space around Nazmiyeh's head. "Right there," she said.

Nazmiyeh came to understand that the inner world of individuals formed a colored halo, which only her little sister Mariam could see. The family spent days after that testing Mariam's ability. "Okay, tell me how I'm feeling now," her brother, Mamdouh, said upon returning home from a fight with the neighborhood boys. "You're red and green," Mariam replied and turned back to whatever she was doing. Nazmiyeh mocked, "Red and green together means you're scared and horny."

"Mariam has no idea what horny is; so I know you're lying, you horrendous unmannered girl!" Mamdouh slapped the back of Nazmiyeh's head and ran for cover.

"You better run, boy!"

"I feel sorry for the poor donkey who marries you," Mamdouh said, taking cover by the door.

Nazmiyeh laughed, which only irritated Mamdouh more.

Although Mariam's special ability waned over time, it remained one of two family secrets, and Nazmiyeh used it to her advantage. When the mother and sisters of a suitor came to their home to meet Nazmiyeh, she treated them with arrogance and sarcasm, because Mariam could intuit that they found Nazmiyeh unworthy of their son. In the market, she shamed many a merchant who tried to cheat her. Mariam's gift was Nazmiyeh's secret weapon and she forbade mention of it outside their household, just as she forbade talk of Sulayman.

THREE

Um Mamdouh, my great-teta, lived before my time. They called her the Crazy Lady, but she was all love, the quiet impenetrable kind. She saw things others couldn't, though not like Mariam did.

THERE WERE FIVE MAJOR family clans in Beit Daras, and each had its neighborhood. The Baroud, Maqademeh, and Abu al-Shamaleh families were the most prestigious. They owned most of the farms, orchards, beehives, and pastures. "Baraka" was Nazmiyeh, Mamdouh, and Mariam's family name, but it was nothing to brag about. They lived in the Masriyeen neighborhood, a ragtag muddle of Palestinians without pedigree who had settled in the poorest part of Beit Daras. They had arrived in Beit Daras from Egypt five centuries earlier and had disguised or dropped their family names because they had escaped the wrath of a tribal feud or had perhaps dishonored their families in some way and had had to leave. No one really knew.

For most of their lives in Beit Daras, Nazmiyeh, Mamdouh, and Mariam were known as the children of Um Mamdouh, the village crazy woman. Even though they had no father, people didn't dare speak ill about their mother in front of them because Nazmiyeh would have appeared at their doorstep, her tongue sharpened with scandal and an alarming lack of inhibition. Although the children lamented their mother's state and fiercely tried to protect her from the scorn of others, they could not always shield her. Um Mamdouh was often found staring off into the distance, engaged with the wind, speaking in a strange language to no one; and she would sometimes laugh inexplicably.

Once, people saw Um Mamdouh hitch up her *thobe* and shit in the river, and Mamdouh, then only eleven years old, pounded a boy much bigger than he for daring to mention it. There were many nights when the three of them would have to coax their mother away from sleeping in the pastures among the goats.

Their father was said to have left them before anyone could remember him, except Nazmiyeh, the oldest. "Our father came back once, and we all ate *ghada* together," Nazmiyeh told them. Mamdouh could not remember, but he believed Nazmiyeh because she swore it on the Quran. Besides, it had to be true. How else could Mariam have been conceived?

Still, Mamdouh wished he had memory of a father.

FOUR

I don't want to get ahead of myself and tell you about Nur. She was still two generations away when my great-khalo Mamdouh went to work for the beekeeper. But if you believe as I do that people are part love, part flesh and blood, and part everything else, then mentioning her name now makes sense, at the source of her love part.

As Mamdouh grew older, his limbs stretched into manhood and his voice deepened in authority. He was able to secure a steady job with a beekeeper, whose jars of honey were sold throughout the country and beyond to Egypt, Turkey, and reaching even to Mali and Senegal. The old beekeeper realized in only a month that he had found the boy whom he could nurture to one day take over the family business that had been passed down to him through multiple generations. He had three wives, two of whom had borne him five daughters and one son, who died shortly after birth. Only one child, his youngest daughter, Yasmine, had shown an aptitude for beekeeping. Little did he know that in less than three years the centuries of bees, apiaries, beeswax, hives, honeycombs, and beekeepers that marshaled his life would be gone, as if history had never been there. All that would remain would be his love of bees, which Yasmine, his favorite child, would carry in her heart and plant in the soil of another continent. But no one could have known that then. The future of the people of Beit Daras was so far from their destiny that even if a clairvoyant had announced their fate, no one would have believed it.

Thus the beekeeper began to teach Mamdouh everything he knew about the art of apiculture. His smile was nearly toothless, owing to rickets, and he never wore protective gloves, insisting that he did not like separation from his bees—although he always wore his hat and veil and kept a smoker nearby in case of a swarm. He insisted that Mamdouh wear gloves until he could feel the connection to bees in every part of his body, beginning with his heart and moving to other vital organs until it reached his skin. "Only then can you stop wearing gloves," he said, patting Mamdouh's shoulder.

In truth, Mamdouh could never have such a visceral connection to beekeeping as his mentor expected. True, he arrived early to work every day and stayed late listening to the beekeeper for hours. But Mamdouh's enthusiam and attentiveness was born from the wound of fatherlessness, and from a desire deep in his thighs. He heard very little of the beekeeper's tales, absorbing instead the warmth of being there and scanning his surroundings for a glimpse of Yasmine, the beekeeper's youngest daughter. And as memory will often succumb to the insistence of longings, Mamdouh invented a memory of a father, whose features took on those of his mentor and his character that of a beekeeper, sitting down to tea after a meal to speak of honey while Mamdouh searched the room for wafts of love.

Before Mamdouh became the apiarist's apprentice, his family had lived on whatever he could peddle or earn from small jobs and what charity they got from mosques. But it was never enough, especially when his mother's strange cravings grew. Once, during Eid when Mamdouh was not yet twelve years old and the mosque had given their family half a lamb, Um Mamdouh got a frightening appetite that no amount of food could satiate. Mamdouh had to slap her before all the meat was gone. The Quran says that heaven lies beneath the feet of mothers, and everyone knows that to slap one's mother is to make a reservation in hell. But surely Allah would forgive him because he had acted not as her son, but as the man of the house who needed to ensure the family might have meat to eat. That was when Mamdouh and his sisters started to turn against Sulayman, the other family secret, because they knew their mother's appetite was his fault. They knew when he was near, by their mother's voracious appetite, her transported eyes that showed only the whites, or by the singed odor of smoke Sulayman brought wherever he was.

FIVE

People who knew my great-teta Um Mamdouh eventually learned of Sulayman. Or they learned of her after they heard of Sulayman. In those days, they all recalled a verse from the Holy Quran (Al Hijr 15:26–27): "And indeed, He created man from sounding clay of altered black smooth mud. And the djinn, He created aforetime from the smokeless flame of fire."

O N A DARK, CLOUDY December evening in 1945, Um Mamdouh wandered in search of the moon until she found it, a thin crescent tangled in the stars over Beit Daras. Sulayman was with her. He always was now. As she gazed at the night sky, she heard moaning and muffled laughter behind a wall of ruins from a Roman bathhouse. She moved toward the sounds and saw outlines of four teenage boys, their skin glistening with the juices of moon and starlight. Shivering and panting in the cold dark, the boys' *galabiyas* were pulled up over their waists and each was masturbating, not with pleasure, but in competition, it seemed. She began to curse them, damn them to hell for such sin. The boys went instantly soft with fear and scrambled to pull down their galabiyas, until one of them saw who it was.

"It's the crazy Um Mamdouh," he shouted, and they sighed with relief, then laughed with malice.

15

"Go back to the Masriyeen neighborhood," yelled one boy. "Crazies are not allowed here," said another. "Are you going to pull up your thobe and shit in the river again?"

Um Mamdouh retreated, frantically waving her hands. "Stop it! Sulayman is getting angry. He never gets angry. Stop it! You must stop."

Their laughter intensified. "Who is Sulayman? Is that your sissy son's nickname? Is he going to shit in the river, too?"

Suddenly, before she could stop him, Sulayman began to emerge through her face. Specks of stars from a black sky glistened on the contours of her head as his presence grew. It expanded to the width of her shoulders, a dark immensity with raging eyes of red fire. It spat gibberish in a voice that thundered from all directions, and a cauterizing smell, like pollution, soaked the air.

Transfixed, their legs held upright only by the fear that stiffened them, their souls limp as their dicks, two of the boys urinated involuntarily, one shat himself, and the oldest among them, Atiyeh, the one who had been most arrogant and cruel to Um Mamdouh, was stunned into a knot of silence.

For the rest of their lives, the boys would compare their memories of that instant, and they would all agree that never had anything terrified them more, not even the Jewish gangs or later the Israeli military that came first with guns and machetes and later with incredible machines of death. They had glimpsed Sulayman in rare anger. A real djinni.

SIX

The Quran says that Allah made the djinn from smokeless fire.
Everyone knew that. Some revered the djinn, others feared them, but
everyone respected and cowered at their power. And those who
communicated with the djinn were avoided by some, revered by
others, and feared by most.

THE NEXT DAY, THE parents and elders of each family
convened and went to Um Mamdouh's house, where they
were welcomed in the Barakas' small stone dwelling. The women
were invited to sit on the carpet inside, while the men, including
the stunned boy, received the hospitality of Mamdouh in the
courtyard, where they were offered tea and dates and *argilehs*,
or hookahs, already packed with tobacco and filled with rose
water and lemons. Clearly, the family had been expecting them.
Sulayman had emerged to protect their mother and, as there
was no way now to contain this family secret, Mamdouh had
surmised that the town would come. So, he had borrowed the
argilehs from the beekeeper, who happily obliged, assuming
they were for Nazmiyeh's suitors.

Inside their hut, little Mariam watched suspiciously as visitors
arrived. Nazmiyeh served the women sweet mint tea. Her headscarf was trimmed in cheap metal coins that chimed shamelessly
when she moved her head, and a brazen portion of her hair
escaped for the world to see a hint of her wild copper curls.
Nazmiyeh walked slowly, aware that the women were watching
her. She had worn her green and orange *dishdasha*, the one that
snugly clung to her large breasts and arrogant buttocks and
thighs that fanned from a small waist. Nazmiyeh had a way of
filling every room she entered, sucking up all the air.

"Welcome to our humble home, ladies. We are honored by your presence," Nazmiyeh finally said with a smile that allowed others in the room to breathe.

"The honor is ours, beautiful young woman," they said in unison.

Nazmiyeh was not beautiful, not instantly attractive to those who looked her way. But for those who saw her, who brushed against her haughty defiance and irreverence, she was irresistible. She had walnut-colored skin that she made no attempt to lighten by keeping away from the sun. She didn't try to straighten her coiled hair by wrapping, pulling, or ironing it for occasions, such as weddings, when women removed their hijabs for one another. Instead, she let her curls just be, enraged and arrogant as they pleased. Whatever people thought of her, she proved difficult to ignore. Indeed, she had been the object of many a fantasy in Beit Daras.

The women of Beit Daras had come bearing gifts of fresh fruit and vegetables, olive oil, honey, and sweets. They apologized on behalf of their children, assuring Um Mamdouh, whom they respectfully addressed as Hajje Um Mamdouh, that each boy had received a hard beating and each would come in to apologize personally, if she would so allow. Hajje Um Mamdouh sat quietly and only spoke when addressed directly. She assured the women that Allah is the One who forgives, and that she had already forgiven the boys. It remained unuttered, though understood by all, that it was Sulayman's forgiveness that was being sought and granted.

Not until hours had passed did one of the women explain the condition of Atiyeh, the stunned boy.

"Bring Atiyeh to me," said the hajje. "I will help him."

As Atiyeh entered, Nazmiyeh bore into him with a stare so indignant and loathful that he stopped for a moment, more unsure of the world than he had ever been. He had just turned fifteen, though he seemed much younger, and Nazmiyeh was seventeen, though she seemed to be so much older. Blistering shame spread through Atiyeh's body and mixed in his organs with the image of Nazmiyeh's orange and green dishdasha stretched by supple rounded flesh at her chest and hips. His ribs pressed down on his heart with embarrassment and, he was sure, with love. Despite all eyes upon him, he felt himself growing hard, and he quickly flung himself at Hajje Um Mamdouh to kiss her hand and hide his predicament. But still, he could not speak. The hajje took the boy's head in her hand, pulled it back, and began to utter her scrambled ramblings. Her eyes rolled in their sockets and her stale breath reached those around her. Suddenly, she stopped, her eyes clear. The boy stood, seemingly taller than before he had knelt, as if in that moment he had crossed the final threshold to manhood. He glanced at Nazmiyeh with eyes that tamed her glare and assured her that he was stronger than she. No one could have perceived that fleeting glance, though it lasted an eternity between the two of them. Then he walked out as if nothing had ever happened to him, and that was proof enough that Um Mamdouh, the strange woman with no husband and three children in the Masriyeen neighborhood, who had once shat in the river and slept in pastures, was in reality among the blessed *asyad*, the gifted mortals who could communicate with the djinn of another realm.

News spread quickly through Beit Daras and the surrounding villages and people began to flock to Hajje Um Mamdouh's home. Many came to explore the world of the unseen. Are there other djinn in Beit Daras? Do the djinn mean us harm? Are they good or bad? Is it true that djinn have free will? Are they like us? Is it true they live more than a thousand years? Most came to search the mysteries of love. Does he love me truly? Which suitor is best for my daughter? Is my husband planning to take a second wife? A third wife? They always brought *bakhour* incense to burn because Hajje Um Mamdouh said the djinn love it. Once, a woman gifted Um Mamdouh a bottle of perfume from Lithuania and Sulayman stayed away until she got rid of it. Such scents based in alcohol repelled the old djinni, which many took as evidence that Sulayman may well have been an angel.

SEVEN

These were the times in Beit Daras when my great-khalto Mariam got her wooden box of dreams and I would traverse time and death, before I was born, to wait for her by the river, where I taught her written language, she talked to me about colors, and we made up songs.

MARIAM WAS DELIGHTED THAT so many visitors now came to her home seeking her mother's advice. They came with gifts and brought the energy of other villages and stories from esteemed families in Beit Daras. Upon seeing Mariam, they would praise Allah for such unique eyes. Nazmiyeh would immediately take her sister aside and read Quranic *muawithat* to shield her sister with the words of Allah, lest the compliments strike her with the curse of hassad. Sometimes Nazmiyeh did it in front of the women to shame them for being so bold with their compliments to anyone but Allah, the Creator who had made her sister's eyes. But Mariam did not care. She loved the attention and wanted the guests all to herself. She fought Nazmiyeh to be the one to serve them tea, going so far as to threaten breaking all the family's dishes if Nazmiyeh did not allow her.

"Okay, little sister. I just thought the tray was too heavy for you," Nazmiyeh relented, and the fierceness in Mariam's mismatched eyes turned to a smile as she carried the serving tray.

Mariam's ability to see auras had lessened over time so that now, at the age of six, she only saw occasional bursts of intense feelings. But her inner world was always sorted by color. So after weeks of working up her courage, she finally asked the women for a pencil, a cobalt blue pencil, the color of Khaled, her friend who was always waiting for her by the river.

The next day, several women came with pencils and note-books and erasers and sharpeners tucked in a carved wooden box with inlaid mother-of-pearl calligraphy of the word *Allah*. Mariam received the gift with awestruck gratitude. It was a wooden box of dreams that Mariam would carry for the rest of her life. She began to spend more time at the river and no amount of threats or whuppings from Nazmiyeh could keep her home during daylight. Mariam had her wooden box to take each day to the river, where Khaled taught her how to write her name and the ninety-nine names of Allah. It was not long before she had unlocked the secrets of language. She had stopped watching the schoolboys walk to school and would leave after her chores every day for the river.

Several times Nazmiyeh followed her to see Khaled. Never finding him, Nazmiyeh concluded that Mariam had made him up to try to explain her self-taught literacy, and they settled into their lives thus. Those were perhaps the happiest days of the Barakas' lives together. Um Mamdouh was respected, Mamdouh was happy in his job keeping bees, and Nazmiyeh became dreamy, looking prettier than ever.

For two years, Mariam would return home daily in the late afternoon, eager to show her sister all that Khaled had taught her, and Nazmiyeh would leaf through the pages, her heart swelling with pride. She was sure her little sister was the first girl in all of Beit Daras to learn to read. Once, in a moment of unbearable love for her brilliant little sister, Nazmiyeh began to cry. She held Mariam's face gently in both her hands, crouched to bring her face close, and said, "You are the most spectacular person I have ever known, my little sister. Remember how special you are, how loved you are. We will always be together."

"Are you okay?" Mariam asked, unaccustomed to this sentimental side of her sister.

"Yes! I'm more than okay. I'm in love," Nazmiyeh whispered. Mariam gasped, wide-eyed.

"Shh, *habibti*," Nazmiyeh put a finger to her smiling lips. "I will tell you later. But for now, this is our secret."

Nazmiyeh had always assumed a motherly role in Mariam's life. Now they were sisters, too, who could conspire and hold each other's secrets. So, almost eight years old now, Mariam resolved to explain who Khaled really was. But not now. They had to pray the day's fourth *salat* and prepare the evening meal before their brother Mamdouh returned home from his work at the apiary.

EIGHT

My great-teta Um Mamdouh could not speak with the unseen except for Sulayman, an old djinni cast out from his tribe for having fallen in love with a mortal. The villagers came to understand this over time, but it did not lessen their respect for her power. Although the villagers' visits eventually dwindled, they continued until history arrived and Beit Daras was carried off by the wind.

IN FEBRUARY 1948, FIVE men arrived at the Baraka home. Village elders and chosen *mukhtars* from each of the main families of Beit Daras, they were pious men who would not ordinarily visit a woman such as Um Mamdouh, who lived with the unseen and without a husband. Their faces were hard and sober, dignified by age and tribal tradition. They greeted the hajje's only son, Mamdouh, with firm handshakes and a kiss on each cheek, a sign of respect for the man of the house, even though Mamdouh was now only seventeen years old. They showed Hajje Um Mamdouh respect and honor by averting their eyes from her and placing their right hands over their hearts.

"Welcome to our home," Mamdouh greeted the men, motioning for them to enter and sit on the carpet cushions near his mother.

"May Allah grant you long life, Hajje. We have come to seek your help and the help of Sulayman," said Abu Nidal, the venerable mukhtar of the Baroud family. Before they could say more, Um Mamdouh closed her eyes, enfolding herself in the climate of another world. She inhaled the severe air surrounding her guests, mumbling incomprehensibly until her body was filled with echoes and her skin exhaled a strong scent of soot. She opened her eyes.

"You come to learn the intentions of the Jews?" she asked. They all nodded, so she continued. "Our peaceful neighbors in the kibbutz are not our friends. They harbor treacherous plans toward Beit Daras."

"Are you sure, Hajje? We have been good neighbors for years. We have given them crops and taught them to till this land. Their own doctor has treated our people and, enshallah, helped them back to health."

"I tell you only what Sulayman tells me. He does not lie."

"Tell us more," they said.

"Only Allah knows the unknown, and only His will shall be done. Our neighbors will come joined by others, and they will spill the blood of the Bedrawasis of Beit Daras," she said of a family known for their bravery and warrior skills. "Beit Daras will be victorious. You will all fight and you will live, but some of your brothers and sons will fall; yet, that will not be the end. More Jews will return and the skies will rain death upon Beit Daras. The big-headed stubborn Bedrawasis of Beit Daras will not surrender. Time and again they will repel the enemy, but the ememy's fury is great. Native blood will pour from these hills into the river, and the war will be lost."

Recognizing the gravity of such a visit, Nazmiyeh, now twenty years old, stood still, listening in the tight space of broken wall between the kitchen and the main room. Eavesdropping next to Nazmiyeh, Mariam did not fully understand her mother's formal words, but she could feel the disquiet they inspired. When she served them coffee, Mariam observed the men sitting straight and stiff, hands clasped in laps. Small, uneasy fidgets and hard swallows that ferried Adam's apples up and back seemed the only movement in the room. They didn't look one another in the eyes, as if doing so would betray the despair they labored to hide. Nazmiyeh pulled her little sister closer and they stayed that way, listening to a trembling silence crawl from the ground, up the walls. Finally, the men sipped their coffee, and Um Mamdouh spoke again. "Only Allah can know the unknown, but if Beit Daras does not surrender, this land will rise again, even if the war is lost."

No one understood the meaning of her words and none dared ask for an explanation. It was enough to hear *this land will rise again*. They grabbed those final words of hope and inhabited them until their final days, which came to some in battle shortly thereafter, and to others in the wreckage of nostalgia that paved refugee camps.

"May Allah grant you long life, Hajje. Take this for your trouble," Abu Nidal said, placing a bundle of Palestinian notes before her. But she refused. "Put your fate in the hands of Allah. Lean on Allah and fight for us, Abu Nidal. I do not accept money. Allah is my provider and my protector. My son will fight with you. I will stay, so Sulayman, too, will remain to help us; but know that the enemy brings *afareet* from *iblis*, demons from the depths of darkness. May Allah grant you long life and may He protect Beit Daras and her people."

NINE

Mariam and my teta Nazmiyeh listened that day behind the broken kitchen wall as their mother spoke to the mukhtars about iblis and afareet. Iblis was the devil, and afareet were his terrible followers, but Mariam could not understand why they were coming to Beit Daras. She buried her face in her sister's chest and clutched her tighter. Nazmiyeh asked Mariam to fetch her wooden box and transcribe a note for her. It said, "If you want to marry me, your family must come tomorrow."

A WEEK AFTER YOUNG ATIYEH'S voice had been liberated from the stun of seeing Sulayman, he and Nazmiyeh had locked eyes again in the *souq*. She tried her meanest stare with eyes outlined in black kohl and underlined by a *niqab* veil she was trying on because it was adorned with pretty jingles, but he didn't flinch. He squinted in a mock attempt to one-up her stare. Then he could see her brow relax and eyes narrow from the force of the smile he knew had formed beneath the veil. She returned the veil to the vendor and looked away, knowing Atiyeh was watching.

They met this way many times, communicating with only their eyes. Six months later, they met by the ruins of the Roman citadel and for two more years, Nazmiyeh refused every suitor, waiting for Atiyeh's older brothers to marry before his turn could come to choose a bride. They met on the first Thursday of every month in a spot they claimed as their own. Anguished by exhausting patience and unredeemed love, they finally agreed it not sinful to hold hands, and from the dexterity of interlacing, squeezing, gripping, and caressing fingers, their hands created an amorous language that spoke of complicity and promise.

In this same place in 332 B.C., Alexander the Great had built fortifications after laying siege to a conquered Gaza, some thirty-five kilometers to the south. Enraged by five months of Gazan resistance to his Macedonian army's march toward Egypt, he finally broke through, killing all male inhabitants and selling the women and children into slavery. Thus had been laid the foundations upon which the Romans, several centuries later, had built their citadel in Beit Daras. Some three thousand years later, they were remote ruins where love between Nazmiyeh and Atiyeh tried to find repose by holding hands on the first Thursday of every month.

But in the days between their meetings, they were pursued and harassed by a panting want that gave them no rest. They did not even notice the unfolding political tumult until the town mukhtars arrived to visit Um Mamdouh, injecting greater urgency to their union.

Family members tried to dissuade Atiyeh's adamant resolve to marry immediately, but it was of no use. Pleased by his grandson's determination, the patriarch gathered the men of the family. Despite the fear convulsing across Palestine as daily news of atrocities committed by Zionist gangs against both the British and the Palestinians emerged, Haj Abu Sarsour brought six men and a dowry of gold to ask for the hand of Nazmiyeh for his grandson, Atiyeh.

Everyone agreed it would be improper to have a wedding celebration under the anxious circumstances. But as soon as calm and order returned to the country, Atiyeh's father and grandfather vowed, they would throw the biggest wedding the

village had ever seen. For now, they brought a *ma'zoon* to offici-
ate the marriage of Atiyeh and Nazmiyeh so their union was
halal in the eyes of Allah. Such a hasty marriage with a deferred
wedding was unusual, but these were unusual times.

Instead, in preparation for the marital bed, Nazmiyeh and
her friends, along with their mothers, spent the day in Gaza's
Turkish bathhouse, exfoliating her skin in steam rooms, where
women scrubbed, plucked, waxed, and massaged every part of
her body in lavender oils. They relaxed on ancient hot tiles,
drinking *karkadeh*, chilled hibiscus tea, and breathing the moist
air infused with eucalyptus.

TEN

I didn't live in these times. But when I went into the blue, when my
condition became as it did, Sulayman revealed all to me. I don't fully
understand it and don't expect you to. But maybe you can believe, as
I do, that there are truths that defy other truths, where time folds on
itself.

THE JEWS CAME, AS Hajje Um Mamhoud said they would,
and they were repelled by the two thousand residents of
Beit Daras and their loyal djinni, Sulayman. They came again
and again, in March and several times in April of 1948, and their
fury grew with incredulity and indignation that a small village
of farmers and beekeepers could overcome the firepower of the
highly trained Haganah, with their mechanized weaponry and
fighter planes, which they had smuggled under British noses
from Czechoslovakia in preparation for conquest. During the last
attack in April, fifty women and children from Beit Daras were
slaughtered in a single day, after which the men ordered their
families to flee to Gaza, while they remained to fight. "Just until

the hostilities subside," they said. "Take enough things for a week or two."

Nazmiyeh hastily packed a bundle of food and belongings to last two weeks and set off toward the river to fetch Mariam. She made her way in the village, walking through walls of fear. The air was heavy, almost unbreathable, and people moved in fitful motions, as if unsure that one leg should follow the other. Women hurried with bundles balanced on heads and children hoisted on hips, pausing occasionally to adjust each. Children struggled to keep pace with their elders, who pulled them by the arms. Bewilderment carved lines in every face that Nazmiyeh passed, and despite the noise and chaos around her, she thought she could hear heartbeats pounding on chest walls.

Near the river, the air became lighter and lifted off the ground, winding into tree branches and rustling leaves. The sky was a soft clear blue with lazy, idling clouds. Mariam sat against her rock, a boulder by the river she had carved her name into the day she learned to write it. Her wooden box of dreams lay next to her and her notebook was open in her lap. Nazmiyeh could see her lips moving, as if she were conversing with herself, even laughing, a pencil in hand.

"There you are. Come, Mariam. We must go," Nazmiyeh said. But Mariam continued in her conversation, as if she had not heard her sister.

Nazmiyeh moved closer. "Who are you talking to, Mariam?"

Mariam leapt to hug her sister. "Khaled," Mariam answered, but Nazmiyeh, seeing no one, despaired that her sister was afflicted with the same madness that jumbled their mother's world.

"Mariam, is Khaled a djinni?"

"No. He's your grandson," Mariam said.

An explosive blast cracked the air.

"We must go, Mariam. Did you hear that explosion? Get up now and come with me." Nazmiyeh pulled her sister's arm. Mariam gathered her things into her wooden box, as she sang the strange song Nazmiyeh had heard her sing before.

> O find me
> I'll be in that blue
> Between sky and water
> Where all time is now
> And we are the forever
> Flowing like a river

"Enough! It's time to leave!" Nazmiyeh yelled. "The men will stay to fight and we will return as soon as the Jews are gone."

Enshallah. By Allah's will.

Back in the village, Mariam begged her sister to allow her to flee the following day with their neighbors who were also going to Gaza. "*Minshan Allah*, please, Nazmiyeh," she pleaded, adding that she wanted more time with her mother and Mamdouh and Atiyeh, who were staying to defend the village if the Jews came back. Unsure and confused as everyone was, Nazmiyeh reluctantly agreed. The neighbors were leaving early the next morning and promised to take Mariam with them, enshallah.

So Nazmiyeh set off with her husband's family, her sister to follow her with the neighbors, her brother and husband staying to fight, and her mother also remaining so Sulayman would be in Beit Daras to help. Without her family to watch over, Nazmiyeh walked with others in the trek toward Gaza, deafened by the screams of her heart wanting to go back and get Mariam.

The next morning, when the neighbor family awoke, Mariam had already left. She had told their daughter in the middle of the night that she was leaving with Nazmiyeh after all. Instead, she had gone to the outskirts of the village to hide in her best hide-and-seek spot, the small shelf inside the water well, just big enough to fit a small crouching child with her wooden box of dreams, inlaid with mother-of-pearl, and a small bag of bread and cheese. She needed to see Khaled, to let him know where she was going so he could find her again.

The well was some distance from the center of the village where most of the fighting had been taking place. On a normal day, Mariam would have taken for granted that the whimpers and cries and claps in the distance were the calls of wild animals—dogs, goats, donkeys, birds—or the shots of hunters. But this was no ordinary day. The thunder of bombs and the way they jarred the earth was unmistakable, and she knew that the muffled sounds that followed reverberated from human agony. For nearly two days, Mariam did not move from the shelf in the water well, not even when strange men speaking in a strange language arrived to fetch water.

ELEVEN

War changed people. It created cowardice and bravery and produced legends. It told the story of my great-teta, a strange woman, made of love, who never told a lie and who moved through the world differently than most. Her story was repeated many times, and in the retelling, she became known as Um Sulayman, the brave old woman of Beit Daras.

THE NAQBA, THE CATASTROPHE that inaugurated the erasure of Palestine, started slowly in 1947, one atrocity at a time throughout the country. For Beit Daras, the decisive battle occurred in May 1948, soon after European Jewish immigrants declared a new state called Israel in place of ancient Palestine. The Haganah and Stern Gang now called themselves the "Israel Defense Forces," and they marched into Beit Daras after hours of sustained bombardment with mortars. A battalion from the Sudanese army came to help, but it arrived too late. The forest was engulfed in flames, swallowing homes to the north. Clouds of smoke hovered low, painting the world black, settling on the dead like dark shrouds and invading the lungs of the living, who heaved and convulsed as they sought refuge. Chaos reigned, perpetuated by more explosions, gratuitous now that Beit Daras was fully consumed by the fog of death and defeat. The villagers who had stayed behind either had been killed or were already fleeing toward Gaza, and the rest were taken prisoner, never to be seen again.

Palestinians escaping from other villages converged on one of several main paths to Gaza that passed Beit Daras. Hajje Um Mamdouh, her son, Mamdouh, and Nazmiyeh's husband, Atiyeh, survived the defeat and were now joining the stream of fleeing humanity. Sulayman helped them escape captivity. Um Mamdouh instructed the two young men to don women's *abayas*, then she pulled two red threads from her thobe and tied one around the crown of each boy's head. "Everything below these strings will elude the awareness of soldiers. Sulayman will see to it. But you mustn't remove the threads until you've reached safety, and then, you must not ever unravel the knot, no matter your circumstances," Hajje Um Mamdouh instructed.

When he stepped outside, dressed as a woman with a thin red thread cutting across his brow, Mamdouh could see and smell through his veil this new world of ash and the smolder of tired fires and expired lives. A rage rising from the black earth through his feet made it hard to move, and the incomprehensible loss of life and country seeped into his lungs, making him cough. He stood in a queue with three more families of women and children who had been rounded up by Zionist soldiers and were now dropping all their valuables into piles of food, jewelry, clothing, even photos. Mamdouh managed to leave with a single photograph, the only one the family ever had, taken by a journalist who had visited Beit Daras occasionally. It had been snapped on one of the days Nazmiyeh had tried to surprise Mariam by the river, to meet Khaled. Mamdouh was standing on the riverbank with his arm around Nazmiyeh, who stood sassily, hand on her hip. Their mother was there in a fine embroidered thobe she had sewn herself, but she was somehow still absent. And Mariam, perhaps eight years old, was captured in an expression of casual conversation with her friend Khaled, a boy of perhaps ten years, with a white streak of hair, as the two of them sat around her wooden box of dreams. When the photographer gave them that photo, the family could not recall seeing Khaled that day at the river and, until holding the photograph, had assumed he was a creation of Mariam's imagination.

Now Mamdouh looked at the photo, trying to touch the past, to compel the clock to reverse its course as they moved in shocked steps sinking in a marsh of sorrow. Without words, they walked away from their lives, away from these new conquering soldiers, who were drunk on an ancient virulence that mixed greed and power with God.

Dazed and confused by an unimagined fate, the villagers continued on the thirty-five kilometers to Gaza. In the distance, they heard the sound of a single shot, followed by the abyss of a woman's scream. Soon, they merged with a larger procession of human despair from other villages. Sometimes, unseen snipers aimed and people dropped. There was nothing to do but collect the dead and injured and continue on. A bullet flew through Mamdouh's leg and he fell, the abaya dropping away. His brother-in-law, still disguised as a woman in an abaya, tried to carry him, but could not. Nor could Mamdouh's mother. But Sulayman could. He entered the old woman's body and lifted her son, nearly twice her weight and height, and walked on toward Gaza with other fleeing souls.

Arab soldiers appeared along the way. What remained of the defeated Arab battalions were stripped to their underwear and huddled in humiliation. Zionist soldiers came, too, shooting above the crowds to ensure no one turned back home. When a group of them happened upon a slight old woman effortlessly carrying a wounded man in her arms, they ordered her to stop. She turned the whites of her eyes at them, and a potent broth of fear foamed in the intestines of the soldiers. One of them shot the woman, and she fell bleeding, dropping her wounded son. But the soldiers did not move, their bones turned to froth, their hearts to ice, and their faces ashened before they burst into flames, writhed, and burned.

Soldiers who came to rescue the killers of Um Mamdouh were also engulfed in the fire until twelve uniformed men of the new Jewish state lay charred on the ground not far from where the old woman and her son also lay, she dead and he with a severely wounded leg. Everyone witnessed it.

The fleeing villagers of Beit Daras needed no explanation for that sudden fire. They knew it was Sulayman but their march was more urgent now, as more soldiers would surely come to exact vengeance for those singed remains. A man discarded the family belongings he was carrying and hoisted Hajje Um Mamdouh's corpse. They could leave the many other bodies that littered their long march to a refugee's life, but leaving Sulayman's friend was out of the question. Hadn't the old djinni fought alongside them?

It was then that the fleeing villagers heard a woman's voice yell "Alwan!" and turned to find Nazmiyeh running toward them, her hair loose and her body exposed beneath torn and bloodied clothes.

TWELVE

Teta Nazmiyeh talked to me about everything in the world, except the day Mariam was gone. The day the name "Alwan" was planted in her heart, which would later be harvested to name my mother.

ONCE THE BEACON CROSSROAD between North Africa, the Middle East, and Europe, the green and sandy terrain of Gaza was the hub of the spice trade, the most lucrative business on earth in medieval times. Palestinians in Gaza were recognized among the finest artisans, producing highly sought-after jewelry as long ago as 2,000 B.C. Noblemen and pilgrims were drawn to Gaza across the ages and scholars from around the world passed through along the "Way of the Sea" that led toward the Great Library in Alexandria.

Those same shores of Gaza had been a place where the Barakas and other villagers had gone for occasional Friday family outings. Once a place of joy, swimming, barbecuing, now it was a morass of anxiety and misery that stuck to Nazmiyeh's every movement, to every effort to find Mariam in the crowds. And when she finally located her neighbors, the realization that Mariam had not left Beit Daras pushed Nazmiyeh farther into desperation. She blamed herself for not having forced Mariam to leave with her. She cursed her little sister for being so stubborn and imagined yanking her by the ear when she found her. She knew what must be done, but she would have to wait for nightfall to elude Atiyeh's family, who would surely stop her. She slept early to rest before another journey, and for the first time in her life, she recalled a dream. It startled her awake amid the sleeping bodies around her. A little girl who looked like Mariam, with dark coiled hair and a foreign name, but without colored eyes, showed Nazmiyeh papers and said, "Teta, these are from Khaled. Want me to read them?" She nodded yes and the little girl said, "It says, Mariam is waiting for you. She left the water well."

Though Nazmiyeh had promised Atiyeh she would wait for him in Gaza, she set out in the darkness back to Beit Daras, stepping over and between the nightmares of families asleep on the ground.

The night was black, thick and smooth, as Nazmiyeh walked the desert path back to her village. Stars tinseled the world above her, but she could see neither what stood before her nor what lay beneath her feet. She stopped to pray, bowing and bending in pleading worship. She asked forgiveness for her sins. She called upon Allah to guide her. She begged to find her sister Mariam alive, then entreated the earth to clear her path of scorpions and wild animals. Soon she could see the glow of a fire in the distance and set out toward it, believing that Allah had illuminated her path.

Along the way, she stumbled upon other Palestinians heading in the opposite direction. They could sense one another in the dark, the way fear immobilized them. "Who is there?" a woman's voice asked in Arabic and Nazmiyeh relaxed upon hearing the Palestinian *fallahi* accent. "I am trying to get back to Beit Daras to find my sister," she replied, and the two women moved closer until they could see one another. Several children clutched the woman's thobe and remained silent as the two, strangers to each other, embraced as if lost family. The woman spoke of unspeakable horrors in her village, warning Nazmiyeh not to return. "I cannot bring myself to describe what they are doing to the women," she said. Nazmiyeh wished her a safe journey and both prayed for themselves and one another before one set off toward the calling waters of Gaza's shore, and the other toward the distant flames.

It was nearly daybreak before Nazmiyeh reached the water well in Beit Daras where Mariam often hid when she played with other children. She called softly into the well, but no response came. She was spent, dirty, and thirsty, with blistered feet and nostrils full of sand. The fire had subsided and Nazmiyeh could see uniformed soldiers meandering on the scorched earth. Most were on the hill, looting the larger homes. Their plunder hadn't yet reached the Masriyeen neighborhood, giving her time to drink from the well before reaching her home undetected. She went into each room, whispering Mariam's name, but there was no answer. She looked in the kitchen and bathroom, then went to the carved-out space in the wall between the kitchen and the big room, their eavesdropping spot. She paused before turning the corner. It was the last place to look. *Please Allah, let her be here.*

And there, curled on herself, Mariam was sleeping with her wooden box of dreams, knees tight against her chest. Nazmiyeh dropped to the floor and embraced her sister. "Oh Mariam, habibti!" she sobbed, fear and exhaustion sliding off her shoulders.

Mariam awoke and clung to Nazmiyeh, burying her own sobs in her sister's bosom.

From the window they could see some villagers in the distance being allowed to leave. Soldiers were taking their belongings and jewelry, but they were allowed to leave. Nazmiyeh felt hopeful. She had been right to come back. To have had faith in Allah. It would be all right. They would give the soldiers whatever they had and go on their way to Gaza. She could walk those thirty-five kilometers again today. They were going to be fine. *Allahu akbar.*

Nazmiyeh pulled her sister closer, as if to tuck Mariam whole into her body. She kissed her sister's face and her tears fell, streaking the soot on Mariam's cheeks.

Neither saw nor heard the two soldiers until one of them yanked Nazmiyeh by her headscarf, pulling it off. Mariam gasped. Nazmiyeh's abundant copper curls breathed, exhaled, and sliced through the air when she swung around to face her attackers. Her penetrating eyes made the soldiers step back, look at each other. And smile. The soldiers spoke in foreign languages and seemed not to understand one another, using hand gestures to communicate. She moved in front of her sister and began taking off her three gold bangles, the *shabka* of her dowry. Her husband had broken with tradition and put them on her wrists before their planned wedding. One of the soldiers took them, but the other was not interested in gold and didn't take his eyes off Nazmiyeh. He moved closer and lifted a fistful of her hair to his face. He inhaled, closed his eyes, grabbed the back of Nazmiyeh's head, and forced her face to rub against his crotch.

As the soldiers handled her, ripping her clothes, forcing her onto her back, baring her flesh, Nazmiyeh ordered Mariam to turn away and close her eyes and ears as tightly as she could. She said it would all be over soon and they would go on their way. She could endure this, she thought.

Nazmiyeh did not understand what the soldier yelled before forcing himself into her. She clenched her teeth, biting the agony of rape lest it escape from her voice and reach Mariam's ears.

"Scream!" the soldier demanded in his language as he shoved himself harder into her. "Scream!" He pulled her body up by the hair, but Nazmiyeh understood neither his words nor his desire to hear her suffering. Instead, she continued to endure the assault as silently as possible. She could not see Mariam and was unsure where her sister had gone. She closed her eyes, remembering her husband, Atiyeh, that beautiful man, on their first night together. She had held her voice then, too, knowing that his mother and sisters were probably listening behind the marital door. It was a devious complicity of memory that provoked her to jerk her head violently, trying to uncouple that image from this reality. The soldier thought she was resisting, which pleased him.

The other soldier took the place of the first one, who now tried to thrust himself into her mouth. He slapped her repeatedly. "Scream!" he ordered. "*Scream!*"

She saw his eyes, gray slits in sacks of fat. His lips were moist with drool and sweat ran from his brow. The grip of her jaw tightened on itself and the soldier grew angry and moved away, mumbling in his language. "I know how to make this whore scream!"

He returned dragging Mariam by her hair, like a limp doll, her wooden box of dreams clutched to her chest. The sisters locked their eyes for an interminable instant, though not long enough to fit a word before the bullet to Mariam's head rang out through eternity, her wooden box of dreams falling open, its contents spilled. From the terrible knowing that the sun would never fully rise again in her life, a wild howl bellowed from the depths of Nazmiyeh.

The soldier with the gray eyes laughed, excited by the scream he had so badly wanted to prise from her, and he pushed aside the other to fuck the bloodied body of this voluptuous Arab woman. Nazmiyeh's wail continued as he ejaculated in her body, then the other moved in to pollute her as she stared at Mariam in an expanding crimson puddle. With an exhausting will, she kept screaming, as if her voice could lacerate reality thoroughly enough that she wouldn't ever have to face it.

Two more soldiers arrived, aroused by the vulgarity, and yanked her by the hair into a new position. Even those defiant locks were defeated and limp with sweat. More soldiers moved in and out of her body, scraping away her life until they had had enough. She lay there, a hollow carved-out thing streaked in spent tears, crusted blood, and dried fear. She listened to the hiss of her breath and surrendered to the silence of wanting to die, waiting for them to kill her, too.

Then, Mariam moved. Her little sister rose from the corpse on the ground and crouched before Nazmiyeh. She cupped her sister's swollen, tearful face in her small bony hands, gently, and repeated words that had passed between them before, "You are the most spectacular person I have ever known, my big sister. Don't ever forget how special you are, or how loved you are. We will always be together."

"I don't understand. How are you talking to me?" Nazmiyeh asked, without uttering a word.

"Everything that happens is as it should be. Someday, this will all end. There will be no more hours, no more soldiers, and no countries. The most anguished pains and blissful triumphs will fade to nothing. All that will matter is this love," Mariam said, though her lifeless body lay in its blood.

Nazmiyeh tried to gather her sister's body into her arms, even as her apparition continued to speak. "Please leave me here. I do not want to leave Beit Daras," Mariam said. "You must go now. Have a daughter, and name her Alwan. Now, go!"

"Go!" An Israeli officer who just arrived at the scene called out to the soldiers to leave the Arab woman and take the body of the child to be burned with the others. Without a word, without looking at anyone, without fear, Nazmiyeh summoned a cold punctilious rage to gather her sister's papers, notebooks, and pencils. She covered her breasts with Mariam's box and what remained of her ripped clothes. She stood on borrowed strength, semen and blood running down her legs, and walked away with broken steps, without looking back.

The soldiers seemed not to care. No one grabbed or called after her. It would not have mattered to her if they had. One foot after the other, Nazmiyeh was carried by her little sister's words. The feel of Mariam's palms on her cheeks. The maturity of Mariam's voice. The love. When she finally became aware of her surroundings, she had already walked six kilometers on the path to Gaza, where other fleeing Palestinians converged. It was then that she saw a group of men engulfed in flames. As she came closer, she realized they were Zionist soldiers, and she saw her mother and Mamdouh lying on the ground. Atiyeh was there, too, trying to lift her brother. Nazmiyeh ran toward them, trying to call out, but sound was still locked in her throat. The rage and resolve that had carried her this far dissolved and her legs felt wobbly. She pushed on, and when her voice was liberated, what emerged from her lips was a promise from another time and another place.

"Alwan!" was all she could yell, and she kept hollering that name into the wind until she reached what remained of her family.

II

But the violence of an alien story burned those
meandering native days, and the Mediterranean Sea
lapped at our history's wounds along the shores
of Gaza

THIRTEEN

My teta Nazmiyeh hung the sky every morning, like a sapphire sheet on a clothesline pirouetting in the breeze.

T HE REFUGEES MOVED ABOUT, beset by confusion for days. Sufficient tents were not distributed for weeks and people slept on the earth, with stones and insects and animals. Bodies accustomed to hard work and pious habits still awoke before sunrise, only to be met with the sluggishness of dormant fate that carved up their days into repeating lines and rows. They lined up five times a day for salat. They lined up twice a day for bread and soup. They lined up for communal toilets. Queues even invaded their dreams and shaped their rebellious thoughts, such that when some imagined fighting back, they thought of lining up first for weapons, then marching off as rows of fighters. And when the United Nations officials arrived, the refugees lined up to put their names in a registry, handwritten entries in thick notebooks. In return, they received small booklets to be stamped once for every ration received. As the reality of their predicament crystallized with every passing year, the refugees held on to every bit of proof of home to pass onto their children. These ration booklets would thus accumulate into pieces of identity and inheritance, sometimes framed in museum halls.

When Nazmiyeh walked away from her rapists on that fateful day in 1948 without once being stopped, she understood that Mariam was still with her, that what she saw had not been a hallucination. Mariam's persistent soul protected her. She was sure of it and she never doubted her sister could hear her. So she spoke to her often. At first it baffled Atiyeh to watch his wife speak to no one while she cleaned, while she bathed, washed their clothes. After each salat, she'd say, "Habibti, Mariam." Before they made love, she would call out to Mariam not to watch. In time, Atiyeh grew accustomed to it and even considered that Mariam was perhaps watching over their family from the unseen realm. After all, Nazmiyeh reminded him, hadn't he once been struck mute by the sight of Sulayman?

"Do not doubt an existence merely because you cannot see or hear it, husband," Nazmiyeh said to him. "I know I saw and heard Mariam that day, as I see and hear you now before me. She is the reason we survived our journey here when Zionists went on a killing spree after Sulayman set their soldiers aflame."

When her first child was born, a boy with gray eyes, Nazmiyeh saw only the eyes of her rapist and she cried out to the shadows, "This one is the son of the devil. Is Allah testing me? How can I love this thing? How do I love a son of the devil?" *Astaghfirullah!* The midwife put the baby to Nazmiyeh's teats, but she pushed him away and continued to beseech what she could not see. "Mariam, tell me!"

"You are delirious right now on account of the labor, but your crazy talk better stop before you let this baby starve, woman!" the midwife warned.

Nazmiyeh turned her head and spied something in a dim corner of the room. She grinned, then laughed. It was knotted up and all-wrong laughter. The midwife, a woman from Beit Daras who could remember the hajje who had shat in the river and spoken to the djinn, surmised that Nazmiyeh was her mother's daughter and was at that moment speaking to the forbidden realm. She looked to the corner of the room to see the object of Nazmiyeh's gaze and saw nothing but random papers with childish drawings in an open wooden box. The midwife quickly collected her things, muttering Quranic verses, and left in such a hurry that she forgot to collect her fee from the husband waiting outside.

Atiyeh swaddled his firstborn and stood over Nazmiyeh's deserted eyes. The infant could not be assuaged and Atiyeh tried to coax his wife to feed her baby. He stroked her hair, put the baby in her unwelcoming limp arms, then took him back. He tried to calm the baby, but the crying hunger clawed at both father and son.

"What shall we name our firstborn, Nazmiyeh? How about Mazen? Do you want to be Um Mazen, my love? Let him eat from his mother now."

"Name him Iblis!" she said. Devil.

Atiyeh paced nervously, unable to console the baby boy whose cries echoed now from the abyss of abandonment. Finally, Atiyeh held their son in one arm and swung the other across his wife's face, slapping her with the full force of his angst. "Nazmiyeh! You will feed this child now, woman, or by Allah, I will divorce you!"

Nazmiyeh looked into her husband's face and saw eyes of steel glistening with tears. She reached out her arms, slowly taking her crying child to her breast, and he latched on with a ferocity that first repulsed Nazmiyeh. But soon, her son's suckling created a rhythm that spilled through her until she was a river, fluid and calm. She rocked herself in a languid cadence of maternity, mesmerized by the attachment of his mouth to her breast. Her body continued swaying, mother and son becoming one, and quiet tears dampened her cheeks. Atiyeh took her hand, and his fingers danced with hers, as they had done in an irretrievable time and place on the first Thursday of each month.

Later, she spoke to Mariam. "Please stay with me, sister."

Sometimes Nazmiyeh would ask Mariam to give her a sign that she was still there. "I will never doubt it, sister," she said, nine months pregnant with her fourth child as she crouched bathing

45

the first three, each separated by ten months in age. They were all boys and with every new pregnancy, Nazmiyeh prayed for the girl she was destined to name Alwan. "Maybe give me a sign, sister." Occasionally she would open Mariam's wooden box and leaf through the papers, which bore writing she could not understand. These were times when Nazmiyeh wished she could read. She would put them back gingerly, careful not to tear anything, and place the box on her highest shelf, out of her children's reach, protected between rows of folded clothing.

By the time she delivered her fifth boy, the pain of childbirth had become akin to the chill of winter or the sweat of summer, sometimes difficult to bear, but well known and dealt with. She paced, squatted, and pushed repeatedly until the child was ready and the midwife could pull it out. Nazmiyeh held her breath. "What is it?" she asked. Another boy. She inhaled the room's stale air and closed her face, eyes tight, forehead furrowed, thinking of the next pregancancy she'd have to endure soon, until her daughter, Alwan, could be born. She slowly exhaled her disappointment and asked Allah that the next one be a girl.

FOURTEEN

The beekeeper's widow was related to us only by love. This childless woman was happy anywhere, as long as she could dig her hands into a fertile earth, let life-giving dirt live under her nails, and talk to the plants she grew.

MAMDOUH STARED AT HIS ration booklet, issued by the United Nations Relief and Works Agency (UNRWA), which indicated he was the head of household. But there was no house and there was nothing to hold. He lived in a tent he shared with his sister Nazmiyeh, her husband, Atiyeh, their children, and

Atiyeh's parents. But Mamdouh was rarely there. For much of the first two years after they were forced from Beit Daras, he slept on the sand of Gaza's shore under a canopy of stars. He found work as an assistant to a local blacksmith and gave one third of his earnings to Nazmiyeh and one third to the old beekeeper's widow. He thought it was the right thing to do to honor the man who had been a surrogate father. There was another reason. During the years he had spent as the apprentice, Mamdouh and the beekeeper's youngest daughter, Yasmine, had fallen in love. They had never spoken of it, and certainly never acted on it, for she had been betrothed and then married. Even after her husband had been killed by the Jews, she and Mamdouh had communicated their feelings only in rare glances, when he would arrive to give money to her stepmother.

The beekeeper's widow was a cheerful woman who loved to cook, and that remained unchanged despite war, dispossession, widowhood, and poverty. She was the beekeeper's third wife, not much older than Yasmine herself. And though the two young women had not cared for one another in better times, they became bound by their past as the only two survivors of their family after the war, and they made a tender home together from shared wounds, loss, and the widow's love of food. Her days were spent cooking and securing the best ingredients for the next day's meals. Within weeks of moving into a refugee's life, she had collected her broken heart and scoured the landscape for an open plot of land where she could plant a small garden.

Daily, the beekeeper's widow picked the fruits of her labor for cooking, making herbal remedies, and bartering. She used her vegetables to haggle and bargain for fresh goat's milk, which she churned into butter, heated into curds and yogurt, strained into *labneh*, and filtered and dried into cheese. She traded her beets, cabbage, cucumbers, and potatoes for chickens and eggs. While other women waited in their tents, burdened by shock, mud, and humiliation, immobilized by stagnant days of waiting for the next day's newspaper, for the next ration, waiting for someone to do something, for the rain to come or the sun to set, waiting to go home to Beit Daras, the beekeeper's widow began to suffuse the air with the smell of normality. She inspired other women to invest themselves in their makeshift dwellings and it was not long before women began to gather as they always had, to wash their laundry, gossip, roll grape leaves, sift through rice to remove rocks and rice bugs. Their husbands put up laundry lines for them and built communal kitchens and underground ovens to make bread. In the congestion of national upheaval and a collective sorrow that would deepen to the roots of history and expand through multiple generations, the refugees of Beit Daras went back to their jokes and scandals. And while they waited to go home, babies were born and weddings were planned. The tug of life's sustaining banalities pulled them from their cots into communal spaces, where they prayed together, drank the morning's coffee and afternoon's tea together. The war had been a great equalizer and put everyone, no matter their family name or fortune, into the same canvas tents lined in equally spaced rows in open, shadeless fields. All the children played together and soon they all, boys and girls alike, attended school taught outdoors or in tents. The scoundrels, saints, gossips, mothers, whores, pious, communists, egoists, pleasurists, and all other *ists* went back to their former ways in this new, misshapen fate.

In time, mud bricks and corrugated metal replaced the cloth tents and the refugee camps gave rise to a subculture marked by adamant pride, defiance, and an unwavering insistence on the dignity of home, no matter how long it took or how high the price. The camps would become the epicenter of one of the world's most tangled troubles, and some of the greatest Arab poets and artists would be born from their crowded midst. And there, in the heart of national homelessness, the love and care that the beekeeper's widow injected into every meal made her domain a source of life from which the aromas of onions, rosemary, cinnamon, cardamom, and cilantro drifted throughout the camp, provoking memory, stories, and hope. At mealtime, her place was always full of people. Neighbors, new and old friends. And of course, once a month, Mamdouh came. He would arrive self-consciously, investing great concentration and will to walk with as much symmetry and grace as he could manage. The bullet to his leg during the Naqba had hit his growth plate, stopping it from growing, while the other had stretched on several centimeters more, warping his gait and making his movements awkward. The lift he added inside one shoe helped, but it was not enough.

The beekeeper's widow would prepare Mamdouh's favorite dishes using a special *hashweh* of her own blend of spices with rice and meat to stuff vegetables from her garden. Mamdouh most loved her *koosa*, stuffed zucchini in spicy tomato sauce. The time he could spend in her home on payday was as much of a reward as his earnings, not only for her flavorsome food, but because it afforded him an opportunity to see Yasmine, for it was well known, although unuttered, that he would come to ask for her hand in marriage some day when he had saved enough to start a family.

Indeed, he put aside the other third of his wages for that very reason, and in less than a year, Mamdouh had accumulated enough to seek work in Cairo, where he landed a job with a large construction contractor. Before leaving for Cairo, which was at that time administering Gaza, he took his sister and her husband with him to ask for Yasmine's hand. He offered a modest dowry of two hundred Egyptian pounds and an engagement shabka of a gold necklace with matching dangling earrings. To welcome Yasmine into the family, Nazmiyeh took off one of her own two shabka bangles, which her husband had bought to replace the ones stolen by the soldiers, and she lovingly slipped it on her future sister-in-law's wrist. The women began *zaghareet*, ululations that spread a heart's joy into the air for all to hear.

The trilling announced to the world that Yasmine had accepted, and a spontaneous celebration now began. Neighbors had already congregated outside Yasmine's home in anticipation, for matters of marriage could never be kept secret in Palestinian communities, and now in the close quarters of the refugee camp, everyone knew nearly everything about everyone. Dancing and singing went on into the night. The beekeeper's widow and Nazmiyeh, as the female representatives of bride and groom, announced the official engagement party would happen in two weeks, after which Mamdouh would travel to Cairo alone to work and save for their wedding and new home.

On the day of the official engagement celebration, the beekeeper's widow bought meat on credit from the butcher, whom she would later repay with fresh produce, and prepared a feast of tender lamb cooked in cumin, cinnamon, and allspice and sprinkled with browned pine nuts over a bed of rice; heaps of rolled grape leaves and stuffed zucchini; various salads; *mezze*; and cucumber in yogurt sauce with mint and garlic. It was a meal that the refugees would speak about for weeks to come. "No one can cook like the beekeeper's widow," they all said. And Mamdouh replied, "Indeed, because she cooks with her heart." The women guests spoke fondly of Mamdouh among themselves. He was a fine choice for Yasmine, even though he was lame and had no family except one sister, they said. One woman sucked through her teeth in irrepressible disapproval toward Nazmiyeh. "Everybody knows that woman can give a tongue-lashing with no shame and it's not anything to be proud of," she said. But another neighbor retorted, "Allah protect us from your tongue. That poor woman has been quiet as a mouse, pushing out one baby after another since the war. Bite your tongue and repent. I won't have you talking about Um Mazen like that on her brother's happy day!"

FIFTEEN

Suddenly homeless refugees after Israel took everything, Palestinians were ripe for both pity and exploitation throughout the Arab world, where the brightest Palestinian minds bore fruit for other nations, and once proud farmers chased the call of bread, becoming desperate workers far from their lands. My great-khalo Mamdouh was swept up in that stream of cheap labor that kept carrying him farther and farther away.

IN CAIRO, MAMDOUH WORKED without respite. He lived in a dormitory with other Palestinian laborers. Every day, he awoke to the call of the *adan* beckoning the faithful to prayer and performed the morning salat before heading to his job, and at the end of the day, he would muster the energy for a cup of tea and a light dinner with his comrades before collapsing into bed. Sometimes, he stayed awake to count his money, which he kept in a small purse strapped to his body at all times until he could deliver his earnings to Yasmine for safekeeping. He took two days off each month to travel back to Gaza, where the beekeeper's widow, Yasmine, and Nazmiyeh would have spent the previous day planning and preparing his favorite foods. They would be waiting for him with water warming over a flame so he could have a proper bath, the only one he got each month because only cold water came out of the dormitory tap. A simple cotton dishdasha would have been washed and kissed by the sun on the lines for him, and when he finally arrived, by taxi or rickshaw, the three women of his heart would wrap him with kisses and blessings.

Each time, he brought them small gifts and tales from Cairo. On one such visit, he spoke of news from Kuwait, where oil was pushing up new cities and industries, and a new society of entitled Bedouins was paying Palestinians to do everything from building and staffing their hospitals and schools to cooking their meals and wiping their asses. Several of his Palestinian comrades in Cairo had already moved to Kuwait and spoke fondly of the desert. "I was thinking maybe we could all go there," he suggested, even though he knew his sister Nazmiyeh would never leave Palestine and he wasn't sure his Yasmine would, either. The beekeeper's widow, on the other hand, was ready to soar wherever the wind would take her, except to desert soil, where food could not grow from the ground; and Kuwait was merely a desert by the sea.

Nazmiyeh was in her fifth pregnancy when Mamdouh and Yasmine moved to Kuwait. Before they left, Nazmiyeh held her bother's face, then Yasmine's. She kissed them with tearing eyes and repeated the words that Mariam had deposited in her being: "We will always be together."

Nazmiyeh felt the sting of being the only one of her family left in Gaza, but she knew Mariam was always there, and so was her husband, Atiyeh, a man who fought his own family to defend her. They had never accepted Nazmiyeh and, as more of his brothers married, the band of women who hated his wife grew more vicious under the lead of his mother, who never let it pass that her son had married beneath him. They said Nazmiyeh was bewitched like her mother, Um Mamdouh, and would invite evil wherever she was. Her sharp tongue was proof of the devil in her, they said. They thought she shook her ass purposefully when she walked and said they felt sorry for Atiyeh to have to endure such shame. They said her hijab wasn't tight enough around her head and that she sometimes let her copper curls fall for all to see.

But the isolation they created for Nazmiyeh and Atiyeh only drew them closer. One baby came after another into a life that barely brought enough food, and evenings spent counting coins from each day's catch of fish. It was a life that blossomed tenderly, with routines, silliness, tears, and demands. When the boys were small, Nazmiyeh would harness them two at a time to her back as she toiled, and as they grew, one by one they would accompany their father on his fishing boat in the Mediterranean Sea, where they learned to see magnificence and wonder, and to bow to Allah in humility and gratitude every day surrounded by water for miles. Nazmiyeh would wait on the shore until they disappeared into the sea's expanse. Sometimes, she would stay there a while longer, staring into the mysterious blue between sky and water, singing Mariam's song.

> *O find me*
> *I'll be in that blue*
> *Between sky and water*
> *Where all time is now*
> *And we are the forever*
> *Flowing like a river*

SIXTEEN

When Teta Nazmiyeh talked about her brother, Mamdouh, or my khalo Mazen, her eyes would change. They became empty rooms that she'd enter and hurry to furnish with their stories. It was not nostalgia, but a chore of memory, a task to keep them near.

THREE YEARS AFTER MAMDOUH and Yasmine left, they returned for a visit with their firstborn, a one-year-old boy they had named Mhammad, after Yasmine's father, the old beekeeper of Beit Daras. Nazmiyeh, of course, always pregnant or nursing, and with children dripping from her arms, took in Mhammad and pleaded with her brother to move back to Gaza where the boy could grow up with his cousins and in his own homeland. Even if it wasn't Beit Daras, it was still Palestine. But

Mamdouh had found a place in Kuwait where he was thriving, having ascended rapidly from a laborer to construction foreman. His lack of sufficient schooling was masked by a natural mathematical and spatial prowess. He was deft at reading blueprints and engineering plans, and a well-known Palestinian architect had taken Mamdouh under his tutelage in Kuwait.

"Palestinians are building Kuwait from the sand up," he told Nazmiyeh. "You should see! My mentor is designing the layout of the entire country. Another Palestinian has already established Kuwait's military and still another Palestinian has established its police force. The leading doctors and surgeons are all Palestinian and they are running nearly every domestic ministry, from education to the interior." Mamdouh paused, then announced proudly, "I am going to be an architect."

With so many childbirths close together, Nazmiyeh was never without babies strapped to her back, clinging to her legs, or dangling from her breasts. Though she complained endlessly of their boundless needs, and she swatted at the older ones like irritating flies when they were too demanding or misbehaved, she was always heartbroken when they left for the sea with their father. She would wait at the sandy Mediterranean shore in the void of their absence, watching the roll of one wave follow another. For the man and boys of Nazmiyeh's heart, the enchantment of fishing was also in the homecoming to the woman waiting for them with exuberant anticipation, large meals, and, for Atiyeh, lovemaking that went long into the night, changing forms until his soul would ache, depleted by his love for her.

But their delight was always hampered by Nazmiyeh's despondency when they left. So, during those early years after the Naqba, when Gaza was ruled by Egypt, it was decided that one of the older sons would stay behind when Atiyeh went for overnight fishing trips. It was during one such time in the winter, when twelve-year-old Mazen, her eldest, had remained home as man of the house, that Nazmiyeh had swept through the Nusseirat refugee camp like a tornado, kicking up dust and fury that reminded everyone who knew her why she should not be crossed.

Earlier, just an hour before, Mazen had stormed through the house, tears and fury pumping through his young body, incredulity shaking his voice as he confronted his mother, "Were you raped? Am I the son of your rapist?"

Nazmiyeh stiffened. She stepped away from the vegetables she had been cutting, looked into her son's eyes, gray, almost as blue as the morning sky. Her firstborn who had suckled at her breast longer than any of the others, now on the doorstep of manhood. She took him into her arms, absorbing his rage and humiliation.

"No," she began, with implacable calm. "Who told you that?"

Mazen gave her a name.

"I know that boy," she said and walked out her front door, Mazen following.

She didn't need to go far before spotting the boy with his friends. He ran when he saw her approach, and Nazmiyeh called to the others, "You better stop him or I'll cut off all your ears! Every last one of you!"

They obeyed, frightened of this woman's legendary ire. As she reached the boy, who was squirming to get away from the group holding him, Nazmiyeh grabbed him by the ear and began beating him with her slipper. The more he cried out, the harder she whupped him. People gathered. An elderly man stepped in, demanding Nazmiyeh stop and proclaiming the oneness of Allah to calm her. *La ellah illa Allah*. She did, for not even Nazmiyeh would violate the social order of respecting the elderly. But she continued yelling at the boy, insisting that he reveal who had told him the filth he was spreading.

Later that evening, the boy and his mother and grandmother arrived at Nazmiyeh's home. His recoiled demeanor reminded

55

Nazmiyeh of the day Atiyeh, stunned to silence by Sulayman, had come to their home in Beit Daras to beg her mother's forgiveness. Nazmiyeh smiled, inviting them in for tea.

"Um Mazen, my son told me what he said, and I came here to tell you two things. First, to finish beating my son if you want. Second, that he heard no such thing from my home. It was the old midwife. She said in front of my son that when she delivered Mazen, you screamed he was the son of the devil," the woman said.

"*Tfadalo*, sisters." Nazmiyeh served the tea. "I will deal with the midwife when my husband and sons are back."

The homecoming Atiyeh and his sons had come to expect was replaced this time with business urgency. The mukhtar of the town had been summoned to settle the matter of the midwife's terrible gossip and Atiyeh's arrival was eagerly awaited.

The men convened. Atiyeh, the mukhtar, the midwife's husband, and several elders. The meeting began with coffee and an expression of repentance from the midwife's husband. He assured Atiyeh that he had put his wife in her place and regretted her tongue that had dishonored them both. To rectify, he offered Atiyeh one of his wife's gold bangles. They hadn't much else to give. The mukhtar recommended that Atiyeh accept the offering, which would end the dispute, and he did. They shook hands, embraced, and greeted each cheek of the other in brotherhood, and the meeting ended with tea and sweets. The next day, Nazmiyeh went to the market, her wrist exposed with a new gold bangle, which she flaunted for a week to teach the old midwife a lesson before giving it back, a magnanimous gesture that earned Nazmiyeh the respect and eternal loyalty of the midwife.

No one dared utter a word on the matter again, and the midwife denied ever having had an ill thought about Nazmiyeh. People quickly forgot about it, but doubt was planted in young Mazen's heart and it would germinate in him a deep sense of solitude and a quiet but fierce impulse of national resistance. He stopped going on the fishing trips and became his mother's protector.

SEVENTEEN

Teta Nazmiyeh's legs would sometimes buckle and she'd have to stop whatever she was doing until movement returned to them. This sudden paralysis usually lasted only a few minutes, sometimes a few days. A traditional medicine woman told her not to worry. She said angels were watching over her, that arresting her legs was their way of protecting her from walking into harm. My teta believed it, sure that Mariam was her angel, and proof came during the Six-Day War.

WHEN NAZMIYEH WAS CARRYING her tenth son, in 1967, Israel attacked Egypt, igniting a war that would last only six days and would bring a new generation of Zionist soldiers parading triumphantly into her life. The first one she saw up close wore thick-rimmed black glasses, an irrelevant innocence misplaced in malevolent militarism. His young face was infected with power and coated with the filth of invasion as he pointed his rifle with forbidding authority. Atiyeh and their older sons had been rounded up and taken away in a truck with other men. So, Nazmiyeh was alone with her terrified small children clinging to her caftan when her eyes set upon the soldier and he barked orders at her to walk along. Seized by a dormant rage that provoked her to rush in attack, her legs went limp and she fell to the ground before the soldier could fire at her. Her legs simply folded beneath her. It would be three years before she could walk again. Now forty years old, Nazmiyeh was certain that Mariam had intervened to save her, for she surely would have been shot. Neighbors lifted and carried her to a designated zone while helmeted soldiers in ominous uniforms and tall boots, identical sons of a Zionist bitch, ransacked and looted their homes, raped and killed, burned the land, and renewed the glory of Arab degradation.

The humiliation of that war soaked into their skins. Everyone staggered about drenched in another loss, new rage, and revived fear. People watched on their televisions as this Jewish army of Poles, Austrians, Germans, French, Brits, Italians, Russians, Ukrainians, Iranians, and others marched into Jerusalem, demolishing neighborhoods of non-Jews. It was a shocking moment that split the world in two: those cheering and those crying.

Palestinians cried, but tears always dry up or turn into something else. Eventually, the abnormal was normalized, and the constant brutality of Israeli soldiers became the cost of living. People persevered, and they fought back, too.

Nazmiyeh's legs were still paralyzed when she gave birth to her eleventh son, provoking chatter that reverberated throughout the camp and entrenched Namiyeh's reputation of mastery in matters of the marital bed. Women recalled how her husband had abandoned his entire family for her sake. How he had never looked at other women in that way, much less taken a second wife as some men had. Even now, when Nazmiyeh could not move her legs, she and Atiyeh had found a way to conceive another child. The women of the camp were mesmerized by the questions they dared not ask. How did she do it? They tried to imagine the mechanical details, and more women now sought her counsel in the particulars of intimacy and adventures of the flesh.

Although most women considered it good fortune to have borne so many sons in succession, Nazmiyeh was devastated by childbirth and her inability to bear the daughter she had promised to name Alwan. She cried when the midwife announced that she had borne another boy. Her womb felt tattered. Her legs felt nothing at all. Her heart ached to see Mariam as she put the newborn at her breast to suckle. She exhaled the exhaustion of the years and began to speak to her unseen sister while the midwife, accustomed now to her friend's peculiar postpartum monologues, boiled the placenta for the curative broth that she sold as treatment for various ailments ranging from influenza to sterility. Nazmiyeh's fertile womb had been a source of good revenue for the midwife, for it was thought to be supremely blessed.

"Oh, Mariam. Do you see, my sister?" Nazmiyeh spoke to the ether. "What shall I do now? I may not survive another one. My teats have not been dry in nearly twenty years." No one understood why Nazmiyeh's legs had stopped working, nor how they just as mysteriously walked again. Whatever the reason, it didn't matter. Stories and explanations abounded, only adding to Nazmiyeh's intrigue and legend.

EIGHTEEN

Destiny was redeemed in Teta Nazmiyeh's twelfth and final pregnancy, from which my mother, Alwan, was at last born. It was the same year that my great-khalo Mamdouh called from Kuwait to tell her that his family would soon be moving to Amreeka. To "North Carolina," he said. My teta didn't know where that was, only that it was farther away from her. One of her sons was already engaged and planning to move to Saudi Arabia for work. Rather than returning and regrouping, family were leaving and dispersing. She thought Palestine was scattering farther away at the same time that Israel was moving closer. They confiscated the hills and assembled Jewish-only settler colonies on the most fertile soil. They uprooted indigenous songs, and planted lies in the ground to grow a new story.

NAZMIYEH HELD HER PRECIOUS jewel to her breast, Alwan, the promised child. "She's here, Mariam! She finally arrived, little sister," Nazmiyeh mumbled during the delivery while the midwife collected the placenta and cleaned up the space. As they did with each newborn, Nazmiyeh and Atiyeh lay together, counting the fingers and toes, looking for birthmarks and committing to memory the inconsequential details in another milestone of love.

"Now that we have Alwan, we're not having sex anymore," Nazmiyeh declared.

Atiyeh gave a smirk, unfazed. "That's what you say now. We both know you can't live without it," he said. "Besides, what will you say to all the ladies coming to you for advice? Your abstinence could affect population growth of Palestinians and we'd no longer threaten Israel demographically."

Nazmiyeh laughed. "Okay. I'll give you some of this good stuff for the greater good of Palestine," she said.

The resistance in Gaza was growing and an underground railroad ferried weapons and organized fighters to join the PLO guerrillas. The plot to sabotage Israeli occupation took on a new urgency. At the same time as Alwan turned one, the fighters managed to destroy several gas pipes supplying nearby Jewish-only colonies, causing havoc for Israelis. In celebration, after three weeks of imposed curfew, Nazmiyeh decided to mark the occasion with a birthday party on the beach for Alwan, who was just learning to walk.

The sons built a fire to grill fish and vegetables. Two of them were engaged and brought their fiancées. Mazen, now twenty, still had not chosen a wife and his brothers joked that he was like Yasser Arafat, "married to the resistance." The family sat on blankets, smoked, laughed, and listened to the call of the water, which was too cold for swimming. Other families picnicked along the beach, too, glad to leave their homes after the forbidding curfew. A group of men walked about without their families, and soldiers stood menacingly as they always did at their posts.

Atiyeh said, "Only my wife is more beautiful than the ocean." Nazmiyeh sucked air through her teeth. "What do you want, my husband? I know you want something when you talk sweet like that."

He smiled, puffing on his argileh, and winked at her. "I'll take one of those fish kebabs for now."

She looked flirtatiously at her husband and reached for a kebab, noticing a group of men behind Atiyeh walking leisurely toward them. One of her sons asked his brother if he knew those men. They were strangers. Nazmiyeh didn't recognize them, either. Then one of the men smiled, waving his arm in greeting, calling out in flawless Palestinian Arabic, "Mazen Atiyeh! *Salaam*, brother! How are you doing?"

Mazen's body turned to stone. His brothers closed rank and hardened their faces, too. Atiyeh stood tall, ordering Nazmiyeh to get the little ones away. The strangers may have looked like locals and had the right language skills, but a true Palestinian would never greet his comrade thus while with his family. If at all, first dues and respect would go to the parents or at least the whole gathering, and even then, only the most familiar of friends would approach a man with his entire family. These men had called Mazen's name to make him identify himself, and when they realized their cover was blown, they pulled out their guns.

The armed undercover Israeli agents rushed up, shouting. The fiancées screamed for help while Nazmiyeh plucked her startled children from their sand creations. The women in other families on the beach collected their young, while nearby Palestinian men coalesced in a futile show of force as more soldiers converged. Sand was kicked up and the food trampled. The argileh was knocked over. One of the brothers was pushed into the smoldering charcoal of the grill and his burns reverberated over the tide. Then, a determined defiance pushed up from the chaos. It was Mazen. He had leapt to protect his father and rose above the melee, and when one of the disguised Zionists put a gun to his head, Mazen hardened with a ruthless resolve. Such an immediate threat to Mazen's life brought an instant hush in the crowd, and it unveiled to him a courage he had always hoped lived in his own heart. Or maybe, he thought, it was a lack of attachment to life, a careless embrace of death.

"THIS!" he slapped his chest hard. "IS JUST A BODY!" He hit the flesh over his heart with every word. His gray eyes seemed so sure of grace, so in possession of fate that even his attackers froze in that unpredictable moment teetering between life and massacre.

People could see that the Israelis realized they had captured a prize. If they had been unsure before, they knew now that it had been Mazen, indeed, who had masterminded the sabotage to cut the pipeline to Israeli colonies. Soldiers were pushing others away, cuffing Mazen, but his voice still reigned.

"SHOOT! YOUR GUNS CANNOT KILL ME!" he shouted. "BUT THEY WILL KILL YOU AS SURELY AS MY BODY DIES!"

In the midst of the tumult of pushing, dragging, cuffing, blind-folding, shoving, beating, there remained a quality of stillness, as if the air had ceased moving and hung by the threads of Mazen's stand that day. As if the sun paused its fall in the sky to listen. And it was clear to everyone who witnessed those moments that Mazen had been a leader of the underground resistance. They understood that his defiance and unwillingness to submit quietly meant that the Jews would torture him all the more.

"YOUR BULLET CANNOT TOUCH MY HUMANITY! IT CANNOT TOUCH MY SOUL! IT CANNOT RIP MY ROOTS FROM THE SOIL OF

THIS LAND YOU COVET! WE WILL NOT LET YOU STEAL OUR LAND!"

Spittle foamed in the corners of Mazen's mouth as he was being dragged away, blindfolded and tied. Nazmiyeh could see the propulsion of blood pumping in his protruding veins as she tried to fight off the soldiers, holding on to her son. There was not enough space on that open shore to contain the love she felt. With all the force of that love, she tried to summon Mariam as she entreated Allah to protect her son, to protect them all from these devils.

A soldier thrust the butt of his rifle into Mazen's ribs, and Mazen winced in pain but would not be silenced. They had difficulty dragging him away, as if his feet had spread roots in the ground, and that emboldened others to try to stop the kidnapping. More converged, shouting "Allahu akbar! Allahu akbar!" Israelis began shooting into the crowd and several men fell as the soldiers hurried to their vehicles, hauling their prisoners. Even as Mazen was being stuffed into the back of their jeep, his voice could still be heard.

"SOMEONE LIED TO YOU! THEY TOLD YOU THAT GUNS MAKE YOU STRONG. REAL POWER DOES NOT USE GUNS. REAL MEN DO NOT USE FORCE AMONG WOMEN AND CHILDREN! ALL OF YOU ARE DEAD INSIDE AND YOUR EMPTY DEAD SOULS ARE WHAT WILL FINALLY KILL THIS CRUEL MILITARY STATE!"

The Israelis sped away. In all, they killed four, injured eleven, and kidnapped eight sons and daughters of Palestine that day. People stood on those shores at the crossroads of three continents, where spices and frankinsense had been traded before history was born. Now there was only the crying of mothers over a terrible nobility of resistance and blood in the sand that would be washed by the tide soon enough. "Allahu akbar! Allahu akbar!" they shouted and went about tending to the tediums of endless defeat, treating the wounded and cleaning the dead for burial, calming the children, walking home, cursing the Jews to hell, making dinner, and finally, finding a way to inhabit the night. Thoughts and talk of Mazen Atiyeh, son of Nazmiyeh, inspired imaginations, jammed the phone lines, and dominated coffeehouse conversations. They all contemplated the notion that they were bigger than bullets, even if their bodies were not, and that the Jews were smaller, precisely because of the guns they used to oppress.

The story of Mazen's stand on the beach against armed Israelis soldiers was passed from mouth to ear, gaining new dimensions each time, until it became local legend. It was confirmed that he had been among the top local underground resistance fighters. Naturally, there was anxiety that he might succumb to Israeli torture; so, many of his comrades went into hiding. But the Israelis never came for them. Mazen did not betray them in Israel's dungeons, and that entrenched his heroism all the more. People spoke of his livid courage that day, and it imbued them with a sense of personal power, however small. No one was surprised three months later when Mazen was charged with plotting against the state, convicted on secret evidence, and sentenced to life in prison.

It was then that Nazmiyeh began trying in earnest to summon Sulayman for help.

III

Destiny was inevitably dislocated, and some
pieces got lost on the other side of the
Atlantic and Pacific oceans

NINETEEN

Nur and I never spoke, except in her dreams, but I brought her home. Then brought her home again. Nur was our missing link, the extra clothespin Teta Nazmiyeh needed when she hung the sky. She saw colors in the ways Mariam had.

THE SUN DID NOT fully shine that morning in Charlotte, North Carolina, as if the day was not yet ready to rise. Rain falling on the roof had pitter-pattered pink and saffron drops in Nur's heart, and now the morning was a wet gray, as her grandfather seemed to be. But his color brightened when he saw her walk down the stairs.

"Good morning, habibti." He smiled at Nur, who stood in her footed pajamas, rubbing her eyes with one hand and holding Mahfouz, her bear, in the other.

"It's CCP Saturday!"

Chocolate chip pancakes for breakfast every Saturday. Her *jiddo* rose from his chair. Nur liked to watch his wobbly walk without his cane and special tall shoe. He had one good leg. The other was shorter because a bad soldier had shot his growing plate. There was a rhythm in the way he would swoop lower to step with the short leg and then rise to his full height on the good leg. When he walked, his body moved up and down, side to side, front and back, in a fluid cadence that seemed to Nur like a song.

"What shall we do today, habibti?" He picked her up and headed back to the kitchen, carrying her in the melody of his gait.

"Jiddo, can we go to the duck park and ride the paddleboats and feed the duckies and will you tell me the story about how your growing plate got broke? And can we please also get ice cream? And then let's go to the pottery place and paint some more ceramics. And—"

"Well, that will be a full day for sure, but your old jiddo is going to need a nap sometime in all that. And it's called a *growth plate*, not a growing plate."

Nur imagined a nicely painted pottery plate growing somewhere inside his leg. Sometimes she worried she might break hers, too.

He sat her at the table and returned with pancakes. It was just the two of them and her bear, whose right eye was a green button her grandmother, Yasmine, had sewn to match Nur's eyes, one green and one brown with hazel accents. Teta Yasmine had been in heaven for a while now, Nur couldn't be sure how long, and she had promised her jiddo, on that day when she had found him crying on the sofa, that she would take care of him like her teta had. But for now, jiddo was the one who took care of most things. She knew how to cook cereal, which they often ate when she insisted on preparing dinner. But the most important things to learn were words, her jiddo said. Already, at five, she could read her picture books.

"Jiddo, did my daddy used to eat chocolate chip pancakes? And what did Mahfouz do?" she asked, wanting to hear the answer he gave her every CCP Saturday morning.

"Yes, habibti. He loved them. And we used to have CCP Saturday mornings just like this. Except that Mahfouz would be sitting right by the table, waiting for us to give him scraps, but we couldn't because chocolate isn't good for dogs. So, we gave him doggie treats instead," he said.

"Why did Mahfouz die, Jiddo?"

"When dogs get old, they die and go to heaven."

"Was my daddy old?"

"No, habibti. Sometimes accidents happen and . . . Why don't we talk about happy things on CCP Saturdays. Okay?"

She thought about his answer, her legs swinging under the chair. "Okay. Listen. This is happy." Nur puckered her lips and blew.

"Wow! I think I heard a little whistle come out!"

She took a large bite of pancake that made her cheeks bulge as she chewed, still swinging her legs, and asked through a mouthful, "Jiddo, how come my daddy couldn't see shine colors?"

"Most people can't, habibti. You know I can't, either."

"I know. But how come? How can people tell if someone is mad at them if they can't see shine colors?"

Her jiddo smiled a brilliant pink with sapphire edges. "Habibti, very few people can see colors the way you do. My sister Mariam could. It's such a special gift, I think we should keep it as our secret. What do you think?"

Later, curled in her jiddo's lap as they picnicked by the pond, she asked, "Will you tell me the story again of how they shot your growing plate?"

Her grandfather wanted to tell her that story and a thousand more from Beit Daras, again and again, and her curiosity pleased him. He wanted her to know and never forget the place that burned in his heart. He also insisted that they only speak in Arabic. He once told Nur, "Stories matter. We are composed of our stories. The human heart is made of the words we put in it. If someone ever says mean things to you, don't let those words go into your heart, and be careful not to put mean words in other people's hearts."

"I won't get upset this time. Please tell me," she begged.

"Okay, habibti. But if any part makes you upset, let me know and I'll stop."

Nur's grandfather straightened his robe and took a sip of his Turkish coffee from the demitasse. He liked to take his small propane cooker to these outings to make his coffee because it reminded him of the old days in Beit Daras, when he was a boy and food was cooked over an open flame outdoors. Her grandfather took in a soft breath, a waft of a time long gone, and began.

"We had no choice but to leave. No matter how hard we fought, we were no match for their weapons. Not even when soldiers from Sudan—that's the name of a country, habibti— came to help us. So, we started to leave with everyone else. It was just me and my mother—"

"What about Sulayman?"

"—Okay, yes, I didn't forget about Sulayman. He was with us, too. No, he's not a real person. More like an angel, but only my mother could see him, except that day. We all saw him."

Nur's eyes grew wide. "Then he got big and went into your mommy and everybody said *wow* and it was scary."

Her jiddo smiled, kissed her head. "You must wait for that part. I'm not there yet. People were coming together from all directions on the same path to Gaza. We could still hear the sounds of guns. Bad soldiers appeared along the way, shooting over our heads to make sure we didn't go back to our homes."

"Why did they do that?"

"Because they stole our country."

"Can they steal America, too?" Nur asked, her small brow furrowed in a way that provoked her jiddo to smile.

"You don't have to worry about soldiers coming here," her jiddo assured her. "Anyway, the next thing I knew, my leg wouldn't take another step and I fell. I had been shot . . . in the growth plate and that's why my leg didn't grow anymore."

"I like the way you walk," Nur said. And before her jiddo could answer, she smiled toothily and said, "And I know that makes you happy."

"Well, you're right, but remember, keep the colors between us because other people don't understand."

"I'm a really good secret keeper, Jiddo!"

"But not from your old jiddo, right?"

"You're not old!" Nur said emphatically, and the slight quiver in her chin betrayed her thoughts about Mahfouz, their dog who had died because he got old.

"If I were old, could I do this?" her jiddo asked and proceeded to tickle his granddaughter, whose laughter grew in his heart.

"What happened after the bad people shot your gross plate?"

They continued that way, in and out of time, as little Nur listened to the days of Beit Daras, when her jiddo was a boy named Mamdouh, the beekeeper's apprentice with two sisters and a mother who communed with the djinn.

TWENTY

Exile in America offered a professional career and financial gains that my great-khalo Mamdouh could have only dreamed about anywhere else. "It's a great country," he told Yasmine, who was not entirely convinced. But he believed it, even though exile made him a foreigner, permanently out of place, everywhere. Exile took his son, first by extricating the homeland from his heart and trashing the Arabic on his tongue, then by taking his life in a car accident. His only consolation then was that his Yasmine had been spared the pain.

WHEN HIS GRANDDAUGHTER WAS born, Mamdouh had wanted his son to name her Mariam, a tribute to his beloved sister. Had he and his Yasmine had the good fortune to have another child who was a girl, he'd have named her Mariam. Though Yasmine survived her first encounter with cancer, it took her womb after their only child. But words and stories and dreams remained, trying to find a place in the next generation. Mamdouh and Yasmine had tried to explain this to their son. They had told him it would mean the world to both of them to name their granddaughter Mariam, or—in desperation he had added a compromise—any Arabic name.

"I don't understand why you deny us this simple joy, Mhammad," Yasmine had pleaded with her son.

"Mama, you know I like to be called Mike."

"Mhammad is your name because I'm your mother and that's what I named you. Where did we go wrong? You deny your identity and marry a woman who looks down on us like we're filth. Straighten up, boy!" Yasmine was rarely so stern. But she had felt death creeping along the edges of her days, and that had changed everything. "A man who denies his roots is not a man," she continued, as if Palestine would simply rise up in her son by the sheer force of her anger and grief.

"This is why it's difficult to talk to you. It's always Arab drama and endless Arab guilt."

"Why, my son?" she pleaded. "Why do you insult me? I did not raise you like this. Why does it embarrass you to be an Arab? It is what you are whether you like it or not."

"Mama, I'll talk to my wife!" he said and left.

His wife, a Castillian woman from Madrid, had first refused an Arabic name for her child. Both she and her husband sought to erase his unfortunate heritage from their lives. Why would she allow her daughter to have an Arabic name? So what if it made his mother happy? She was likely to die soon and they would be stuck calling their child by a name that reminded them both of what they'd prefer not to remember. Navigating life in America was hard enough with a name like Mhammad, why would they want their child to suffer, too? "Why do Arabs love to suffer? It's like it gives them more drama to guilt people," she said.

"I know, darling. But you should have seen my mother. She was different this time. I think she believes her end is near."

A compromise was reached. "Mariam" was out of the question because it would give her in-laws too much control. But she agreed to consider another Arabic name, as long as the child's last name would be hers.

Yasmine suggested the name Nur, because that baby was the *nur* of her life, the light of her days, and she died a year later never knowing that her Nur's last name was Valdez.

TWENTY-ONE

There was a time, after his wife had passed away and his son had died, when my great-khalo Mamdouh despaired. Nur was all he had left, and her mother would surely never allow him to see her again. He pleaded with her, crying like a child. He hired lawyers and went to court. In the end, money got him what he wanted. It took all he had, everything he had worked for and saved up. But he had his Nur, and that was enough. He called his sister, my teta Nazmiyeh, to tell her they were coming home, at last.

A S THE WORLD GOT cold and snow began to fall, Nur and her jiddo made the special soup they prepared every year in a large vat and froze in small servings to thaw for winter meals. Her jiddo's cold was making him cough more than usual, so Nur took it upon herself to help out. She already knew how to operate the microwave, and she could get the frozen soup from the freezer by standing on a chair. She felt grown up to make dinner and take it to her jiddo when he was too sick from his cold to get out of bed, where they would play games, read books, and watch television together as they ate. When the special prayer alarm went off, he would climb out of bed so they could perform salat together.

That winter, when the papers cleared and her jiddo got full custody of her, he made two important decisions. First, he said it was time for them to go home to Palestine where they belonged.

He had already bought their tickets and was hoping his car would sell before they were due to leave in three weeks. The second important decision was that their new and very urgent project together was to write a love story, which Nur decided to call *Jiddo and Me*. Her grandfather instructed her to write about her favorite things they did together. She drew pictures and dictated what she wanted to write, since she couldn't yet spell all the words. On several pages, they chronicled the highlights of their frequent trips to the duck park, featuring Nur's artwork of the two of them in a paddleboat and another of her jiddo pushing her on a swing at the castle playground. On other pages, she drew them reading a bedtime story together. Mahfouz, her bear, featured in most pictures, and she wrote a special story about Mahfouz's green and brown button eyes. A full chapter was dedicated to CCP Saturday mornings, a drawing of giant chocolate chip pancakes with a scoop of ice cream on the side. She was certain no other little girl in the world got to eat ice cream every Saturday morning. It was such a privilege that she willingly ate vegetables throughout the week. And some chapters were dedicated to the black-and-white past, where they fixed the only picture her jiddo had of that time. "Is that really you, Jiddo?" Nur asked.

"Yes, I was young then."

"Your legs are the same size."

"Yes, that picture is before I was hurt."

"Is that Mariam?"

"Yes, it is."

"I knew it!"

"And that is my other sister, Nazmiyeh. And this little boy . . . well, it was very strange. We didn't remember seeing him, but we knew all about him and thought he was imaginary. His name was Khaled. He was your great-amto Mariam's friend."

"Yes, I know him. I like the white streak in his hair."

Her jiddo stared more intently at the photo and wiped it to remove any dust. "I never noticed that before."

A week into writing their book, her jiddo's cold became so bad that he couldn't get out of bed for prayers and had to sleep at the hospital. That was when Nur met Nzinga, from the Department of Social Services, or "DSS," who took her to live with a foster family until her jiddo could get better. Daily, she went to the hospital with Nzinga, a tall, beautiful woman who wore a colorful wrap called a *gele*, and who spoke in a funny way because, as Nzinga explained, she came from a country far away called South Africa. On these rides to the hospital, Nur learned phrases in isiZulu and she, in turn, taught Nzinga Arabic words. She would remain there most of the day, talking with her jiddo and working on their book. When her jiddo napped, she chatted with the nurses, pushing all the buttons she was allowed to push, from the vending machines to the elevators. And daily, she shared the progress of her book with various hospital staff, and with Nzinga when she would arrive to take Nur back to her foster family.

As the pages grew thick with stories and pictures, Nur suggested to her jiddo that they make lists of good words for their hearts to hold. "What a wonderful, wonderful idea, Nur!" her jiddo exclaimed, his color brightening to a jubilant yellow that delighted Nur to see, for the shine colors were becoming less and less frequent. Her jiddo had told her that Great-Amto Mariam had stopped seeing colors as she got older, even though occasionally it would still happen when things were "very emotional." She had asked what that meant and her jiddo had explained that emotional things were ones that made her heart feel as if it got warmer, beat faster, or were going to fly out of her chest. Things that made her feel like there was a lump in her throat or that made her want to cry. Nur considered all of those very emotional things now and asked her jiddo which one he felt about her idea to make a list of words to put in their hearts for each other.

He replied, "My heart got warmer and felt like it was flying high in the sky. That's how I always feel when I'm around you, Nur."

They made their lists for each other. She started but ran out of words after, "Nice, Funny, My Favorite Person Ever, and The Best."

Her Jiddo started. "Beautiful, Loving, Light of Jiddo's Life—"

"You're those ones, too. Jiddo, can boys be beautiful? I want that one on my list," she said.

"Boys can be beautiful, of course. Do you think your old jiddo is beautiful?"

"Yeah! Especially when you walk without your special shoe and cane."

"Smart, Caring, Kind, Thoughtful . . ." her jiddo wrote them down slowly, his hand shaking.

"Me too! I mean you, too! I want those on my list. Spell them for me, please. Jiddo, you're good at this list game!" She beamed.

Her jiddo began coughing and pushed the button that made the nurse come in to ask how he was doing. Nur liked to do that, so her jiddo usually told her when it was time so she could push the button herself. But he must have forgotten this time. The nurse made Nur wait on the couch outside the room, just like when it was time for her jiddo to go pee or poo. It made Nur giggle to think about her jiddo going poo.

More nurses rushed past Nur into her jiddo's room. They were taking a long time and would not allow her back in. She thought maybe it was one of those poos that are really hard to get out, when you have to push really hard.

"Not yet," one of the orderlies said. "Why don't you go get something from the vending machine?"

"Sure! I know how to do it myself," she bragged.

Nur had a snack. She went to the hospital chapel to see if Pastor Doug was there, but he wasn't. She stayed in the cafeteria for a while, helping the cafeteria ladies stock up the salad bar, until they told her she needed to run along. When she had gone up and down the elevator several times, insisting she push the buttons for all the passengers, she heard Nzinga yell to hold the elevator.

"Nur! There you are! I've been looking all over for you. We need to go back to your foster family," she said.

"Hi, Nzinga. I have to get my book and my stuff," Nur said.

"I already got everything for you. See," Nzinga said, opening a plastic bag, revealing their handmade book tied with a blue ribbon.

"No! I have to go say bye to Jiddo first," Nur protested, feeling something new inside her, a strange tightness in her heart, moving toward her throat, like a lump.

Nzinga crouched close to Nur's face. "I'm afraid we can't do that, little angel," she said.

Nur could no longer see the colors around people to understand if what they were saying was nice or mean. The lump had gotten bigger and was now stuck in her throat. Her chin quivered and tears formed in her eyes. She couldn't say another word, nor did she know why.

Nur walked out of the hospital, her small arms reaching up to hold Nzinga's hand. She turned her head back, instinctively, to see if her grandfather might have come out of his room and down the elevator to the lobby to say good-bye. But he was not there, and his absence made her heart hurt. It hurt so much that she froze and the lump in her throat exploded in a loud cry. The glass doors ahead of her inspired dread and fear she could not yet understand, and for which she had no vocabulary.

The security guard, who had been Nur's friend at the hospital, walked over to them and Nzinga picked her up.

"I don't want to leave. Please don't make me leave," Nur managed to say, crying. "There's very emotional things."

The guard looked pleadingly at Nzinga, who was equally moved, "Why don't we go to the cafeteria for a while. Would that be okay, Miss?" he said.

Nzinga agreed.

The security guard added, "And I'm going to get your favorite." The immediate thought of a chocolate mousse with whipped cream distracted Nur from the hurting thing in her chest. But she did not smile and she wrapped her arms around Nzinga's neck, afraid to let go. The thing in her chest now felt like a monster. Her jiddo was the person in her life to make monsters disappear from under the bed and banish them from closets. He made everything softer and brighter. And now, when the world was growing darker and a scary thing lurked all around and inside her, Nur pleaded with Nzinga, "Can I please go see my jiddo?"

Although Nzinga did not return her to her jiddo's room, she managed to calm Nur and assuage her fears. They talked about her favorite things. Nur showed her the progress with *Jiddo and Me*, until exhaustion crept into the child's body, and Nzinga carried her to the car.

Two months passed before Nur learned the fate of her jiddo. In that time, she waited patiently for permission to visit him again. "When he's feeling better," her foster mother continued to say. Nur wrote letters to her jiddo in their shared book with the blue ribbon. She added more adjectives to her list of him. Eventually, Nzinga would explain what had happened, but for now, Nur continued praying for him to get better soon, until one of the older girls who shared her room overheard Nur's nightly prayer and said, "Your grandfather is dead. He ain't getting better, stupid. Grow up!"

The earth shook. The moon fell. The stars went out. And the mean girl's words would echo forever in Nur's heart. Faint moonlight seeped in parallel lines through the blinds and fell across the stricken child. Nur's hands were pressed together in prayer and tears streamed from her eyes. She wanted to reach for Mahfouz, her bear, but she was immobilized. She could already feel pieces inside of her loosening and falling, the way beads of a necklace fall apart when the string is broken. If she stayed perfectly still, perhaps her jiddo, the string that connected all the pieces of her, would not be pulled completely away. She knew the mean girl was right. Her jiddo was dead.

At last, she moved. She scooped up Mahfouz, squeezing the stuffed bear her jiddo had given her, and she lived a night of silent, sleepless sorrow, the beaded necklace of her young life unstrung and scattered on the floor.

TWENTY-TWO

My great-khalo Mamdouh had planned to return to Gaza for a visit after Yasmine passed away. He hoped to convince his son to travel with him, to mourn in the bosom of family, where Teta Nazmiyeh, Jiddo Atiyeh, and the old beekeeper's widow held a wake for their Yasmine, whose prolonged absence made her passing all the more painful. But they were happy that Mamdouh would be there soon, until news came that his son was also gone. The accident that had killed Mhammad had broken Mamdouh when he was already broken. He called his sister in Gaza. "There is nothing in the world I want more than to be home now. There is nothing left for me here, but I have to wait a while longer so I can return with Nur." My teta and her brother spoke several times a week after that. Their conversations were almost exclusively about Nur. Teta believed that Mariam lived in her. There could be no other explanation for her mismatched eyes. Then the calls stopped.

WHENEVER NUR HAD ASKED her jiddo about her mother, he would simply say, "She had to leave and I don't know where she went, darling." Soon after he passed away,

Nzinga found her mommy, and the two of them went to meet her in the park.

"You look just like me when I was your age," her mother said and took Nur's hand in hers, then continued speaking with Nzinga. Her mother withdrew her hand for a while to wave it in Nzinga's face to show how angry she was, but Nur grabbed it again as soon as it was within her reach. She concentrated on keeping their hands together as the grown-ups argued about "trust." Her mother was going to have to move back to North Carolina from Texas in order to get any of it. Her mother said, "It's her money. I'm her mother. I should be in charge of the trust. How else can I take care of her? I'm not rich."

Nzinga, who had remained calm, lowered herself to Nur's height and asked her gently to go play while the grown-ups talked.

She was allowed to spend the night with her mother at the motel on that first night, but then she had to wait with the foster family until her mother could move back to North Carolina.

"See what I do for you, Nur," her mother had said from very red lips. "It's because I love you so much." She kissed the child. Nur beamed. She had a real mommy who loved her so much, whose kiss left a red mark on her cheek. Proof.

"We need to do something about your name, though. Nuria is the closest, but that's Catalan, which isn't much better than Arab. Let's call you Nubia," she said. Nur only shook her head, unsure how it was possible to change someone's name. "But that will be our secret. Don't tell the lady from DSS, okay?"

"I won't, Mommy." It was nice to say that word. Mommy. "I'm a good secret keeper."

That night, Nur added that trait to her list: Keeper of Seekrets. And when her mommy agreed to read her a bedtime story, she did not mention the secret book with the blue ribbon that she and her jiddo had written. She knew, in the way that small children just know things, that her mommy would not like *Jiddo and Me*.

It took several months for Nur's mother to move to North Carolina and there were no visits to Texas, just occasional calls to Nur in which her mother gave updates on the lawsuit she had filed to gain control of a trust fund from a large insurance policy. There wasn't enough money, her mother said, to have Nur travel to Texas, even for visits, "until we get the trust."

Nur started school living with her foster family, and it would be many years before she would begin to roam her memories and taste the empty adequacy of foster care: the three sufficient daily meals, white walls and clean floors, chores and strictly enforced regimens, and a room she shared with three other foster girls, much older than she, who spoke with such profanity that Nur tried to stay away from them. Twice she woke up to find writing all over her body. The girls told her she should learn to take a joke and not be a tattletale. They reminded her that she claimed to be a Keeper of Seekrets. So, she stopped sleeping well, lying in fear of what the night might bring. And she was overjoyed when Nzinga came with news that her mother had finally moved to North Carolina, and that Nur would be living with her as soon as DSS could inspect the new home.

The new house had two bedrooms. One was for Nur alone and the other for her mother and Sam, the boyfriend. They all shared one bathroom and spent most of their time in the big room just off the kitchen, where they put a new extra-big television set with wood paneling. "I always wanted a big-ass TV," her mother said.

When the next monthly check came from the trust, Sam

insisted that they use part of it to buy new linens for Nur's room, instead of the oversized white sheet and tattered blanket that her mother had placed on her bed. The mother hesitated. "We still need things for the house."

"We're getting bedding for her," Sam insisted, winking at Nur, who stood smiling, imagining how she would decorate her room to match the new comforter, wondering if she might get sheets with pictures of Wonder Woman, or maybe Cinderella.

"Playing daddy to my daughter is so sexy, baby," her mother said, grabbing between his legs.

Nur squeezed her eyes shut. When she opened them, Sam was smiling at her. Then he and her mother went into their room and closed the door. They made terrible sounds that Nur drowned out with the big-ass TV.

Still, it was better to have a real mommy and her own room, and Nur worked hard to be worthy. She helped clean and learned to make coffee, which was then added to her chores. By the time her mother shuffled out of bed, Nur would already be dressed for school and fresh coffee would be waiting for the adults. Her diligence at home was matched only by her good grades at school. Only in first grade, she was reading and writing at a third-grade level. She had found a way to shine, a space where she could feel love and admiration, if she worked for it. And so she worked and studied as much as she could.

But her happiness didn't feel happy. Suffused in this new life was a longing for something not there. An old man whose walk was a song. Bedtime stories of another world. A duck park and a castle playground. A kind of love that does not require completed chores or exemplary grades. That yearning embedded in her body, and when it stirred, it felt like a bellyache that started in her tummy and went all the way behind her eyes.

TWENTY-THREE

Mama was fourteen years older than Nur. She had already met my father when Teta announced that little Nur was coming to Gaza with my great-khalo Mamdouh. But that didn't stop her from being excited by the prospect of having a little sister around. Teta Nazmiyeh kept calling and calling her brother. She had lived through all manner of disappointment and heartache, but those days of waiting by the phone and dialing endlessly were especially hard on her heart. The nagging panic that she had lost her brother was matched only by the worry that Nur was alone in Amreeka. She prayed constantly, and secretly tried again to summon Sulayman, but answers were not forthcoming, not from the telephone, God, angels, or djinn.

NO ONE TOLD THE news to Nur directly. She plucked bits from conversations and from the new ways that bodies moved around her: her mother's wide-open face, excited phone calls, the hands and attention on her mother's belly. Not only was Nur going to have a new sibling, Sam was going to be her stepdaddy. The wedding date would be set soon.

To celebrate, Sam gave her mommy a fancy catalogue to order whatever she wanted. Nur waited patiently for her turn while her mother went through it. When Nur tried to help, her mother shooed her away.

At last, the catalogue, marked throughout with circles and notes, its pages folded at the edges, was on the coffee table. Nur opened it to the section with models who looked her age. There was much to choose from. Dresses, shoes, socks, skirts, shirts, shorts, sandals, bows, dolls, toys. But she knew to be reasonable. "Not Greedy" was already on her list of good traits. Her mother had gone out and Nur spent her time home alone ruminating over what to pick. Before falling asleep with the catalogue in her arms, she had chosen four items: a blue and white striped dress with a red sash that tied into a big bow in the back, red patent leather shoes with one strap across the top, white stockings, and a stuffed brown dog she already named Malcolm, to be a friend to Mahfouz, her bear. It occurred to her to call them "M&M," and she imagined taking them to school for show and tell.

The doorbell rang repeatedly and loud banging woke Nur on the sofa, the television on and catalogue still in her hands. Her mother was home.

"You shouldn't be up this late," her mother said when she came through the door.

"Mommy, I circled the things I want in the catalogue," Nur began.

"Okay, go to bed, Nubia."

"I only circled four things. I wasn't greedy, at all," she added. "Want to see what I picked?"

"Show me in the morning."

The day finally arrived when the catalogue order was delivered. There were three boxes, two large and one smaller one. Nur's mommy opened one at a time, insisting only grown-ups could open packages. Nur waited as her mother pulled out one item at a time. She unfolded each article of clothing, inspected each pair of shoes and each tube of lipstick. Nur fidgeted, craned her neck to peek inside the open box, each time hoping an item would be for her.

"Yes, it's beautiful," she said when her mother asked if Nur liked the matching baby hat, gloves, and booties. The same scene repeated as the boxes were slowly emptied. Nur did not despair, not even when she realized all the items had been taken out. She began looking through the new clothes; perhaps she had accidentally missed her new dress.

"Where are the things I circled, Mommy?"

"Oh, sweetie. I forgot to tell you!" her mother said. "When I called to place the order they said they were out of the items you picked."

The hard thing that lived in Nur's belly stirred. It moved upward and started clumping in her throat, pushing behind her eyes. The last time Nur had cried, her mother had told her to stop being a crybaby. She had written "Not A Crybaby" on her list. Now, as her mother left the room and Nur stood alone with three empty boxes and the new things strewn about, the memory of that undesirable trait helped to stop the tears. She wanted to ask if the catalogue people would send her things when they got more in, but she knew not to and went to her room instead. There, a silence crept along her edges, wrapping around her small body. The familiar bellyache ran amok inside her. Only when the pain became intense did Nur give herself permission to cry. *Because you're not a crybaby if something is really wrong.* She cried, and cried harder and louder when no one came to check on her. She could hear Sam had returned home. She kept crying out, even though the pain had dissolved, until eventually, her mother came in.

"Mommy, my stomach and my head hurt really bad," she said, relieved to stop crying.

"Nubia, how much attention do you need? You do this kind of stuff every time I make plans. Please try to go to sleep," her mother said, closing the door behind her.

Late into the night, Nur awoke to find Sam sitting on her bed.

"Hi there," he said. "How is your tummy feeling?"

"Better," she said, rubbing sleep from her eyes.

"Let's see here." Sam lifted her gown. "Poor belly." He rubbed her skin. "It's a very pretty belly." He leaned to kiss it, on her belly button, then above it. Then, around it. "And you have the most beautiful and unusual eyes I've ever seen."

He put her gown back, covering her. "Do you think your mommy is mean sometimes?"

Nur shook her head no.

"Come on, tell the truth." He tickled her slightly, making Nur laugh. "Oh, so you're ticklish, too? I'll have to tickle you silly soon."

Nur decided that she loved Sam.

"So, tell me," he asked again.

"Yeah, sometimes Mommy is mean," she admitted.

"Don't worry. I'm going to take good care of you," he said. He tucked her back in, kissed her forehead, then her cheek, and left.

Indeed, Sam began to intervene on Nur's behalf. He took her to buy new clothes to replace what never came from the catalogue. When Sam's niece, who was Nur's age, wanted to be the flower girl at the wedding, Sam insisted that honor was for Nur alone. At a dinner gathering with family, Nur climbed into Sam's lap, taking possession of him, and stuck her tongue out at the niece. Sam squeezed her waist, affirming their secret alliance. He stopped going shopping in the evenings with her mother, staying home instead to babysit. On the first such evening, as they played checkers and Nur tried to cheat, Sam began tickling her. When she could catch her breath between fits of laughter, she begged him to stop. But as soon as he did, she taunted him to provoke more tickling.

"I know a special tickle spot you've never even thought of," he said. "It's a little spot that you tickle and then you feel it all over your body."

"No, you don't! Where?"

"It's a secret. Do you know how to keep a secret? Or are you the kind of little girl that tattles?"

"No way. I never tattle. I'm the best secret keeper." She remembered her list. Keeper of Seekrets.

TWENTY-FOUR

Teta Nazmiyeh woke up one morning in the smog of the previous night, the specters of a terrible dream still clinging to her. In the caverns of sleep, she had walked back to Beit Daras, this time in search of Nur. She found Mariam as before, maneuvered the walls to hide them completely as she could only do in a dream, and said, "This time, we will outsmart them." Then Mariam pointed to an open field hemmed with smoke rising from burning life. A small child stood in the center. "It's Nur," Mariam said. A woman appeared next to her, seated with a phone receiver at her ear, and a man came to undress Nur, fondling her indecently. In the dream Nazmiyeh instinctively leapt across the distance from wall to field, to save Nur. But the soldiers hidden in memory entered, reenacting an old trauma. She sat up in bed when the gun rang out and Mariam fell. My jiddo Atiyeh held her in their bed. "I couldn't outsmart them. Mariam is dead again and Nur is alone and frightened," she sobbed, pursued by the dream.

Nur's third-grade report card arrived studded with gold stars. Sam read it aloud. "It says, 'Nur is a remarkably bright little girl. I am impressed by her reading and writing skills, which exceed her grade level. I would like to propose that she move into the fourth-grade reading class.'"

Pride danced on Nur's face, but then something else immobilized it when her mother reacted. "That's nice. I was a good student in school, too. So you must get that from me. You don't need that fancy school anyway. I went to public school and so can you. Won't that be nice? You can be just like me."

The thing that lived in Nur's belly moved.

"Now that the tuition from the trust is coming to me, we can put that money to better use, for things we really need," her mother added.

Tears rose up and Nur went to her room so no one would call her a crybaby. She remained in her room for hours, listening to the house beyond her door. Her mother's chatter on the phone. The big-ass television. Sam. The two of them doing what they did in their bedroom. She put her hands over her ears. She thought about the fourth-grade reading class. Of an old man's voice in her head, *Words are so important, Nur.* She looked around her room, attentive to irregularities in the paint, slight layers of dust settling on the surfaces of furniture, wrinkles in the curtain, smudges on the door, and details in the fabric of her dress. And a while later, she heard her mother leave.

Then, there was quiet. The quiet of a spooned-out hole in the heart. She pulled out her secret book, untied the blue ribbon, and stared at her list. Stared hard. A void meandered and grew in her belly until two large, bold words rose up, and she added them to her list. There, just under "Never Tattle" and "Never Squeal," Nur wrote "Dirty" and "Bad."

She put her book away, walked out of her room, and went into her mother's bedroom, where she knew Sam was waiting for her.

TWENTY-FIVE

History took us away from our rightful destiny. But with Nur, life hurled her so far that nothing around her resembled anything Palestinian, not even the dislocated lives of exiles. So it was ironic that her life reflected the most basic truth of what it means to be Palestinian, dispossessed, disinherited, and exiled. That to be alone in the world without a family or a clan or land or country means that one must live at the mercy of others. There are those who might take pity and those who will exploit and harm. One lives by the whims of the host, rarely treated with the dignity of a person, nearly always put in place.

A S THE FREQUENCY OF Nur's mysterious illness increased, so did her mother's anger. The school nurse called her once to pick up Nur early because she had a high fever. Her mother arrived shortly afterward, expressing shared concern with the nurse. But as they got to the car, her mother grabbed and squeezed her arm with an unnatural ire.

"There's nothing you won't do for attention! Is there?" Her mother burrowed those words with her nails into Nur's flesh.

"I'm sorry," Nur shrank.

"Shut up and get in."

Nur climbed quietly into the car, dragging the heavy furnace of her body. She knew better than to cry, but she couldn't stop the tears. Her eyes felt heavy and her heart cowered somewhere in a depletion spreading through her.

"I said shush. You're not fooling me with your tears. On top of everything, now you wanna act like the victim?" Her voice rose and words sprayed a now familiar random rage. "THIS IS MY FUCKING WEDDING. I WILL NOT ALLOW YOU TO MAKE IT ALL ABOUT YOU!"

Nur turned her head to look out the window, sucked in one long breath, and there were no more tears. Just like that. At the age of eight. Nur's tears dried up and they would not form again until she was an adult standing on Gaza's shore, the Mediterranean caressing her feet, a folded and refolded letter in her hand.

Later that evening, Nur's mother came into her room, gently asking if she wanted to eat dinner, but she didn't wait for an answer. "I know I was hard on you today, but it's only because I love you. I'm trying to make you a better person. See all the nice things I bought so I can give you a good life? Nobody ever did anything like that for me. I just need you to think about how I feel sometimes. I'm trying to make a good life for all of us, but that means you have to help. Your grandparents and the rest of the family are coming in for the wedding and I'm going to need you to behave and obey, okay? Do you think you can be a good daughter and show everybody what a happy family we are?"

Nur nodded yes.

"Good girl."

The "big day" fell on June 1, the day before Nur's ninth birthday. "I did that on purpose so I could give you the best present ever! The gift of a father and soon twin baby brothers," her mother said.

Various family members arrived from Texas, and Nur's grandparents, her abuelo and abuela, flew in from Florida. "Look at you! You're so pretty!" her abuela exclaimed and continued speaking in Spanish. They seemed happy to see Nur again, and they didn't call her Nubia. Her tía Martina and tío Umberto even remembered her birthday and brought a wrapped gift with a note that said *To our niece, Nur. Love, Tía and Tío.*

"To be honest, Santiago is the one who reminded us!" Nur overheard Tía Martina tell her mother. Nur perked up at the mention of Tío Santiago. Although she had only met him once before, Tío Santiago had instantly become her favorite relative. He had visited for only a few days, spending most of that time with Nur. He had given her guitar lessons and had taken her to the park. Nur had latched on to the attention with all the force she had, and when Tío Santiago had left, she had fallen ill with the familiar bellyache.

Now, a commotion at the front door pulled Nur to the living room. She saw the guitar case first. It was worn, held together with duct tape and bright stickers. Santiago ignored everyone and came to Nur, lifting her off her feet. "Nur! Look how much you have grown! I'm so happy to see you, my awesome rock-star neice!" Although Nur could no longer see feelings in color, she knew this was a vibrant blue moment. Almost like being lifted off the ground by her jiddo. Almost love. Her face, her eyes, heart, skin, hands, and toes smiled.

She stayed by her tío Santiago's side for the rest of the day, even though her abuela remarked that he should tell "the little girl" to go play with kids her own age. But she pretended not to understand, especially because Tío Santiago ignored the comment, too.

On one of the rare occasions when Nur was not with her tío Santiago, she saw him across the room chatting with Sam. Desperation suffused her body, and she felt a sudden and intense hatred of Sam. Nur ran to Tío Santiago, pulling him away, taking full and sole ownership of him with such resolve that Santiago went with her outside where they could speak in private.

"Nur, are you okay, darling?" Santiago said.

Tears that formed behind her eyes but refused to fall were gathering in her belly.

"I have a bellyache," she said.

Santiago crouched to face his niece. "Is there something else, Nurita?"

"I don't want you to talk to Sam!" Nur blurted those words, unsure where they came from.

"Okay, I won't talk to him. But can you tell me why?"

The full weight of her secret pressed on her. Her lips quivered, as if her body's way of coaxing tears that needed to fall. Her breathing quickened and she stiffened. All the words she wanted to say collected in a stagnant cesspool inside her belly. "I don't know. My stomach really hurts, Tío," was all she could muster.

"Have you eaten, Nurita?" Santiago asked and she answered with a slight shake of her head.

"Let's sneak off to the park and get some hot dogs. But we can't be gone long or your mom will be upset with me," Santiago said.

They left through the backyard and walked two blocks to the park. While they were eating their hot dogs, Santiago asked gently, "Nurita, has Sam or anyone ever hurt you or asked you to do something you didn't think was good?"

"No."

Keeper of Seekrets. Never Tattle. Never Squeal.

"Nurita, this is our family, but no matter what they say to you, only believe that you are wonderful."

Nur nodded. "Okay, Tío."

He smiled and added, "And when you're older, do what I did. Get away from them as quickly and as far as you can."

Tío Santiago left that night, without saying good-bye to Nur. She heard the big fight and knew that it was at least partly about her. It happened after Tío Santiago tucked her into bed. She could hear loud voices alternating between English and Spanish. Her mother said Santiago didn't know shit about shit and should stick to being a loser, drug-addict hippie. She said he could talk about her parenting when he became a real man and had kids or at least got a job. Tío Santiago asked her if she knew when was the last time Nur had a meal or even a bath. He said she smelled as if she hadn't bathed in a while. Nur's mother told him to fuck off.

"What is wrong with this family?" Santiago yelled, and then he said the words that became solid objects the moment they hit the air. Words that became a fixture in Nur's life: "She's not an old shoe you can tuck away or throw out when you feel like it."

There it was. An old shoe. The lurking thing inside her, always there, ready to be a bellyache, suddenly took form in the shape of a tattered old shoe. It walked up and down Nur's body as she lay motionless. The old shoe stopped precisely on her belly. There were more voices and then she heard Sam say, "Why is a grown man like you spending time with a pretty little girl, anyway?"

There was a long silence, then a thud and the sound of things breaking before Nur heard her mother scream, "Get the fuck out of my house!"

Doors were slammed and anger seeped into Nur's room from the space under the door and through the keyhole, crawling along the walls, curling her body on itself, and painting her sleep with dread of "the big day" tomorrow.

In the morning, she walked slowly into the hair-raising silence of the house, where she was first greeted by Sam. He was pouring juice into a glass; his left eye was swollen and bruised. The rest of the family was sitting around the table and they all turned to look at Nur.

"Where's Tío Santiago?" Nur asked, her words tiptoeing amid the stillness.

Her mother turned away. Nur didn't know if she should sit down or retreat. Her heart beat faster and harder in her chest. Sam did not speak. She had messed everything up with Sam, and now Tío Santiago was gone. What had she done? Her body trembled.

"I'm sorry, Mommy," Nur said.

"Go back to your room. You were determined to ruin this day from the start and now you got what you wanted." The words clawed at Nur and thickened the air as she sat on her bed, hungry, then lay down, then sat again. The old shoe walked around in her stomach and everything began to hurt. But she stayed in her room, until Sam came hours later with a sandwich, chips, juice, and cookies. She stared at him apologetically, sorry for turning on him. Sorry for hating him.

"I'm sorry, Sam," she said.

"It's okay, my princess. It's good this happened so you can see for yourself who really loves you and who is going to stick by you," Sam said, and Nur flung her arms around him.

"I've missed you," he continued, but Nur did not react. "They're leaving for the rehearsal in a little while and you and I can join them late, okay?"

"Okay."

"Good girl."

He left. Nur ate in her room, happy to ignore the commotion downstairs until there was the sound of a front door opening and closing, followed by car doors opening and closing, car engines starting and fading. Then, there was a silence cracking with the creak of stairs under the weight of someone's feet. She put her book on the bedside stand, *Roll of Thunder, Hear My Cry* by Mildred Taylor. She steadied her fists in her lap, staring at them as the footsteps reached the top step, which creaked the loudest.

Sam walked into her room, "Hey, princess," he said.

Nur was ill throughout the wedding but didn't dare mention the pains in her belly or the fire in her pee, and the next day, she was immobilized by fever. Sam brought her soup and kept checking on her.

"I love you, Nur, you know that, right?"

"I love you, too." Even at the young age of nine, Nur wondered how love could occupy the same space as hatred.

"You remember that lady from the DSS?" Sam asked.

"Yeah."

"She came to the house earlier. Your uncle Santiago is trying to cause trouble between us. He's jealous of what you and I have."

"No he's not!" Nur mustered as much defiance as her limp body would allow.

"Well, you saw how he abandoned you. Who is the person who always stands by you and sticks up for you, Nur? No one will love you like I do, and you have to make sure that you don't say anything that is going to break up our family," Sam said.

"Where's Mom?"

"She's jealous that I love you so much."

"Sam, my stomach really hurts and the walls are moving."

"I'll go get you some ginger ale. That usually helps."

A while later, it could have been minutes or hours, Nur awoke to shouts downstairs. She could hear her mother, Sam, and other strange voices, but she didn't have the strength to get up. The voices came nearer and began up the stairs. She thought she recognized the voice insisting, "Sir, we have a court order. If you don't get out of my way, you will be arrested."

The source of those words came into Nur's room. "Nzinga!" Nur yelled her name, but no sound came out. Nzinga rushed to her bedside, "Jesus lord! Nur?" Then she turned and yelled in her wonderful accent, "Call an ambulance. She's burning up."

Nur blinked, feeling the warmth of her lids slide over her eyes.

"Jesus lord, she's soaking in sweat and urine. What's wrong with you people!" Nzinga panted as someone lifted Nur from the bed.

"I'm really cold," Nur whispered. As she was carried down the stairs, she glimpsed Sam, tears in his eyes. Outside, she caught sight of a policewoman holding her mother's arms. Her mother was screaming at someone. It was Tío Santiago.

Nur closed her heavy eyelids again, returning to the dream that had been interrupted by the commotion. There was a river. A girl named Mariam and a boy named Khaled with a streak of white hair who was teaching Mariam to read. She knew them well from her jiddo's stories long ago. "Nur, it's good to see you again!" Mariam said.

"Will you teach me, too?" Nur asked Khaled.

"You'll learn to read Arabic in college, Nur," Khaled said, and he pointed in the distance to a handsome young man tending to bees. "There's your jiddo." Nur's heart swelled. It burst from her chest and flew. She chased after it, calling to the young beekeeper in the distance, "Jiddo, jiddo! Jiddo, jiddo! It's me, Nur."

She kept calling for him and felt a hand on hers. A woman with an accent called to her, "Oh, baby girl . . ." She looked around and saw Nzinga's metallic blue gele first, then her kind face. There were beeps and lights and white walls. Tío Santiago was there, too.

They spoke, then he kissed Nur's forehead. "You're going to be all right, Nur."

Doctors kept her two more days in the hospital to "make sure the infection has completely cleared." It had been "pretty bad," they said. She was a "lucky girl," because the infection had gone from her tushie all the way into her "kidneys." Her "vagina was bruised inside," like someone had "done something to it." Could she tell them "how that happened"?

She mustered an emphatic "No!" when they asked if her Tío Santiago had hurt her. "It was Sam!"

They didn't make her tell everything. She was allowed to draw pictures to show what Sam had done to her. She thought she had to draw what she had done to Sam, too, so she did, and it made Nzinga cry.

Soon it was time to leave the hospital, with Nzinga once again in her life. This time, at the ripe age of nine, she refused to go until someone brought her secret book and Mahfouz, her bear. Nzinga got them. And on her first night in a new foster home, Nur snuggled with Mahfouz, staring at the cover of her book, contemplating the words *Jiddo and Me*, trying to remember the tenderness that had been. She thought of an old shoe and sensed inside her body there littered so many islands of crusted uncried tears. She looked at the still unopened book and put it aside. Nearly fifteen years would pass before Nur would open that book again, as she searched her memories for Tío Santiago, Jiddo, and a boy named Khaled with a streak of white hair.

TWENTY-SIX

More than two decades would pass before Teta Nazmiyeh finally heard the stories of Nur's life. When Teta looked into those mismatched eyes, she felt as if time had folded on itself, and she gave glory to Allah. She said the most luminous light is found at the other end of darkness. And she said that Nzinga was one of us, that she would always have a home in Gaza.

NZINGA HAD BEEN IN the United States almost two years when she was assigned the case of a little girl named Nur whose sole guardian, her grandfather, was seriously ill. Her task was to secure temporary housing for the girl while she attempted reunification or placement with relatives.

The first time she met Mr. Mamdouh Baraka and his grand-daughter at Charlotte Mercy Hospital, the old man said things to her like, "Thank you, my daughter," and "Yes, my child." It surprised her to hear an Arab man use African linguistic mores that make relatives of strangers. They spoke for a while, and when the little girl had gone out of the room, he gripped her hand, begging with all the force he could gather, "Please help my granddaughter get to our family in Gaza if I don't make it out of here." He showed her the paperwork and flight arrangements, and gave her the name of an old friend in California who could communicate with his sister in Gaza, since Nazmiyeh couldn't speak English.

Nzinga looked at him, unsure of herself, and in the shadows trampling his face was the weight of exile's untouchable loneliness. Specks of age pushed into skin, Muslim Palestinian skin, consigned to peripheries and inferiorities. Displacement had warped his soul and the possibility of leaving his granddaughter alone there deposited in his eyes a wild fear.

Nzinga saw it all and stayed at the hospital longer than she had planned. "I will do everything I can for Nur," she said to the grandfather, "I promise you."

When the sad day came and went, and Nzinga finally met Nur's mother, she understood why Mamdouh had insisted that Nur be sent to her family in Gaza. The mother had little interest in her daughter, claiming to be financially unable to care for Nur, until Nzinga was obliged to inform her that Nur's grandfather had a significant life insurance policy put into a trust fund for Nur's sustenance and education.

Nzinga tried, but she could not make a compelling case for Nur to be sent to live with relatives in another country when her biological mother would take her. Besides, the state would not allow Nur's travel outside of the United States as long as she was a ward of the court. There was nothing Nzinga could do but hand Nur over to her mother. And it pained Nzinga, even if it did not surprise her, that four years later, she was tasked, once again, with finding a home for Nur. After six temporary foster homes and six different schools over the course of two years, a permanent space opened up for Nur at a Southern Baptist children's home in Thomasville, North Carolina, called Mills Home.

TWENTY-SEVEN

Nur had everything we wanted. We thought all Americans did. But for all the security and freedom and opportunity she had; for all the learning and good grades; for all the ways she excelled, Nur was the most devastated person we knew. There was no place in the world for her to be. She could be tolerated, maybe even accepted, as long as she was good. But when she wasn't, she was sent away, abandoned. So she was always trying to be good, submissive, and she panicked when someone got upset with her. Life burrowed holes and tunnels in her. It filled her with an immense silence that grew teeth and claws that cut her from the inside.

MILLS HOME WAS A campus of twenty "cottages" set up by the Southern Baptist Church. Each cottage had a set of "house parents" who cooked for ten to fifteen children.

Nur was twelve years old when Nzinga drove her there on a warm summer day. She noticed that Nzinga had put on weight since the last time she had seen her and she wanted to call her a fatty. She thought about all the mean things she could say to Nzinga. Something about her stupid braids, maybe. But words always got stuck in her throat. She could write them down later. On paper she could tell herself how much she hated Nzinga for moving her from one shitty foster home to another.

"Nur, I know there is terrible hurt inside of you," Nzinga broke the cold silence. "And it didn't help that it has taken so long to find a permanent placement for you."

Placement. Nur was fluent in the jargon of Child Welfare. She was a case of "neglect and sexual abuse without possibility of reunification." It had taken a lot of effort on Nzinga's part to get that classification for Nur so she didn't have to go back to live with her mother. But Nur wondered sometimes if that wouldn't be better than bouncing from one school to another. Always being the new kid who either got bullied or who made friendships that were torn like paper in short order.

Before Nur went to her first foster home, Nzinga had given her a prayer mat with salat clothes. "Your grandfather wanted you to continue to pray as you did together and I gave your mama the mat and clothes he had entrusted to me," Nzinga had said. "But I figure you never got it since I haven't seen you pray like you used to in the hospital with your grandfather."

Nur thanked her for the gift. But her new foster mother made it clear that hers was a Christian home and demanded Nur hand over the rolled up mat. Nur never got it back.

"I'll get a requisition from the county to get you a new prayer mat and salat clothes," Nzinga said the day she picked Nur up to take her to the second foster home. "I should have known better than to put you with that family. I'm sorry, Nur."

"I don't care. I don't want a stupid prayer mat anyway," Nur said.

The second foster home was a three-story row home in Charlotte, where six other foster children lived under the care of a kind elderly woman from Jamaica. She and Nzinga embraced when they arrived. Nur did not react or respond. She stared at whatever inanimate object she could find, a place for her eyes to sit and rest. Her foster mother was kind and Nur adapted to her new home, which started to feel like family. She made friends at her new school and soon began to thrive.

But eight months later, Nzinga arrived to move her once more. All the kids were being moved. Their foster mother's trip to the hospital the day before had left her disabled from a stroke. None of the kids were allowed to visit her and Nur never saw her again. Just like that, family was formed and dismantled, forever.

The third through sixth foster homes were a blur, blending together into a single incident where some older kids pissed in a cup and poured it on her while she slept, then accused her of wetting the bed. Nur didn't know how to retaliate. Everything inside of her, words, rage, humiliation, even joy would try to find a way out, but it all got stuck. In her throat, her belly, behind her eyes. Nothing made its way out. Clots of unuttered words and uncried tears formed and took root, spawning a silence that spread to all her parts, such that everything about her seemed quiet. She breathed and ate quietly. Her eyes were remote, without language. That's how she was the first day she arrived at Mills Home. Mrs. Whitter, her new housemother, a desiccated white woman with exceptionally thin lips, was delighted, "Praise Jesus!" that the "first Muslim child on campus" had been delivered to them. "We love and accept everybody here," she said.

Nur didn't react. She plopped her sights on something insignificant and waited for the greetings, the introductions, the rule readings, the importance of God and Jesus in each cottage, the formalities of yet another "family," to be over. And when Nzinga left, Nur didn't say good-bye.

For the next six years, Nzinga would make the two-hour drive every six months to visit Nur. Only when Nur was fourteen years old did she realize that no other case worker did such a thing for any other kid on campus.

"Why do you always come? It's not even your job," Nur asked, taking a bite of her burger at a local diner where the two usually went on these visits.

Nzinga looked up from her plate, a penetrating smile in her eyes. "You're right that I don't have to come. Why do you think I come?"

"How the hell would I know!" Nur rolled her eyes.

"I already told you not to use curse words around me, little girl!" Nzinga snapped, but even such agitation or anger did not dimish the thing in her eyes that always seemed to smile at Nur.

"I'm sorry, Zingie."

"I liked your grandfather and maybe I like you, too. When you're nice and when you don't use bad words, I like you more," Nzinga said. "How are your grades?"

"Fine."

"Yeah, I know," Nzinga winked at her. "Mrs. Whitter said you were the best student they've had in their cottage."

"Whatever," Nur said, and Nzinga laughed.

Still laughing, Nzinga tucked her lips under her teeth, imitating Mrs. Whitter. "Praise Jesus!" And they both laughed.

"Laughter looks good on you," Nzinga said. "That's how you were when I first met you. The way you and your grandfather were together was probably one of the best love stories I've ever seen. Maybe that's why you're one of the few cases I can't let go of."

Nur looked down, moving food around on her plate. "I can hardly remember what he looks like," she said. "He doesn't even seem real. Like it was all a dream."

"I know what it's like to come from so much love and one day find yourself alone in strange places, without love to hold you together. I had five brothers and every one of them is gone."

Nur smiled and said, "We're cursed." Nzinga smiled, too.

"That's kinda how I feel, Nzinga. Like there's nothing holding me together. Like I'm just made up of a bunch of pieces from different places and it's all taped together and is gonna rip apart if I move too hard or talk too loud or something," Nur said.

Nzinga reached across the table, gently lifting Nur's chin and cradling her cheek in her palm. "You are not going to fall apart. You are more whole and sturdy than most people. Want me to tell you how I know?"

"How?"

"Because I have never met a fourteen-year-old who recognizes the details of their own feelings the way you do. And I have never met a fourteen-year-old who can put language to those feelings the way you just did. In fact, I don't meet too many adults who can do that, either," Nzinga said, narrowing her eyes and concentrating her brow. "Some day, you're gonna make your own family, Nur. I hope you will find your way to the world in your grandfather's heart. He wanted you to know Arabic and know your people in Palestine."

Palestine seemed another planet to Nur. She barely remembered the Arabic she had known as a child. "Whatever," she said.

That night, after Nzinga left, Nur asked Mrs. Whitter to retrieve her book from the cottage safe, but Mrs. Whitter knew nothing of it. She would later learn that Nzinga had rescued it from one of the last foster homes where other kids had gotten their hands on it, scribbling obscenities in it, crossing out Nur's drawings. But for now, Nur thought she had lost it in the moving from one foster home to another, and she despaired. Mrs. Whitter said, "Whatever is wrong, just ask Jesus for help. He loves everybody. But he will love you more if you accept him as your savior." Nur let those words fall on the floor behind her and she didn't turn around to pick them up. She went into her room, turned off the light, and circled her body around memories wrapped in a blue ribbon, entitled *Jiddo and Me*. She thought of the letters to her mother that had gone unanswered, and it occurred to her that Nzinga was the nearest she had ever had to a mother.

She dreamed again that night—as she would repeatedly for years—of a river, a boy named Khaled with a white streak of hair, and a girl named Mariam with a wooden box of papers and pencils, who would greet her in Arabic: "*Salaam ya nur oyoon Mamdouh*." Greetings, light of Mamdouh's eyes. Nur would ask, in Arabic, what they were doing. "Learning language," they would say. "Will you teach me?" Nur would ask. But the boy, Khaled, would shake his head sorrowfully, saying, "You must learn to blink first," then he and Mariam would return to a conversation in Arabic that she could not understand. In the dream Nur would try to blink, but her eyes would dry out, and she would wake in panic.

The strange dream that haunted Nur changed when she began Arabic studies in college. From the first day of class, the children of her dreams by the river were there, with the same words, but this time, she could blink. Khaled held up a chart of the Arabic alphabet and from that point forward, Nur could communicate with them only by blinking. In the dream, Khaled's fingers moved along the letters and she would blink when he came to the letter she needed. Letter by letter, she assembled Arabic words and sentences to communicate with Mariam and Khaled.

Nur would close her eyes each night and open them on the other side, where she could blink and blink to unlock words that lived deep in her, slowly understanding the conversations between Mariam and Khaled. These encounters in her sleep were vivid and became more animated when Nur spent a semester at the American University in Cairo for language immersion. But always in the morning, she would awake in the mist of a vague sense of it all, grasping at threads of a fading dream she knew had been living just moments before. In vain, she would close her eyes to conjure it all again.

IV

We made do with the remains of the day, built
homes from debris, bathed where the fish swam,
created love out of thin air, loaded our slingshots
and scavenged for power in Molotov cocktails

TWENTY-EIGHT

Alwan was my mother; heaven lay beneath her feet. For years after they took her brother Mazen away, she watched my teta Nazmiyeh try to summon Sulayman. But Teta didn't have the gift, so Mama pretended she did. She was only a child but it took Teta a few days to realize her little Alwan was making it all up. Teta pinched her daughter's ear and told her Allah does not like children who lie to their mothers.

ALWAN WAS NOT CONSIDERED beautiful. She was slender, with long features that gave the impression of height, though she was not tall. Her face was made of geometric shapes, with a long triangle for a nose. Her body, too, was angled, with thin limbs and few curves. "Not much for a man to hold on to," her mother-in-law said. Although her individual features were oddly put together, she was not unattractive. Her solitary manner endowed her with a mystery that intrigued the boys, like a puzzle to solve. She was known to be pious and became the only woman in her family to wear niqab, although her mother, Nazmiyeh, eventually convinced her that niqab was un-Islamic. But rumors that she spoke with the djinn followed her from childhood and kept some would-be suitors away.

It was make-believe that she spoke to Sulayman. But when her mother yanked her ear for lying, Alwan sulked for the rest of the day, until Atiyeh returned from the sea. Unlike her mother, who discharged her emotional bile and forgot about it, Alwan held on to hers.

"What's wrong, Alwan?" her father asked.

"Mama twisted my ear because she doesn't believe that I can speak to Sulayman," she said, immediately regretting her words as her father's eyes widened, astonished by a memory resurrected of a long-ago night of terror in the pastures of Beit Daras.

"You speak with djinn? May the devil be banned from this home!"

"Nazmiyyyyyyyeh," Atiyeh called to his wife and immediately began reciting prayers. Alwan started to cry.

He glared at his wife and daughter in silence as they assured him that neither of them could speak with Sulayman or any other djinn. And in this domestic tribunal, the bond of mother and daughter was reinforced with complicity and their shared wish to speak with Sulayman. The next morning, her father called to her after breakfast. "Slip on your sandals, Alwan. We're going."

"Where, Baba? Amto Suraya's?"

"No."

"To buy things?"

He did not answer. She walked along, understanding that now was a time for silence.

They arrived at a sheikh's home and Alwan clutched her father's caftan when she saw the carved-out space where the sheikh's right eye should have been and the white cloud that sheathed his left eye.

"Come here, daughter," the sheikh said, and her father nudged Alwan toward him.

She sat on the cushion next to the scary blind man, fingers buried in her mouth, her eyes beseeching her father to please, please take her home.

The scary man traced her features, trying to see her with his knobbly hands.

Alwan's fingers were still curled into her mouth, and her bottom lip quivered and turned outward as she whimpered.

The blind man read Quranic verses over her for what seemed an eternity. After a while she was not afraid of him but continued to contemplate the space without an eye and the eye with a cloud. She was tired and hungry, but she drank the special water he gave her and stepped over the *babboor* seven times as he instructed. She recited the Fatiha and felt proud when the nice old sheikh with one cloudy eye and an eye-hole complimented her for having memorized an important Quranic chapter at such a young age. He said she must be very smart and she recited more to prove him correct.

"Bravo, Alwan!" said the sweet old man. Her father thanked him and gave him an envelope before they left.

On their way home, they stopped to buy sticky sesame treats, Alwan's favorite.

"Forgive me if I was harsh. You can have whatever candy you want in the store," Atiyeh said, carrying Alwan, whose small arms squeezed her father's neck tighter.

As passing years knead the heart, time would soften Atiyeh, and age would find him an old man telling his grandson Khaled, "All the men who survived the massacre in Beit Daras swore that Sulayman had helped them. Some even said they had seen him strike at the enemies. But I just couldn't have djinn in my house."

Over time, and following the stern instructions she was given that day, thoughts or conversations of the djinn disappeared from Alwan's world. But an aspect of otherworldliness clung to her reserved character, and mothers of would-be suitors, who would rather be safe than sorry, avoided her. On the other hand, Alwan was the daughter of Atiyeh, Abu Mazen, a respectable fisherman and observant Muslim, and her brother, Mazen Atiyeh, was a legendary political prisoner. But Alwan wanted to marry for love, as her mother had. She wanted to live out a story of seduction and romance that grows from a glance to a gaze to breathless longing, and maybe to a forbidden dance of the hands, like her parents had done in Beit Daras on the old rubble of

Greek and Roman glory. Alwan manufactured love stories and lived them out in her imagination, but only there, beneath a disinterested surface.

When Abdel Qader came with his father to ask for her hand in marriage, she was nearly eighteen years old. Her parents, brothers, and friends advised her to accept. He was handsome enough, from a good family, and a hard worker. He too was a refugee in the Nusseirat camp and came with a modest dowry. Best of all, he was a fisherman like her father.

Alwan accepted, and Nazmiyeh erupted in zaghareet, rushing out to share the news with family and neighbors, who added the trilling of their own zaghareet into the air. This spontaneous call among women brought inquiring neighbors and visitors to their home, curious to learn who Alwan would finally marry. Later in the evening, as Nazmiyeh was preparing for bed, she said to Alwan, "I'm too tired right now, but tomorrow we are going to talk about the private affairs of marriage. I have so much to tell you about things I learned with your father."

"*Yumma*, please don't," Alwan pleaded, scandalized.

"You'll change your mind once Abdel Qader gets hold of you and you don't know what the hell to do." Nazmiyeh laughed and turned on her side to sleep.

Abdel Qader had left school at the age of thirteen to help his father on the family boat and since then, he had known few days away from the sea. Even during the Eid holidays when no one worked, Abdel Qader nonetheless sought the rhythm of the ocean rolling beneath him. On shore, he kept the steady pace of a laborer's hands, whether patching or painting the hull or deck of his boat, fixing the plumbing of the two running taps of their home, or building, perhaps, new shelves for his family's belongings that lined the thin walls separating them from the neighbors. Everyone agreed that he was a good and hardworking man, and Alwan could see no reason to refuse when he came to ask for her hand. Alwan's brothers, too, liked Abdel Qader, even though they did not know him well. In fact, few knew him well, not even his fellow fishermen who understood the way the ocean calls a man to solitude. Beneath his kind manners and calm temperament was an impenetrable quietude, like the sea itself, and other fishermen loved him as they loved the sea, knowing they would never plumb the depths or secrets of either.

Before the family could grant final acceptance, however, decency required that Mazen also give his blessing.

TWENTY-NINE

It took three years after Khalo Mazen was arrested before Teta Nazmiyeh could see him again. Thenceforward, her life was metered by visits to the Ramon Prison, and the events of life were counted relative to their proximity to each visit.

ALTHOUGH MAZEN WAS ALLOWED one family visit every six to eight months, Nazmiyeh renewed her application monthly with the Red Cross to travel to the Ramon Prison. Since Mazen was unmarried and without children, only his mother was allowed. On every trip, Nazmiyeh would lament the injustice. "What's going to happen when I die? There will be no one who can visit my son." The prison authorities were unmoved.

On these long-awaited days twice a year, Nazmiyeh would wake at three A.M. Atiyeh and all her children would rise with her in a quiet expectation imbued with prayers they made throughout the night. *Please, our Lord, make it possible for my wife, my mother, to visit my son, our brother. Please allow them a moment of love. Please do not send her home without his voice renewed in her heart.*

Atiyeh would make breakfast for her, and the boys would pack food for the long journey and photographs for Mazen. They would travel with her through the darkness before the sun, across two checkpoints lit with high-beam spotlights from guard towers, wild cats foraging nearby in garbage piles, until they reached the chartered Red Cross bus, which other families of prisoners with the same prayers in their eyes would also board.

On the day she made the journey with news of Alwan's pending engagement, Abdel Qader's family joined them to see Hajje Nazmiyeh off. They brought sweets and letters, even though Nazmiyeh could take neither with her through Israeli security. Atiyeh touched her hand, invoking their private language, and they watched their fingers move in an ancient dance before he kissed Nazmiyeh's forehead. "*Allah ma'ek,* habibti," he said. Allah be with you, my love.

The bus was full, some seats doubled up with mother and child or two siblings huddled together, alternating sleep and anticipation of seeing their kin. Women from various villages, who met only twice a year on these trips, would fill the hours unpacking news of births, scandals, marriages, deaths, gossip, recipes. The children would play games. Some of them would get out of hand running through the bus and inevitably get whacked by a mother or grandmother who had had enough. Hajje Nazmiyeh chided a young boy running up and down the aisle, ordering him to calm down. One dreadful checkpoint after another rose on the horizon. Young soldiers with big guns would get on and off the bus, demanding to see ID cards, sometimes making everyone disembark, line up against this or that. Wait. And wait. Unpack what they were carrying. Wait. Show ID. Wait. Sweat or shiver. Wait. Answer questions:

Why do you cover your hair? Why do you waste your time going through this? Have you ever tasted Jewish dick? It's like candy.

Some soldiers were excessively polite, embarrassed by their jobs. One gave a piece of bubble gum to a little girl. "I am sorry you have to wait so long," he said. The little girl smiled. The mother's eyes were vacant. They all waited. Then they were back on the bus and the thought of seeing the men they love postponed the humiliations. But not for Nazmiyeh. Blocks of hatred stacked up inside her, building in the vast terrain of her thoughts prisons where she could put these soldiers and their heartless mothers to live in darkness forever.

Five hours later, they were waiting outside the prison. They entered and went into small rooms, where they were ordered to disrobe. They waited together in nakedness, trying to keep their eyes on walls and floor tiles. But not Nazmiyeh. She surveyed other women and made comments on the relative firmness of their breasts. "May Allah curse all the Jews for denying your poor husband the juices of those ripe apples." She picked up her own breasts. "Mine used to stand at attention, too. But my hungry husband and babies sucked them dry," she laughed awkwardly, aware and disapproving of her own inappropriate remarks. But no one reproached her. Women have a right to handle these moments in their own ways. Another woman shorn of her hijab, with wilted breasts flattened against her body, muttered a prayer with rote piety, asking Allah for strength for herself and for forgiveness for the *thalemeen*, the oppressors.

Every woman has a right to handle these moments in her own way, indeed. Except this way. "Shut up, woman!" Nazmiyeh's nervous banter turned to ice. "Forgive them? Stupid woman! They have stolen our lives and the lives of our sons. We're standing here like cows ready to be milked, or fucked if they please, and you want Allah to forgive them? Pray He burn them all, or say nothing loud enough for me to hear or so help me with all that burns in my heart now. We are trying to get through this to see our sons. Do not pollute my mood." Nazmiyeh was grateful for this new contempt and she deposited it where breast measurements had been, which she had been clumsily using to fill the space of humiliation carved out with nakedness and a metal detector running between her legs and over her skin by a nonperson soldier. The woman with wilted breasts began to sob quietly as others consoled her and banished the devil with disapproving eyes at Nazmiyeh—*a'ootho billah min al shaytan*—when a female soldier wheeled in a large box of their clothes, and with a gesture of her hand, gave the naked women permission to get dressed.

Another two hours passed before the visitors were called, one by one, to see the prisoners. Women would spring to their feet weightless and disappear behind metal bars and doors. Nazmiyeh leapt when her name was called, and queued up to pass through metal and wood and and guns and soldiers and walls and metal detectors until she could sit in a plastic chair before a thick pane of smudged glass, through which her son looked back at her. He was still so handsome. His hair was dusted with the ash of age and the desolation of his skin was a plea for sun. And though his gray eyes had darkened and deepened, hooded by tired eyelids, they still smoldered with life. For thirty glorious minutes, Nazmiyeh swam in her son's beautiful face. She watched his lips move and heard him through a receiver she pushed hard against her ear, the better to feel his voice. He gave his blessing for Alwan's marriage, pressed his palm against the glass to align with his mother's hand, smiled and reassured her that he was steadfast in fine spirit. Nazmiyeh held up photographs against the glass and he squinted to see the faces of new nephews and nieces, growing siblings and old friends. He told his mother of new and old inmates and some legendary political prisoners, but they never delved deeper because everything they discussed was recorded. Whatever the weather outside, in that small room with plastic chairs and a glass barrier between mother and son, the sky was clear and the air fresh. The sun shone and the moon smiled and the stars winked. Rivers flowed clean and the trees danced with the wind. Nazmiyeh greedily soaked it all up, committing to memory every word from her son. Every love note from his eyes. She concentrated on recording it all so she could replay it for herself and count the hairs of his mustache if she wanted. To replay the lyrics of his face.

The buzz of the alarm went off, signaling that their time together was over. Mother and son held one another in the tight grip of sight, safeguarding the memory of the previous thirty minutes.

The women were searched again before they left. The nakedness, box of clothes, metal detectors, bars and doors and walls and wasted time were the same, but humiliation did not penetrate them. They stood silently inside themselves, in the dignity of small rooms they built in their hearts, with plastic chairs, smudgy glass, and love songs. They remained in that space for the hours that followed on the bus, through checkpoints and a dimming sky. The mischievous boy who had been chided by Nazmiyeh was at it again on the way home. Nazmiyeh smiled this time and pulled him near. "You're a handsome boy, my son. Here," she said, giving him a sweet from her bag.

THIRTY

Teta Nazmiyeh and Jiddo Atiyeh had a special dance they did with their hands. Teta said it was how they told each other secrets. I wasn't born yet, but I know their hands danced the day my parents married. And I know they interlaced in languid foreboding after the wedding.

LIKE ALL WEDDINGS IN the camp, Alwan and Abdel Qader's union brought hundreds of guests and thousands of onlookers into the streets and alleyways. There seemed to be much curiosity and anticipation for this union. Two separate *zaffehs* danced throughout the streets, one holding up the bride in white on a chair and one for the groom on a horse, both chair and horse adorned with flowers and flags. Women and men sang and hollered their prayers to the heavens, leaving a charmed wake that rose to the balconies filled with onlookers lining the alleyways.

It was Hajje Nazmiyeh's joy, most of all. She danced and sang throughout the streets. Had people not been accustomed to her outrageous ways and kind heart, they'd have been scandalized by a grown woman in a traditional embroidered thobe trying to shake her hips in public. Instead, they clapped and sang with her. She carried two framed photos—a portrait of Mazen and a photo of Mamdouh and Yasmine—and held them up at times when she danced, to include absent family in the only way she knew how.

Mamdouh had been expected to arrive from America in time for the wedding. He had finally received the papers for full custody he needed to leave the country with his granddaughter, Nur. He was returning to Palestine with the newest member of their family, for good. From photographs he had sent, Nazmiyeh had been astonished to see that Nur had inherited Mariam's eyes. She held a photo of little Nur and cried, believing that Mariam somehow lived in her. Mamdouh had also confided that he thought Nur saw colors in the way their sister had years earlier, which only intrigued Nazmiyeh more and increased her anticipation to meet her grand-niece. At last everything was falling into place. Falling into love.

It had been nearly eight years since she had seen her brother and Yasmine. They had come for a visit with great longing, hungry for home, and they brought two suitcases of gifts from America. When they heard the adan beckon, Yasmine cried. They closed their eyes and inhaled deeply the smells of the souq and they drank in the breeze off Gaza's sea. Nazmiyeh doted on them and kept them close. The old beekeeper's widow came and went daily, cooking for them. Nazmiyeh and Yasmine held hands like school-girls when they walked and stayed up late talking night after night. They smoked argileh every evening and filled the hours reliving stories of people and places in a time just under the thin skin of the eyelid. Nazmiyeh's grandchildren, not much younger than Alwan, who was a still a young girl, consumed those stories, protesting when their mothers pulled them away to go home, and then dreaming of Beit Daras. Of a river. Of a woman who spoke with the djinn and a girl named Mariam who taught herself to read.

When the inevitable day of their departure arrived, the family was inconsolable. Mamdouh and Yasmine would have stayed and never gone back to America, but for their son, who had refused to return with them. He was in college, engaged to a Spanish woman. Both Nazmiyeh and Yasmine prayed hard to hasten a breakup between them. Their son, Mhammad, had been to Gaza before Alwan could remember. He could not, or was unwilling to, speak Arabic and complained about everything from the food to what he perceived as a lack of sanitation.

Alwan's brothers wanted to give him a well-earned beating but Nazmiyeh intervened, though later regretted it. "That's what happens when you only have one child. They never get the mean and nasty beaten out of them by their parents or siblings. I should have let our boys whup him. Would have done him some good," she had said to Atiyeh.

In the years after that visit, their son married the Spanish woman and had a daughter, Nur. Yasmine's cancer returned and she soon passed away. Then Mhammad died in a car accident and Mamdouh bowed in gratitude to Allah for sparing his beloved Yasmine the heartbreak of losing her only child. It was then that Mamdouh resolved to return to Gaza for good, but not without Nur. "Come home, brother," Nazmiyeh had pleaded. "There is no dignity in life or death away from your home and family."

It had taken a few years, all his money, and long legal procedures to gain full custody of Nur. And when he finally did, Nazmiyeh's happiness was as big as God's outdoors. Now, her only daughter was going to be married, her brother was finally coming home, bringing Nur, her only niece, who was perhaps inhabited by Mariam's spirit—and someday, she was sure of it, Allah would bring Mazen home, too. Allahu akbar!

Although Nazmiyeh was disappointed when her brother called to say he had fallen ill and had to delay his trip, she was not too concerned. He assured her their reunion was a matter of short time. She proposed delaying the wedding, but Mamdouh insisted that everything go on as planned; he would be there soon enough. "Enshallah, our family will be whole again."

Shortly after the wedding, Mamdouh began to call several times a week. He was in the hospital, and though he tried to assure Nazmiyeh that all would be well, she sensed otherwise. He had a lung infection, he said. Infections always clear up with antibiotics. He said he would be home soon. His long exile would be over. Exile, he said, had stolen everything. It had excised his home and heritage and language from his only son. It had taken his Yasmine. Exile had made him an old man in a place that had never become familiar. But life had been merciful, too, for he had a gift of this miracle granddaughter, who could now return home to Gaza with him. Already, she could speak Arabic and her appetite for stories of Palestine was endless. They were making a book together, of all the things they loved. "It's called *Jiddo and Me*," he told his sister.

"May God keep you both in the palms of love and extend your life, brother, to be both father and grandfather to her," Nazmiyeh had replied, but in her heart she wanted to ask why the urgency for such nostalgia.

Then the calls stopped.

Nazmiyeh dialed his number, but only heard an automated message in English, which she could not understand. She asked Alwan to give it a try and got the same effect, then she demanded one of her sons try, believing that both she and Alwan were dialing incorrectly. He got the same message and Nazmiyeh stomped off, cursing her children for their inability to perform the simplest task of getting another person on the phone. She would get up several times at night to check the yellow phone in the big room. Then she laid a makeshift bed, a mat and pillow, next to the yellow phone and slept in the family room, waking frequently to check it for a dial tone. She would dream that Mamdouh called and would rise grasping at the smoke of that dream, trying to will it into reality. At meals, they pulled the phone beside her. When one of her grandchildren bragged about his report card, she immediately demanded he try dialing her brother's telephone number. "You're the smartest of everyone. I'm sure you can dial properly," she said.

The boy, only eleven years old, looked around at the equally bewildered adults as he dialed the yellow rotary phone, one number arc at a time.

"It's okay, son. We just keep trying and then it will work eventually," she said at the sound of that wretched American automated message, and she took the phone back, checking the receiver again to ensure a dial tone.

Finally, the yellow telephone rang. Nazmiyeh, two of her daughters-in-law, and the newlywed Alwan were in the local market buying fruits and vegetables for their *jomaa* meal the following day. She had agreed to leave her yellow telephone because Abu Bara'a, the spice merchant, had a red telephone. Atiyeh had promised that he'd direct any caller there, and he was hurrying to the market as the red telephone rang. A disbelieving Abu Bara'a handed it to Nazmiyeh, who was seated in his shop, sipping tea. Nazmiyeh's eyes widened and she yelled for everyone who could hear to quiet as she answered.

"Mamdouuuh. Mamdouuuh. Is that you, my brother? Mamdouh?" Those moments appeared on her face as an inconceivable smile and as they passed, the smile fell. The sky fell. Beit Daras fell. Nazmiyeh fell to her knees and slumped to the floor. She held her face in her hands, the telephone at her ear.

From the epicenter of Nazmiyeh's body, flanked by her daughter and daughters-in-law, concentric rings of silence rippled through the bustle of the market. Merchants left their customers to look on helplessly, and haggling was transformed into hushed whispers that Hajje Nazmiyeh had received The Call, and the news it brought was what they all had feared.

The call had come from an old friend of Mamdouh in California. He was a Palestinian who had known Mamdouh since he first arrived in the United States. Nazmiyeh knew of him and had even spoken to him before on the telephone once when Mamdouh and Yasmine had called her years earlier. The man was deeply saddened and sorry to have to make such a call. There was a package of Mamdouh's personal belongings that could not be kept with Nur because she was too young.

He promised to send the package he had received from the child welfare department. Mamdouh had asked him to make sure that Nur was sent to Gaza to live with her family, instead of foster care, but Nur was being reunited with her mother. There was nothing he could do. Nazmiyeh could hear tears in his words. There was no way to take Nur out of the country. He was sure that she was being raised Christian. Her mother would not allow him to speak with Nur. "I'm an old man here. A foreigner. I wish I could do more," he said.

Nazmiyeh sat in that place on earth and the weight of her heartbreak conspired with gravity, collapsing her further, turning her into a body of dense silence.

A woman whispered in the crowd, "What's going on?"

"Hajje Nazmiyeh got the call. *Enna lillah wa inna elayhi raji'oon.* May He have mercy on her brother's soul," someone responded.

THIRTY-ONE

My mother loved quietly and lived as if she watched the world through slits in the curtains. People thought piety provoked her to don the niqab when she was young, but it was to complete her invisibility—to take the curtains with her while she roamed her own life. But my father saw her. He stepped behind the curtain and loved her there. When she decided to take off the niqab, people thought it was because of Teta Nazmiyeh's nagging. It was really for Baba. He never asked for it, but she knew he wanted the assurance of her face, all of it, in all the spaces of his life.

THE YEARS BROUGHT ALWAN several miscarriages and a stillborn baby. They brought expropriation of land and Israeli settlers and more soldiers. Jewish-only settlements and checkpoints carved the hills, and fate excavated Alwan's womb.

Though the early years of her marriage to Abdel Qader were hopeful and loving and sweet, shadows began to accumulate in the corners, and the disapproving eyes of his mother collected in her empty belly. The desert of her womb swelled until it occupied the whole of her thoughts and filled the rooms where she stood. "I understand if you want to take another wife, my love. I just ask that you not divorce me," she said to her husband five years after their wedding.

"We get in life only what Allah wills, habibti. Let's just put this in His hands for now," Abdel Qader said.

He had indeed considered the matter of a second wife, mostly because his mother had become increasingly more vocal in lamenting his childless fate, but he feared that his seed, not Alwan's womb, might be the problem. It was in those days that Abdel Qader agreed to move into Alwan's family home. Her brothers had built their dwellings nearby and one had made his home by building a new floor on the family home. Only Alwan's parents lived in their house now and Alwan's bedroom was still empty. The choice to live there brought renewed vigor and optimism to them both. A raw decision had been made somewhere along the way, in the quiet places of the heart that do not know words, that they would be content with Allah's will. They communicated this acceptance of fate in the marital language of intimacy. It was unuttered, but understood from the way they made love on their first night in Alwan's old bed— disengaged from expectation, passionate. Alwan saw it in her husband's eyes and cried from the pleasure of it. Abdel Qader held her tight, caressed her hard, kissed her deeply. It was a hunger, almost violent, that awakened in her an unfamiliar and unrestrained appetite. They consumed one another that night and carved with their mouths, teeth, and nails places of refuge in the other, where they left pieces of their hearts in each other's body.

It happened again that Alwan became pregnant, but they dared not hope. Her belly continued to grow, unimpeded by the assumption of birth, even in the ninth month of gestation. Atiyeh and Abdel Qader were at sea when Alwan went into labor, but she forbade her mother to send word to them. She wanted to spare her husband, to bear the disappointment alone. She refused to go to the hospital, insisting on privacy in another hour of misfortune. So Nazmiyeh called the midwife and together they delivered a baby boy after only four hours of labor.

Thus I was born. On December 27, 1998, three weeks before Teta's next scheduled visit with Khalo Mazen.

THIRTY-TWO

I don't know who named me, or when. Mariam called me Khaled, but I don't know if I told her that was my name or if she called me that so my teta would name Khaled when I was born. In that way, it was Mariam who named me before I was born, after I went into the blue at the age of ten. I know it doesn't make sense. I'm sorry I can't tell it any other way.

NAZMIYEH LIFTED THE CRYING baby boy grandchild and Alwan's heart sank when she saw her mother's stricken face. "What's wrong with him?" Alwan demanded.

Nazmiyeh looked at her daughter, then back at the infant. "Khaled. Name him Khaled. He's a beautiful healthy boy," Nazmiyeh said, putting her grandson to her daughter's chest. Allahu akbar!

Overjoyed, Alwan took her precious boy. Khaled. She liked the name, but she insisted they wait for Abdel Qader.

Nazmiyeh immediately sent word for Atiyeh and Abdel Qader to return at once. News reached those closest first and soon their home was crowded with friends and relatives. Alwan's brothers, their families, and their in-laws came, as did Abdel Qader's siblings and their families. Alwan's mother-in-law abandoned her grouchiness and came with good cheer. Neighbors flocked to see. *Allahu akbar*, they all said. Congratulations, may Allah bless and protect this child. Allah is all knowing and merciful. And while they mingled in the big room, spilling outside into the alleyways, they were allowed to see Alwan briefly, but not baby Khaled. Hajje Nazmiyeh forbade anyone from seeing or holding Khaled, except the mother-in-law and later Atiyeh and Abdel Qader. She claimed it was about germs, but in truth she was afraid to tempt fate. She feared the curse of hassad, the malice of hot, envious eyes. Not until she could dress her grandson with a blue amulet to ward off the evil eye, and recite protective Quranic verses over him, would she permit others near him.

Atiyeh and Abdel Qader returned to shore as quickly as they could. By the time they arrived, their home was full and the name Khaled had stuck, even though Abdel Qader had originally planned to name him Mhammad, after his own father.

Abdel Qader held his boy, his eyes brimming, and others cleared the room, making space for a new family's togetherness. In a tender solitude of their own making, Alwan and Abdel Qader marveled at their baby, inspected his pinched placenta cord, playfully praised Allah for the healthy endowment between his legs, watched him suckle from Alwan's breast, kissed him and consumed his scent, and gave boundless thanks for Allah's generosity. Allahu akbar.

As is the Arab way, Khaled's second name was his father's name, his third name was his grandfather's, and so on, followed by the family name. So he was Khaled Abdel Qader Mhammad Ghassan Maqademeh. And just as children take their names from their fathers and grandfathers, they in turn name their parents. Thus, from that day forward, Abdel Qader became known as Abu Khaled and Alwan was Um Khaled.

THIRTY-THREE

Teta Nazmiyeh was the one who cut my umbilical cord. She said she knew I would be her favorite grandson from the moment she held me. But that was our secret and I kept it.

WHEN ALWAN AND ABDEL Qader's son, Khaled, was born, Hajje Nazmiyeh thought he had been in the world far longer. She was the first to get a good look at him. Holding her newborn grandson in the name of Allah, the most merciful, most forgiving, she nearly dropped him when she saw the tuft of white hair at the top of his black mane, remembering her sister Mariam's words: *Khaled has a white streak in his hair.* Allah was all knowing and mysterious in His ways. She tried to contemplate what it meant, but she became tangled and confused in her own thoughts. *Foolish old woman* was her final word to herself on the matter, but that did not prevent her years later, as Khaled learned to speak, from asking him if he knew or dreamed about a girl named Mariam.

"No" was the consistent answer, however creatively she framed the question.

Despite the growing encroachment of Israeli colonies and menacing guard towers, the family lived their days sustained by gifts of the sea, daily chores and toils, rumors and gossip, politics and defiance, and love. As all of Hajje Nazmiyeh's sons married and began having children, she was surrounded daily by a regiment of grandchildren who petted her and competed for her affection. They were cousins who divided, fought, and united according to the current alignments of their mothers, whose jealousies and arguments provided a shifting landscape of allegiances. The wars of the daughters-in-law were sometimes firestorms of curses and sometimes icebergs that got dragged into Hajje Nazmiyeh's kitchen on Fridays when they all gathered for the jomaa family meal after the noon prayers. And just as much as these jomaa gatherings were occasions for treaties, they were also battlegrounds, where biting remarks and gloating stares were flung across furniture, eyes were rolled, brows were furrowed, and feet were stomped. But there were lines they dared not cross. Allah's name could never be invoked except in reverence, vulgar curses were not allowed, and Hajje Nazmiyeh's word was always final, her authority absolute in matters of family disputes.

The jomaa ghada at Hajje Nazmiyeh's would set the tone for the rest of the week. When one of the sisters-in-law came flaunting a new dress—"My husband bought it for me for no reason at all"—the others pouted for days, demanding of their husbands, "Why can't you be like your brother and buy me presents every once in a while for no reason?"

The same happened with new furniture and appliances. It happened often enough that the brothers finally implored one another to ensure their wives would not provoke such jealous havoc. But in vain. When one of them became pregnant, Nazmiyeh joked to the other wives, "Looks like the rest of my sons are going to be happy in the coming weeks because I know the rest of you will try to get pregnant, too." Alwan begged her mother to stop speaking like that. "They might think you're serious," she said.

"Who said I wasn't serious, my daughter?" Nazmiyeh smirked. "You just wait. In a few weeks' time, at least two of them are gonna come back and say they're pregnant."

Alwan read the Quran more often, as if to offset her mother's unseemly speech. In the domestic wars between the sisters-in-law, Alwan was neutral ground. Nothing in her nature provoked the others. She was Hajje Nazmiyeh's only daughter, not very attractive, and she had only one son and a husband who was odd and remote. She was also the closest to Hajje Nazmiyeh, the glue that held all the siblings together and forced the wives to share their lives and children with one another. Hajje Nazmiyeh was the wisecracking matriarch that the other matriarchs loved and hated in equal measure. She was perhaps the only matriarch who was referred to by her first name. All mothers were addressed as Um so and so. It was not a sign of disrespect that Nazmiyeh was not identified by her relation to anyone else, but a testament to the force of her being, a mixture of defiance, motherliness, kindness, sexuality, and sassiness. No son or husband could rename her. People were drawn to her. Her children and grandchildren doted on her and kissed her hands when they joined or left her presence. She was the mother-in-law who taught her new daughters how to cook meals the way their husbands liked them. She made them all blush with her questions. "Does my son know what he's doing in bed? If he doesn't, you shouldn't be afraid to teach him." She made them laugh. And when they needed to cry, they found a tender place to do so on her shoulder. Without realizing it, these women who thought they disliked one another became bound in sisterhood under Hajje Nazmiyeh's aegis, and it showed in times of trial, like the day Hajje Nazmiyeh got the call about her brother, or in the coming years, when the sky crumbled, raining death on their roofs.

THIRTY-FOUR

No one noticed my first "episode," when I went in and out of the quiet blue. It was a day like any other. I was perhaps six, walking to school with my cousins and friends, when settlers descended from their perch. Jewish women pushing their babies in strollers, their older children marching along. I saw it immediately, the jubilant venom of bullies out for fun. We all scattered to take cover as the settler kids, under the watch of their mothers, hurled stones and broken bottles at us. Just before the world drenched me in a silent blue, I felt the hot wetness of my urine stream down my pants, against my leg. The next thing I recalled was my cousin chastising me as we huddled behind a boulder, "Next time don't just stand there like a dumb donkey. If I hadn't dragged you away, the Jews would have gotten you."

T HE DAY CAME WHEN Israel removed its settlers. The world said it was as if Israel had cut off one of its limbs for the sake of peace. Palestinians in Gaza sucked air through their teeth and rolled their eyes. Isn't that something, they said. They steal and steal, kill and maim, and they're so brave for giving it back after they've depleted the soil of clean water and nutrients. To hell with them, they said, roaming the refreshing absence where settlers had been. Hajje Nazmiyeh started speaking with Mariam again, asking for signs. She didn't know for what. She warned against so much celebration. "Light will cast shadows," she reminded people.

Soon thereafter, Atiyeh passed quietly in his sleep. It was not unexpected, for he had already acquired the qualities of the dying—endless patience and deep wisdom, shuffling feet, trembling hands, and random smiles. Sometimes, with no apparent provocation, his hands and Nazmiyeh's would find one another—watching television, eating, cleaning the dishes, or in bed—and their fingers would engage in their ageless private tango, born so long ago of forbidden longing amid remnants of a bygone castle and citadel. They both knew an ending was near, but they never spoke of it except in the quiet dance of their hands. Still, his death was shattering. It made Nazmiyeh suddenly an old woman, the youth she spent in love now buried in a grave. Nazmiyeh removed her colorful scarf and tied black grief in its place. She watched in anguished nostalgia as her sons washed, carried, and buried their father. They gathered around their mother and kissed her feet as the Quran intoned from the sound box, its hypnotic melody moving through mourning bodies. People came with condolences and left in respect.

Around the slow motion of the family's loss, Palestinian factions fought one another and when the faction less conciliatory to Israel won, Israel locked down the whole of Gaza, cordoning off even the sea.

From that day onward, Hajje Nazmiyeh slipped into the soothing blackness of widowhood, and she never added color except the embroidered stitches of heritage on her thobe. Abdel Qader kissed his mother-in-law's hand, asking Allah to add many years to her life, and from the sea that lived inside him, he said, "At least Abu Mazen died naturally." At least Zionists had not killed him.

THIRTY-FIVE

An American girl named Rachel Corrie came to live in Gaza. Her beauty touched us all. All twelve million of us Palestinians around the world. In a letter she wrote from Gaza to her mama in America, she said, "I spent a lot of time writing about the disappointment of discovering, somewhat first-hand, the degree of evil of which we are still capable . . . I am also discovering a degree of strength and of basic ability for humans to remain human in the direst of circumstances . . . I think the word is dignity."

ALWAN, UM KHALED, HAD another pregnancy in 2003, which progressed late enough to identify the gender before she miscarried. Her husband had been telling his fishing comrades he was having a girl. And that's why Abdel Qader blamed himself for the miscarriage. He had spoken with authority of things that are the exclusive domain of Allah. Still, he grieved, but he soon resigned to his characteristic surrender to Allah's will.

"It was not our lot to have this child, Um Khaled," Abdel Qader tried to console his wife. "We will try again. Enshallah, we will have our Rachel, habibti," he said, as he sought Allah's pardon.

Alwan took courage and protested, "Everyone is naming their daughters Rachel, Abu Khaled. I don't want that name. It's not even Arabic and we don't know what the English name actually means."

"Alwan, we agreed. You named the first one. I will name the next," he said, sure of victory in this domestic disagreement.

Alwan said nothing more.

"Trust me, Um Khaled. Whatever the name means in English, here, it means purity of heart, unfailing faith, and deep courage."

"Abu Khaled, let us not name a child we don't even yet have. It's bad luck."

He agreed wholeheartedly, embracing his wife.

THIRTY-SIX

Once, Baba returned carrying the sea in wet hair and soggy clothes. On that day, Mama had sent me to trade with the neighbors a lemon and garlic for onions that Teta and I chopped up for our meal. A year later, when I went into the blue for good, Sulayman took me back in time to witness what had happened that day in the ocean. And in the going-back, we became part of that day. We, Sulayman and I, were the ones who had cajoled the fish to shallow waters.

ABDEL QADER BADE AN unceremonious farewell to the sea one day. The Mediterranean was calm and the sky endless. He and his fishermen comrades inhaled the expanse as they reached the limits of the three nautical miles imposed by Israel. It was as far as they were allowed before gunboats would fire, so they cast their nets and waited. They were four men in Abdel Qader's boat, and Murad, his cousin, pulled out a deck of cards, worn and tattered from many games of *Tarneeb* in the moist, salty air of the sea.

The fishermen bantered in the world of men at sea, cigarettes dangling from the sides of their mouths, unshaven hard faces in the sun, a contented brotherhood floating on a silent immensity, waiting for it to deliver their sustenance. They stayed that way for hours before reeling in nets of small fish. They knew the catch would not be bountiful so close to shore, but they thanked Allah for what they had, as a pile of writhing sea creatures glistened in the sun. They cast their nets once more, and this time, they caught a miracle. Prime sea bass, grouper, bream, snapper, red mullet, striped mullet, sardines, tuna. The fishermen could hardly believe it. Where were all these fish coming from? Answered prayers, the mysterious ways of Allah's mercy. And the excited cries of fishermen in boats near and far filled the air over the water.

The elation at sea was suddenly muted as Israeli naval vessels sped toward the fleet of small fishing boats fanning Gaza's shore. Most boats quickly gathered their nets and sped off with their good fortunes toward land. Abdel Qader and his comrades were closest to the vessel and could not flee the Israeli boat heading toward them. As they stood folding their nets, one of the fishermen exclaimed, "Check that we've not drifted beyond three miles!"

"We're fine. Just stay calm. We've done nothing wrong," Abdel Qader said, and suddenly, the ocean became a small room with a small fishing boat, a naval vessel, and no windows or doors. Abdel Qader shouted over the water, "We are not beyond three miles."

Soldiers laughed and shot a hole in the boat. The fishermen scrambled to plug it. "You say you want freedom, but you are oppressing the fish," one of the soldiers said, laughing. "Maybe we should tangle you in a net to show you how the fish feel." They ordered the fishermen to throw their catch back into the sea, and they all watched those sea creatures swim away. Then the soldiers ordered the men to strip and get out of the boat, making them count to a hundred while treading water. When they finished, the soldiers ordered them to start counting all over. The minutiae of cruelty alleviated the languor of patrolling the sea; so the soldiers were amused, but then they grew bored, though they waited and took bets as the fishermen counted in the water.

Abdel Qader and his cousin Murad were flanked by two of their comrades, Abu Michele, a Christian, and Abu al Banat, a man who had six daughters and no boys. People called him "father of the girls." He was the first to succumb to exhaustion and as he sank, some soldiers cheered as others paid out money to them. Abdel Qader and Abu Michele tried to hold him up, but they could barely hold themselves. Abdel Qader pleaded, "Have mercy. We have children and families."

Murad quietly closed his eyes and melted like despair into the sea, then one of the soldiers took aim and shot Abu Michele's shoulder. Abdel Qader uttered the *shehadeh*, preparing to meet his end. But the soldiers were done. They sped away, their wake flapping against remnants of the boat. Abdel Qader relaxed his body and let it glide through the water, holding his breath, holding off the compulsion to breathe water deeply into his lungs, until a hand reached for him. He climbed in the water and cut through the surface with a loud gasp of air. Abu Michele floated next to him, nearly passed out, and said, "Don't leave me to die, Abu Khaled."

Several families from Khan Younis were grilling food, having a picnic on the beach, when some of the children came panting from the water, pointing to something in the distance. The adults rose to their feet, squinting their eyes to make out the approaching shapes. There was at least one man, in distress. They saw hands waving, then heard the man's calls for help. Two young men from the family had already jumped into the water, swimming to the rescue. Closer, they saw another, injured, clinging to wooden remnants of what was probably a boat. Others dove in with abayas to cover the naked men before they limped out of the water. The injured man had been shot in his shoulder and had lost blood and consciousness. They rushed him to the hospital. There, they questioned the men.

"What's your name, brother?" someone asked.

"Abdel Qader, Abu Khaled," the man said and added only this much more: "We're fishermen. The Jews came. There were two others, returned to God's sea. I have to go tell their families now. I will be back for my friend with his family."

THIRTY-SEVEN

When Jiddo Atiyeh passed away, Baba stood in the front row of the prayer lines for the deceased. Like everyone else, he said to Mama and Teta, "May his remaining years be added to yours." And when it was just us at home in the evening, when he was smoking an argileh, when he exhaled his thoughts in a cloud of smoke that stared back at him, he said, "I am glad for Ammi Atiyeh to have died of age. It's a blessing to die naturally."

THERE WAS NO WORK on land. Israel's siege of Gaza saw unemployment rise to eighty percent and malnutrition began a slow creep into the new generation. Abdel Qader joined the growing number of jobless men, who gathered in their neighborhoods every morning. These were laborers, accustomed to rising before the sun to wait in Israeli checkpoint queues to get to their jobs. They were men with large calloused hands, damaged nails, and the scars of hard work. With strong, if not young, backs. They'd gather, compelled by the pull of a bread-winner's habit to leave their families early and return late, tired and proud from the hours of backbreaking toil. They'd gather to escape the shame of idleness. To avoid the eyes of their hungry children. Few of them ever stood in the UN ration queues. They could count on their wives and daughters and sons to accomplish the humiliation of waiting for hours to haul back the bags of rice and flour. But Abdel Qader had only one son, barely seven years old, and a pregnant wife who had already had too many miscarriages to risk another one by carrying the heavy rations.

He delayed going to the handout lines as long as he could. He even tried to get his nephews and nieces to help, but they were already getting their own families' allotments. When there was no work to be found and nothing was left to eat, he hung his head and waited in the ration lines with women and children, who looked at him with pity, fueling his sense of impotence and uselessness.

His shame shape-shifted to anger, and Alwan was the easiest target. Her weakness and inability to deliver healthy children sooner was to blame. He questioned his choice of a wife with narrow hips who had taken so long to bear him a child. Luckily, the firstborn had been a son, sure to carry on his name. Still, if she had been a better wife, he would already have many children who could have stood in these lines to spare their father such disgrace. He should have listened to his mother and sisters when they had tried to dissuade him from marrying Alwan, whose grandmother had been the crazy lady of Beit Daras. And whose mother, Nazmiyeh—though he loved the woman, God bless her—was the most crass hajje he had ever known. He should have been more pragmatic in choosing a wife. It was all Alwan's fault. The fault of her deficiency and her cursed family.

Abdel Qader left in the morning and returned in the early afternoon with two bags of rations flung over his shoulder. He threw them in the middle of the family room for his wife to deal with. Alwan stared at the heavy bags and touched a hand to her swollen belly. She grabbed the rice bag and leaned her weight to drag it into the corner. The effort caused her to wince. She made a silent plea to Allah to protect her pregnancy and admonished her unborn child to behave and not try to come out too early before grabbing the bag of flour to move it to the corner with the rice. Then she gave thanks for the solitude of her suffering, relieved that Hajje Nazmiyeh was making bread in the outdoor *taboons* under the orange trees where the matriarchs gathered daily.

Still reeling from the humiliation, and still blaming Alwan for it, Abdel Qader did not look at his wife as she struggled with the sacks. He walked out, unsure where to go. He wanted to walk out of his skin, out of his anger and his impotence. There was no job to go to. There was no boat. The sea had betrayed him. He was too ashamed to join the men. Too bored with them. He walked. Nearby, he saw his son Khaled with other small boys, listening to horrible English songs and dancing like a girl. The sight renewed his anger, which finally gave him purpose and authority, if only briefly.

Though he'd have liked to have smashed the tape player for the momentary sense of power, he was not so rash as to destroy a material object he could not afford to replace. He pushed the stop button and stood with stern eyes that made his son cower.

"How can you listen to this trash?"

"Baba, this is rap. It's not Israeli."

"They're all the same, and don't talk back to me when I speak." He slapped the small face of his son, knocking him to the ground. "Go help your mother, boy!"

With tortured eyes, Abdel Qader turned slowly away, toward aimlessness. Toward the sea.

When he finally returned, Abdel Qader was drenched in seawater, his eyes swollen and red. He entered their home silently and went to change his clothes. Something in the way he moved, in the way his head seemed too heavy, dissuaded his wife and child from asking why his clothes were sopping wet. Alwan had done the best she could for their meal but Abdel Qader didn't compliment her. He didn't speak at all, and she wished for one of his rare affectionate moments. Instead, he sat in a pile of his own thoughts, next to his son but somehow very far away. He tried to summon the virility of anger by thinking he should have a bigger family by now. More children around the meal. But the truer part of him was ashamed of his thoughts and grateful for fewer mouths to feed. The previous hours in the ocean and the cowardly path he had contemplated still clung to him. He remembered that fateful day at sea when his boat and comrades had been devoured. The familiar brew of fear, helplessness, anger, and bewilderment began frothing in his body. He squeezed his eyes shut and clenched his fists to stave it off.

"What's wrong, Baba?"

Abdel Qader opened his eyes, relaxing his fists at his son's touch. Just then the adan beckoned the faithful to the evening prayer. He kissed his son's cheek, the one he had slapped earlier. "May Allah cut my hand off if it hits your face again."

"Let's pray the *magreb* together, son," he said, and the two stood close on their prayer mats, one large, one small, bending, kneeling, and prostrating themselves together before Allah.

The family ate and sat watching the news, then tuned in to Hajje Nazmiyeh's favorite evening soap opera. Khaled went off to bed, and soon Hajje Nazmiyeh's snoring in the big room suffused the house. Alwan finished the dishes and joined Abdel Qader, who sat outside smoking his argileh. Years into their marriage, with one child and too many miscarriages to show for it, Alwan understood that her husband blamed her for the degradation he felt.

"What can I do?" she said.

He didn't look at her, continued puffing.

She sat by his feet for a while and mustered the courage to speak again, "I'm sorry, Abdel Qader. Hit me if you want. I can take it. But please do not turn away from me."

Her words moved him to bend closer to his wife. He put his hands to her face and pulled her closer to him. He kissed her forehead, hesitantly at first, then forcefully, squeezing her close. "It's not your fault, Alwan. By Allah's will and mercy, we will get through this." That was all he said. He held his wife and they slept that night in an embrace that held the world together.

THIRTY-EIGHT

When my sister Rhet Shel was born, Teta told me not to worry. I would always be her favorite, even though Rhet Shel was named after the only brave American she had ever heard of. "The rest of them just make weapons to kill, or junk to sell to people," Teta Nazmiyeh said. "I don't know why Allah made them so pretty with yellow hair and such." She contemplated her own words. "Maybe to offset the badness in their hearts."

GIRLS WERE OFTEN NAMED after their grandmothers or some other beloved woman in the family, the Quran, or history. But Alwan and Abdel Qader's daughter was named after an American young woman named Rachel Corrie, an international activist who had been run over by an Israeli bulldozer as she tried to prevent the demolition of a Palestinian family's home. Witnesses all swore the driver had crushed her intentionally, and Gaza poured into the streets to honor her as a martyr. Corrie's funeral marked the first and only time in Gaza that the American flag was carried through the streets with reverence, as it draped a mock coffin after her body was returned to her family in Olympia, Washington.

Soon, there were hundreds of little girls in Gaza named Rachel even though Gaza's best efforts at the American pronunciation were two-syllable approximations that came out Arabized as *Ra-Shel* or *Rhet Shel*, the latter more attentive to the English *ch* sound. Abdel Qader swore that honoring Rachel Corrie in such a way had been his idea first, and he held on to the name until Alwan gave birth to their second child.

The months leading up to Rhet Shel's birth were hard times, but Abdel Qader's patience and prayers were answered with money and chickens soon after his daughter's birth. He managed to secure a microloan from an aid organization for five hundred dollars, which he used to purchase lumber, wire mesh, and chicken feed. What remained would be spent buying live chickens and chicks for a family business.

It seemed to Khaled that his mother had been pregnant for years. When he was seven years old, his sister, Rhet Shel, arrived. He had wanted a brother and sucked air through his teeth as family and friends delighted in the new arrival. "She's ugly, with no hair and yellow skin," he told his friends Wasim and Tawfiq. "All she does is cry. Baba keeps talking to her as if she can understand. Why does he do that? Like he's losing his mind," Khaled complained.

Before Rhet Shel arrived, his baba had been wallowing in a collection of bad tempers and moods. He had lost his boat and refused to talk about it. Israel had shut the world down, making some people go hungry. Khaled heard his father say, "May God punish the Jews for what they have done to us."

That same day, Khaled watched an Israeli football team on television and repeated his father's words as his eyes followed the lithe, muscular limbs moving in nice blue uniforms with shiny gold stripes. He repeated the plea to Allah when the camera panned across the fans in the stadium and he saw boys his age enjoying what seemed to be the most thrilling day imaginable. He continued his prayer to Allah. "And when the Jews are punished, please bring their uniforms to Gaza," he said, adding for clarity, "the blue uniforms with the shiny gold stripes."

Khaled thought it was he who brought the family good luck, not this newborn. After all, he was the one who worshiped five times a day and made *dua'a* to Allah. He resented the credit going to his infant sister, and he tried to outshine Rhet Shel in other ways. He helped his baba build the chicken house on the roof. He learned very quickly and soon his baba allowed him to take charge of the hammer, which, as everyone knows, is the most important job in building things. His father was a mere helper who sawed the wood and held it in place while Khaled hammered the nails.

Alwan smiled as she bandaged her husband's battered hands, listening to him recount the day building the chicken coop with their son.

"Khaled was in such command that I just couldn't bring myself to take the hammer away from him," Abdel Qader said. "I don't know how I will manage tomorrow, though. We still need another full day to finish everything."

"I'll pad the bandages more. Enshallah, your hands will heal quickly. The body heals very quickly, Allah be praised." Alwan said, smiling coyly at her husband, and Abdel Qader began to grow hard in that instant.

"Is it healed down there? I'm sure it has been more than the required forty days," he whispered.

"It has only been twenty-two days," she said and lifted her eyes flirtatiously, adding, "but my body is completely healed."

Abdel Qader started toward Alwan, his erection in full disregard of the scriptures that dictate a man shall not touch his wife for forty days after the birth of a child. Alwan hesitated, the weight of religion upon her. "Let me at least feed Rhet Shel first. My breasts are engorged," she said, trying to hold off her husband and her own desire, but Abdel Qader was already pulling at her.

"Let her sleep. I can help you," he said, wrapping his mouth around her breast. He suckled from one, then the other, and back again. The more he indulged that sin, the harder he became. Soon he was moving inside of her, making his world right again.

Later, as he lay smoking a cigarette next to his wife, Abdel Qader went through the inventory of blessings, beginning with

Alwan. She had given him Khaled, who would, enshallah, grow into a strong man to carry his name. The chicken coop was nearly complete and he had not even used up a third of the loan, which meant that he could buy more chickens than he had initially calculated. He puffed on his cigarette and did the math over and over, rearranging numbers of chickens and chicks to discern the greatest return in as short a period as possible. He finally decided on fourteen chickens, twenty chicks, and a rooster, estimating that if all went as planned, enshallah, he could provide for the family and pay off the loan within sixteen months. The dance with these numbers, however meager, satisfied him. He inhaled the last of his cigarette in a long and contented breath, put it out in the ashtray, and turned on his side to sleep. *Allah is generous*, he thought, and concluded that his enduring faith in those trying times had earned him divine favor. Just then little Rhet Shel began to stir. Another blessing to be counted.

THIRTY-NINE

When the sky, land, and sea were barricaded, we burrowed our bodies into the earth, like rodents, so we didn't die. The tunnels spread under our feet, like story lines that history wrote, erased, and rewrote. Our family still had chickens, I made money delivering their eggs, and I was in love with Yusra. Once, I found a single Kinder Egg at a store and bought it immediately. I put it amid the delivery to Yusra's house and felt proud to give such a gift to the girl I loved, but I couldn't help feeling guilty that I hadn't given it to Rhet Shel instead. She always wanted one.

KHALED FED THE CHICKENS daily before and after school and watched their numbers multiply. He delivered orders to customers, which was the best of his chores because occasionally, some let him keep the change. He always picked the biggest eggs for Yusra's house because it was never too early to start currying favor with his sweetheart's family for the eventual day when he'd grow up and ask for her hand. On these days, he made a special effort to tame his hair with a dab of olive oil, making a perfect side part to divide his shiny black mane. He wore his best blue jeans and a white shirt buttoned to the collar, perfectly tucked into his trousers. He knew it would be years before hair would appear on his face, but he inspected his jawline nonetheless, in case he was an early bloomer.

Much to his irritation, his teta Nazmiyeh watched him with a knowing grin. "You delivering to Yusra's family today, son?" she asked.

"No!" he lied.

"That's good, because you look so good, I don't want that girl getting sweet on you."

Khaled contemplated the idea of Yusra being sweet on him, and he prayed that she be the one to answer the door. Usually, she did. Khaled would use his own money to make up the shortage in their payment. Life had become more hopeful for his family. There was enough money for what they needed. They stopped going to the UNRWA ration lines and could afford luxuries, like chocolate and pasta, which were smuggled through the tunnels from Egypt.

If he hadn't already had a job, Khaled might have succumbed to the seduction of the tunnels. It was one of the few jobs that paid well and the Gaza businessmen who owned the tunnels usually hired boys and young men small and limber enough to crawl in the narrow passages back and forth, dragging, pushing, pulling baskets of goods and shuttling the empty containers back for more. They smuggled a vast list of banned items, like diapers, sugar, pencils, petrol, chocolate, phones, eating utensils, books.

One enterprising tunnel owner even started delivering Kentucky Fried Chicken from Egypt. It was not long before Khaled saw his own friends leave school to work there. The first to go was Tawfiq, a slight boy of twelve years. His older brother had already been working there, but he was of no use after he lost his left eye and badly damaged his right one. Tawfiq was the next in line to help the family.

On that first day, as teachers marked Tawfiq and Khaled absent, the two friends were sitting in an orientation class with five other boys their age in the tunnel village, listening to instructions on how to operate the levers and pulleys used to move containers, and what to do if the earth shook from bombs or tunnel collapse. Khaled had gone even though he knew his mother and teta would take turns whupping him for leaving school if they found out. He was also sure they'd not tell his father, unless he did it again. He always got at least one warning.

Khaled went that day on an errand of friendship for Tawfiq, whose face ashened before he set foot in the tunnel. Each new boy was to be accompanied by an older, more experienced one their first week of work.

The tunnel village was an eerie town with closed doors and shuttered windows. There were no trees and children were rarely seen playing in the streets. The children here worked and almost everyone's face was swathed to protect from the pervasive dust of excavation that hovered in the air like perpetual dry fog. Tawfiq knew to bring his *kaffiyeh* and wrapped it across his face. "I'm ready," he said.

A gravel path led to the opening of the tunnel, which lay inside a goat shed in a deserted, brown garden. The newer tunnels were more sophisticated than this one. *Five-star tunnels*, they were called. One could walk nearly upright the full length of them. Lanterns lined the paths and structural beams added safety. But this tunnel was narrow and dark, with just one system of levers and pulleys. That's why the owner only hired boys with slight bodies.

Tawfiq gripped the rope as he sat atop the plastic basket, and he looked back at Khaled as the rope slowly lowered him into the bowels of the earth. Standing at the lip of the tunnel, Khaled watched his friend tremble, then disappear into the dark hole.

"How can he see where he's going down there?" Khaled asked a worker next to him.

"There are lanterns at the bottom."

"What's it like?"

"It's cold as your mama's pussy. Stop asking stupid questions."

Khaled waited silently for hours until Tawfiq finally emerged, his face coated with filth. It was late enough that Khaled was assured a whupping, but not so late that his mama and teta would worry just yet. Tawfiq was given a day's pay right then, and the two friends, one nine, the other twelve years old, had in their pockets the honest pay of working men.

"What was it like?" Khaled asked as they walked to a local store.

Tawfiq blew his nose and showed the tissue to Khaled. "It's like that."

Khaled looked at the muddy snot.

"There was another boy at the bottom. Mahmood. Real nice. We're friends now. The shit that came out of his nose was even worse," Tawfiq said, with something like envy. "You know what surprised me the most?"

"What?" Khaled's face opened.

"It's really cold underground," Tawfiq screwed his face. "I thought it would be a lot hotter since down there is closer to hell."

The two friends held that riddle on their young faces in contemplative silence until it faded into other thoughts.

"Mahmood is already growing hair on his face. He showed me. He has a bunch on his chin but not much for a mustache," Tawfiq said. "But he has a big gap between his front teeth. I bet girls make fun of it. Poor guy."

Khaled did, indeed, get a whupping from his mother. His teta was not at all sympathetic, especially when he admitted going to the tunnels. "I better not ever hear of you going there. People die every day down there!" Alwan yelled. His teta Nazmiyeh added, "Every damn day!" They threatened to tell his father if he ever went to the tunnels again.

He promised he wouldn't, but he continued to meet up with Tawfiq after school by the store whose owner said he'd try to get more Kinder Eggs.

On a day two weeks later, Tawfiq did not arrive at the usual spot where Khaled waited. Instead, Tawfiq had gone to the ocean, and the next day, he explained the reason.

Tawfiq had hopped into the plastic basket to be lowered into the tunnel as usual. But on this day, an intense rush of earth surged from the opening, tossing Tawfiq high into the air. He didn't know what had happened or how or when he had landed sitting forty feet from where he had just been. He sat there in a haze, unable to see in front of him, but he heard people gathering, running, shouting, "The tunnel is collapsing!" The wail of ambulance sirens mixed with the wails of women running toward the familiar sounds of disaster. His friend Mahmood had been in the tunnel. The boy with the cheery smile, big gap in his front teeth, and sparse facial hair, of which Tawfiq had been envious, was no more. People ran to help Tawfiq, gave him water, then turned to help the others as they tried to dig.

Tawfiq walked away, then ran. And found himself alone with the blue expanse of the Mediterranean. "I just sat there for a while," he told Khaled. "Then I went home."

FORTY

I was too young and jealous at first to see the enchantment that Rhet Shel brought to our world. I blamed her for my own hurt. When Baba killed Simsim, my favorite chicken, he yelled at me to stiffen my spine, grow up, be a man. He said, "Boy, you can't name a chicken. This is meat, Allah's blessing that keeps us alive." He said, "Here, come help me pluck these feathers, son." I did, and then I was in charge of slaughtering the chickens. Rhet Shel got my job of feeding them. It was not long afterward that the world changed, and I went into the blue.

KHALED WOULD STEADY HIS being, invoke the name of Allah, and mumble to himself before moving the blade deftly in one swift motion across the slender bird neck.

Rhet Shel, now three years old, was given charge of feeding the chickens. She would throw the feed with the fitful and feeble skill of a toddler, spreading the seeds only around her little feet, and sometimes in her braided hair, a daily spectacle her father loved to observe. Abdel Qader would stand in the doorway with his coffee and cigarette, watching Rhet Shel delight as the chickens flocked around her to eat. She tried to impose order. "No, no, no, chicken!" she would scold her feathery friends, pointing her chubby index finger for authority. "Let the baby chickens eat, too. Move, move. No, no, no. Bad chicken!"

Everyone who knew Abdel Qader understood that Rhet Shel was the song that made his heart dance. She was perhaps his greatest love. To Khaled, Rhet Shel was a nuisance who could get away with anything, praised for everything she did, no matter how infantile. She had no chores except feeding the chickens, which she couldn't do properly, and when Khaled tried to correct her, his father yelled at him. Worse, Khaled was warned not to allow Rhet Shel to see him slaughtering chickens. "I don't want her to be sad," his baba said. And Khaled resented them both because nobody ever worried about his feelings. Did his father think it was easy for Khaled to kill and pluck? So what if Rhet Shel was a girl and so little? She wasn't so innocent. It would be good for her to stiffen her spine, grow up. She should understand that chickens were not pets. They were meat, a blessing from Allah. So, he was only doing her a favor when he arranged it so she accidentally saw him killing her favorite chicken on the roof. It was the one with the white ribbon around its neck.

"I told you to spare that one, didn't I?" Abdel Qader screamed at Khaled.

"Yes, Baba. But . . ."

"Don't talk back to me! You did this on purpose. I specifically told you not to slaughter that chicken, and I tied the ribbon on it to make sure you didn't make a mistake."

"The ribbon fell off, Baba," Khaled begged, then felt the hot slap of his father's fury across his face.

"Don't lie. Never lie, boy! NEVER lie!" Abdel Qader removed his belt to strike Khaled again.

I feel a kind of stillness, as if my body itself has become a moment of silence. A hollowed-out cave of a life within a life. I see my father; his rage has turned to alarm. Then to fear. Then to terror.

"Khaled! Khaled!" Abdel Qader cried, dropping the belt.

Rhet Shel had run into the room, crying, to save me when she saw Baba hit me.

"My son! My son! What is wrong? I am sorry, my son. I am sorry. I didn't mean to hurt you. Khaled! Please answer me, son. What have I done?" Abdel Qader was pleading now and Rhet Shel was crying. Alwan rushed in.

"Abu Khaled, this happened the other day, too, and he snapped out of it," Alwan said to her husband.

"What's happening to him?" he asked, horrified and spiritually unhinged by the rolling eyes and blank expression settling on his son's face.

"Lay him down. This happened before. He was okay when I rubbed his chest like this," Alwan said, trembling.

The way my mother rubs my chest is soothing, and I feel love surge through me. My sister, Rhet Shel, is still sobbing. She has attached herself to me and I feel compassion bind us. I feel sorry and ashamed for killing her chicken.

"Tawfiq and Wasim brought him like this a few weeks ago. They said his eyes just started rolling in the middle of a convesation," Alwan said to her husband.

"He needs to see a doctor, Alwan. You should have told me about this," he said.

"I thought it was just because he's sensitive. It only lasted a few minutes." Alwan was now rubbing more vigorously, with a mother's deepest dread. She looked at her husband, the same anxiety passing back and forth between them, when Khaled's eyes seemed to focus as he blinked a few times.

"What's going on? I don't need to see a doctor," Khaled said.

Khaled

"You feel like a child playing around with a magnifying glass, burning up ants."

—Israeli soldier, on attacking Gaza

I knew December 27, 2008, would be no ordinary day. It would mark the first full decade of my life, that important passage from single to double-digit age.

Coming from large families where birthdays passed like any other day, Alwan and Abdel Qader did not concern themselves with such fancies. Besides, Hajje Nazmiyeh was superstitiously opposed to birthday celebrations, given that Mazen had been kidnapped the only time she ever threw a birthday party. But Khaled had made such a fuss of his birthday, counting down the days for months, that he inspired a sense of expectancy in the family, and plans for a party materialized. Even Abdel Qader joined. "So, son, how many days left?" he would ask whenever the spirit moved him.

Tawfiq and Wasim, who were already in the double-digit age, told me that turning ten was magical. They said it would give me sudden powers. I asked like what. They snickered and told me I had to wait. But I could tell they were pranking me. They did that sometimes because I was the youngest of them.

When the kids went off to school, Alwan began baking a cake. Hajje Nazmiyeh reluctantly agreed not to forbid the party. "You were too young to remember the last time we had a birthday hafla in this family," Hajje Nazmiyeh said to Alwan.

"Yumma, the Jews didn't take Mazen because you threw a party for my first birthday. Please be reasonable. This will make Khaled so happy," Alwan pleaded.

"May Allah touch our lives with His mercy, daughter," Hajje Nazmiyeh said, giving in to reason despite the vapors of premonition in her breath.

I thought Wasim and Tawfiq were lying to me. But they were telling the truth. Turning ten was everything they said and more. It was magical, like they said. Even the Jews came to celebrate with me. The whole of Gaza, and I think the whole world, celebrated my tenth birthday.

Classes were just letting out the first shift and the streets were filled with children either coming or going to school when Israel dropped the first bombs. Explosions shook the earth, hurtling buildings and bodies and all the things of living in broken parts that sailed through the air in all directions. There was no place to run.

Gaza burned.

Khaled stood where he was, going into the place his mother called "episodes," for which she had sought help from doctors who had no help. It was a quiet place of refuge, deep inside him. A place of blue.

Great fireworks made the ground shake. Cars drove through the streets blaring their horns and people ran everywhere, yelling and waving their hands in the air. Ambulances turned on their sirens and raced through the streets. Israel sent planes for me, flying so low that buildings shook and all the windows broke open. I had been wrong about the Jews. They are wonderful. Baba is wrong about them, and I ask Allah to forget all my prayers to punish them.

Blood poured and dust rose. Smoke painted lungs and hearts raced. The remaining flour mill, the last source for bread, was bombed. Schools, homes, mosques, and universities, too. Then Israel sprayed Gaza with white phosphorous.

They brought helicopters that sent out enormous streams of white confetti that streaked the sky like a spiderweb. And the confetti landed like a million candles with a million flames. Some people caught the confetti flames and ran around with them on their bodies, yelling. What an invention! Everyone knows that the Jews are the smartest people in the world. I became nearly weightless and floated around Gaza. I slid over the sea, even. Such is the magic of the age of ten.

From the tremendous noise in Gaza, it became quiet here, inside the age of ten. As I hovered in the center of that silence, I could see Rhet Shel inside a strange cave at the base of our house. Baba was holding up a wall with his back, yelling for Rhet Shel to leave him, and I knew that I should call for Rhet Shel. So I did, and I continued to roam the world, as if I were a breeze.

Rhet Shel did not answer my call, but a man emerged from my father's body and whisked Rhet Shel toward me. I knew that man was not a man at all. It was Sulayman. This is what I want to tell you about being ten: You know things without knowing how you know them. Then all the men in town carried me through the streets to my mother, who was so happy to see me that she just held me and cried.

FORTY-ONE

*Stories were written in my Teta Nazmiyeh's skin. When I was a
small boy of four or five, the wrinkles on her face were part of a game
we played together. She would mark two random dots on her face
and take a nap. I could wake her at any time, but only after I had
figured out a path of face lines that connected the two dots. Teta
could get half an hour's worth of shut-eye, knowing I would be fully
engaged by the map of her face. My favorite was connecting the left
ear to the corner of her right eye. It was nearly a straight path, with
one long wrinkle across her forehead that scooped down to join three
more large lines emerging from the corner of her eye, especially when
she laughed. Those games etched Teta's face in my memory, like
lanes leading home.*

ISRAEL'S BOMBING OF GAZA altered the clock. As if time
had been wounded, it now moved in a crawl, its daily passage
impeded by the rubble that carpeted the terrain, its presence so
thick that Hajje Nazmiyeh felt the sun dragging along the heavy
weight of each hour. So much needed to be done, yet there was
nothing to do. People gathered with nothing to say. Even when
they spoke, their words were coated in a silence that stared into
a chasm as they picked out and buried their dead. Even rage and
calls for revenge seemed perfunctory. Tears made for a sort of
refuge. A place to go to feel something in a wreckage that demanded numbness. For many, it was simply a waiting to die. Hope
seemed vulgar in this hour, and the idea of death was so comforting and alluring that no one spoke, lest words do away with the
seduction of a quiet ending.

But time did pass, however painstakingly. Slowly, people
returned to themselves, salvaging life. Hajje Nazmiyeh collected

some of her pots, random papers flying about that could be used for schoolwork, broken pencils that might still be of use. Perhaps a shoe that could be coupled with another, even if it didn't match. For some children—because, Allah be praised, children are resilient—the rummaging was turned into games and contests. But for most, the landscape of destruction hid the broken parts of them—memories of bombs, fear, and the recently dead—and no one wanted to find those. So, they sat on the peripheries of their own lives, on rocks, huddling around fires for warmth, waiting for time to limp along. Someone threw a plank over a large rock to make a seesaw and children played, their laughter small suns. The harsh winter spent outdoors in tents amid the rubble gave way to springtime pushing up from the scorched ground, absorbing the pollution of bombs and grief. Insects reappeared, then birds, then butterflies.

Nazmiyeh's home was partially destroyed. She and Alwan could still walk through the front door and recognize their home, but the top floor where one of her sons and his family had lived was torn off, and the door leading to Alwan and Abdel Qader's bedroom opened now to the outdoors choked with rubble. The bathroom, too, was gone and they were given tents, along with fourteen other families whose homes had been bombed. The tent came with lanterns and blue cots, each bearing a white outline of Earth, the symbol of the United Nations. But Hajje Nazmiyeh didn't use their tent, instead taking refuge with another of her sons on that first night, while they tried to retrieve the body of Abdel Qader. And so the melancholy requiems of the Quran poured from every speaker, every minaret, every soul.

It took several days to dig Abdel Qader's body out from under a collapsed building. That's why Alwan forbade Rhet Shel from joining in the salvage competitions with the other children. Once again, Nazmiyeh's sons abandoned their individual lives and coalesced at their mother's feet, a workforce of strong, able men who had felt helpless during the invasion, running and huddling for shelter from the whims of death. They labored, propelled by rage, humiliation, resolve, and love, first to retrieve Abdel Qader's body and wash and bury his corpse; then to rebuild their mother's and sister's home.

Israel had long ago blocked building materials from entering Gaza, but a local entrepreneur had started a profitable enterprise recycling rocks and rubble into new building bricks. The brothers pitched in to buy what they could of these bricks and used various mud mixtures instead of cement, which was impossible to find in Gaza. Their wives and children would also come, bringing food and solemnity that eventually turned into the familiar chaos, laughter, and bickering of large families.

In the rhythm of this restorative daily toil, the constancy of regimented prayers, the serial burials as bodies were recovered, the poetic hymns of the Quran, the gatherings of families and neighbors, the conversations, tears, and children's play, homes were restored as much as possible, grudges faded away, scandals were no more, and slates were wiped clean. Men reclaimed masculinity from the grateful eyes of the women who tended to their tired bodies and sweat-drenched clothes. They found solace from the mothers, like Hajje Nazmiyeh, who preempted any silence with dua'as to Allah to keep and bless their sons; from wives, who made love to them; and from children, who clung to their limbs, chests, and necks for the comforts a strong father could impart. The women worked alongside the men, clearing rubble, repairing, and building anew. They cleaned and cooked and baked and organized the children's chores. The constant movement and ache of muscles and bones rocked their wounded souls, at least to distraction.

But there was nothing anyone could do for Alwan. She was like a tree in endless autumn, standing still, leaves drying, weakening, then falling. She became an island unto herself and for some time it was hard to find her in her eyes. She wanted to return to wearing niqab, but Hajje Nazmiyeh said, "Nonsense! It's not even Islamic. You don't get to hide your grief behind pretend piety."

On the surface, life looked like decay. The destruction of buildings and infrastructure was so immense that debris and dust painted the air gray for days. The green earth was scorched then layered with the fragments of broken things and broken bodies. But after the dead were buried and all the tears had fallen, time thinned out to a liquid that rushed over Gaza like a stream over rocks, smoothing the jagged corners and coating them with a new moss of life. The legion of able bodies clearing rubble, rebuilding, recycling, cooking, and gathering was an industry that reconstituted community.

Nazmiyeh and Alwan placed Khaled at the center of it all. Weeks after the assault, he still had not emerged from his episode. Between futile visits to doctors, the family kept constant prayers over him. He breathed in and out. That part worked, thanks be to Allah. A kindly Norwegian doctor named Mads put tubes in and out of him connected to plastic bladders for nutrition and waste. The doctor said that everything on the inside worked and he taught Alwan and Nazmiyeh how to fill his bag with "food" and how to empty his waste.

"Does that mean that he can hear and understand us?"

"I don't know. There are no resources to check for brain activity. This is all I can do for now," the doctor apologized.

Khaled

"Where could I cry out the despair and rage I felt for all this terrible fate we saw at such close quarters?"
—Dr. Mads Gilbert

Time does not exist here. Everything is now, but when I am with Sulayman I cannot also be with Mama and Rhet Shel and Teta Nazmiyeh. I leave Sulayman when I feel my mother. I hear her speaking to someone I do not know. She is telling this stranger that my eyes usually roll in my head. But now, "Look!" she says.

"His eyes are set and he is blinking. It's like he's awake," she says.

She is trying to convince someone that I can hear her. But of course I can. I yell, YES! But I already understand that they do not hear me. I stopped trying when Sulayman said that my words roam in my mind with no way out.

I hear a man's voice. "We are all one, Hajje," he says to my teta. I wish he would come into my view so I could see him fully.

There he is. With a camera. Will I be on television? He asks Mama what happened. He wants to know if there was anything wrong with me before the invasion. Mama tells him that I had episodes and spells that came and went.

"They found him like this and brought him here," Mama says.

"Then he started shaking. He was having seizures. We had taken refuge at the school. We left the house because the bombs were getting too close. Everybody was running for safety to the UN school. Khaled and Rhet Shel were with me," Mama says, and yet I wonder if she is speaking of me at all because I do not remember any of that.

"My husband, Abu Khaled, left us there and went back to save the chickens." Mama's voice is cracking, like she will cry. Then she does. She cries and Teta thanks Allah for his mercy and asks Him for strength to endure His will. Mama speaks again.

"We were in the UN school and Rhet Shel wandered off when I fell asleep. We couldn't find her and Khaled went to look for her. We were sure she was in one of the classrooms with the other children and Khaled was just looking in the school."

But I don't recall going to look for Rhet Shel. I see the top of Mama's head in my peripheral vision moving back and forth against the mustard-colored curtains my uncles had hung for us. Mama is wearing a black hijab and from the corner of my eye I see a black line formed by the back-and-forth motion of her head. She always rocks herself when she cries.

The man speaks, asking what happened next. Mama doesn't answer. The black line is mesmerizing and I think I should leave to be with Sulayman. The man tells Mama to lean on Allah because our strength is in Him, and Mama and Teta proclaim the Oneness of Allah in response.

"And then both children were gone. I got everyone in the school to look for them. Then Israeli helicopters started firing," Mama says. Only now do I realize that nothing I saw then was real. There was no birthday celebration. I replay it all, roam the details of memory, and see the face of horror. Of merciless terror. The Jews had destroyed Gaza again and killed my father. Teta says, "May Allah bomb them, too, for the sake of the Prophet."

I want to leave now. The black line of Mama's hijab is gone and she is no longer crying. I can hear Teta making coffee.

"We finally found Rhet Shel roaming in the ashes of the school-yard. She was sucking her thumb wildly and I had to yank it out of her mouth to understand her. But all she said was that Khaled had brought her back and then left. She didn't know where he had gone, and she refused to say anything else."

I don't remember that.
"A few hours later the men came running, carrying Khaled."
I remember that. They carried me to Mama and she was . . .
"I was so happy to see him I just held him and cried."

V

We worried when the sun sank into the sky. Then darkness illuminated the stars, as only darkness can, and we lay in dirt, gazing at the splendor and immortality above

Nur loved in a way that was adamant, persistent, and reckless. Her heart wasn't smart enough to set limits on its generosity. Maybe that's what rejection by one's mother does. It retards the heart. Makes it love wrong, love too fast, without limits.

THEY STILL TALKED. Even after Nzinga married and had kids; after Nur aged out of the child welfare system, graduated from college, then graduate school; after South Africa's apartheid system fell and Nzinga returned to Durban with her family, the thing between them remained. It changed as they needed it to. Its parts were made of motherhood, sisterhood, womanhood, comradeship in struggle, political activism, mentorship, friendship.

When Israel began a devastating assault on Gaza in December 2008, Nur had been working as a psychotherapist for the City of Charlotte, helping teens confront histories of rape, incest, abuse, neglect, drug use, and inconceivable traumas.

"Makes sense you go into that field," Nzinga had said on Skype. "All us wounded women make a career of trying to put other people back together."

Shortly after Israel's assault, Nzinga emailed a video link to Nur.

Darling Nur,
Howzit?
Here's the video I told you about. I remembered you did a paper on Locked-In Syndrome in college and thought you might want to take a look at this. I checked the last name, of course, as I always do with stories from Gaza.

Unfortunately, it is not the same as your grandfather's name.

I was very moved by the extraordinary things being done to care for this boy by his mother and grandmother, who have clearly lost so much.

Let me know how things turn out at your fund-raiser. You are doing wonderful things, Boo. I am very proud of you.

Love,

Zingie

Nur clicked on the link and watched the eight-minute documentary. It showed a close-up of the boy in the film, and she stared at his face, the white streak of hair. He seemed familiar. His name was Khaled. Two women sat against mustard-colored curtains. The older one was his grandmother. His mother refused to believe that he was comatose, insisting, "I know he can hear me. Sometimes he blinks when I ask him to."

The phone rang in Nur's office. It was nearly eight in the evening. Someone from the organizing committee for the Palestine Children's Relief Fund fund-raiser was letting her know that they finally had confirmed the speaker's attendance. He was a Palestinian psychologist, one of a handful in Gaza. After six months of calling, writing, and meeting with elected officials and State Department bureaucrats to secure travel permission from Israel for the speaker to leave Gaza, they received news that Dr. Musmar would be allowed to cross the Rafah border and fly to the United States from Cairo.

"Great," Nur said, reaching for a bag of potato chips as she hung up.

FORTY-THREE

Nur was orderly and neat. She was even methodical in the excavation of her stomach, filling it with junk and emptying it by provoking a gag reflex with two fingers, then brushing her teeth immediately in a consistent pattern that brought regimen and precision to self-abuse and self-loathing. She worked endless hours, paid or volunteer, perfecting the habits of loneliness and escape by rescuing others. And daily she tamed her wild mismatched eyes with the strict symmetry of brown contact lenses.

T HE ENERGY OF THE day was hurried and expectant. Nur managed the volunteers, ensuring that each aspect of the fund-raiser was well staffed. Organizations always sought Nur's help with events because she brought order, if not imagination, to everything she did.

She put three volunteers at the registration desk, ten at catering, and two were coming to run the babysitting service. The sales tables were manned, ushers were in place with seating charts, and she assigned several volunteers the task of filling donor gift bags at a corner table, where a man she did not recognize was helping. Tall, with dark features and a substantial mustache, the unfamiliar volunteer created a gravity where he sat. His presence tugged at Nur until she finally approached, ostensibly to check up on progress with the envelopes.

Months later, she would probe that compulsion toward him. What had been so special about him? There had been many people she did not know or recognize at the event, most also Arab with features like his. Why had he caught her attention?

"Hi, Nur! We're almost done," said one of the volunteers.

"Great! Looks like you've cruised through. We still have a couple of hours before the patrons arrive," Nur said. The stranger at the table stood up, tall indeed, and shy. "My name is Jamal." He extended his hand.

His voice was strong but gentle, accented with the lilts and timbre of Arabic. He was slender, almost concave, as if deliberately trying not to assume more space. His clothes fell loosely, somewhat wrinkled against his brown skin, and his hair was disheveled, perhaps too long. His brown eyes were intent, set under drooping eyelids that gave him a quality of sadness. In contrast to the general disorder of him, his mustache was meticulous. Symmetrical, trimmed, combed, perfect. Nur thought him beautiful.

"I'm Nur," she said, extending her hand.

Touching his skin thrilled her, however briefly their hands met. Then words were lost and the silence between them grew awkward.

"Nur, do you want us to distribute the envelopes to each seat?" asked a volunteer.

"Oh, yes. Thank you so much!" Nur responded with more enthusiasm than was warranted.

As the volunteers left the table, Nur thanked Jamal for helping out.

"It was my pleasure," he said, shifting his weight.

"So, what brings you here?"

"I'm just visiting," he said, with more self-assurance now.

"Well, you're in for a treat. The speaker is amazing. I'm sure his talk will be very inspiring."

A smile climbing one side of his face, he asked, "Who is the speaker?"

"He's a psychologist from Gaza. Doctor Musmar. It was a nightmare trying to get permission for him to leave Gaza."

He raised his brow, as if with curiosity. "I'm looking forward to hearing him."

Nur looked around. "He must be here by now."

"You know him?"

Strangely eager to impress, a lie spilled from her lips. "Yes."

She quickly tried to retract, but could only do so with another lie. "Well, only by e-mail." Fabrications formed faster than she could think, and the more she spoke, the more entangled she became in random forgery. "We've corresponded about a particular patient that I was interested in. It's a very sad case . . ." She searched her memory of the video. The white streak of hair. She couldn't remember the boy's name. ". . . a young boy in Nusseirat . . ." She was glad to at least recall the name of the refugee camp. "He's in a coma. Well, not a coma . . ."

"Are you a mental health clinician?" he interrupted.

"Yes, I work with DSS in Charlotte," Nur said, relieved by that small truth.

"DSS?"

"Department of Social Services. I work with teens transitioning into the foster care system from difficult circumstances."

"But tell me about, please, what is your interest. I mean, sorry, my English is out of practice. I just am curious why you are interested in this patient particularly. He is so far away." Now, he was the clumsy one.

Nur leaned into the authority of knowledge and conjured the documentary video. Using the jargon of her profession, she spoke of the boy's mother, who believed her son could hear her. "Locked-In Syndrome," she called it, explaining that it was rare. That a part of the brain—the brain stem, she said—is injured and disrupts all muscle movement without affecting cognition or perception.

And when he did not immediately respond, fidgeting uncomfortably, Nur stepped deeper into the morass of impromptu dishonesty. "I am planning to go to Gaza to work with this patient and others at a psychotherapy center there," she said.

He looked down, shuffled his feet uneasily, almost guiltily.

"Doctor Musmar! There you are!" the committee president yelled from across the room. Nur looked behind her in search of Dr. Musmar, but there was no one there. When she turned back, he tried to smile apologetically. Her face reddened and she hurried away.

"Nur, wait, please," he called, trying to stop her, but several committee members were already gathering around him, reaching out to shake his hand.

Nur found a corner away from the crowd, from where she could see him occasionally searching the room. Was he looking for her? She slid deeper into the corner until it was safe to leave early.

At home now, she ate, then vomited.

The Tuesday following the fund-raiser, she received a brief e-mail from him.

Dear Nur,
I looked for you immediately after the talk and for the rest of the evening without luck. I finally manage to track down this e-mail address. I hope it is correct. I want to apologize, sincerely, for not telling you immediately who I was. I don't know why I just played along, and I'm ashamed for it. I will be a happy man to know that you have forgiven me. Please at least let me know that you received this e-mail.
Sincerely,
Jamal

She read it several times, wrote, edited, and erased a response, and spent the day thinking of little else. She wanted to talk to Nzinga, but it was too late in Durban to call by the time she signed in to Skype.

Dear Dr. Musmar,

There's nothing to apologize for. I'm glad you wrote to me. I was terribly embarrassed after our conversation and decided to leave early. I hope you had an enjoyable time in Charlotte.

Kind Regards,

Nur

Her e-mail was time-stamped 4:30 A.M. and the response she received was at 4:38 A.M.

Dear Nur,

Please call me Jamal and please do not feel embarrassed. You were delightful and charming. Truly, I can't tell you how happy I was to have met you. I would really like to correspond with you more, especially regarding your theory on the boy in the documentary. I am aware of this video because the boy—his name is Khaled—was brought to our clinic by his mother, and I have a file for him. A local filmmaker interviewed Um Khaled when he heard about her son and the mysterious circumstances of his condition. (He had no significant cuts or trauma to any part of his body or brain that might give doctors a clue to understand how he went into this coma; or perhaps it is not a coma, as you said.) There just wasn't much we could do for him, but perhaps I can learn something from you that may help him.

I don't know if you are still planning to come to Gaza, but I have a grant that could pay you a small stipend for a year, with modest accommodation at our hostel. I've attached an application if you're interested. I hope you will consider it.

Warmly,

Jamal

Their correspondence continued, a daily construction of an epistolary refuge where Nur went for a sense of purpose. On the edges of memory, Nur found a moment when her grandfather had told her that her mismatched eyes were just like his sister's eyes. "I think you're the only one in the family who inherited her eyes," he had told her so long ago. "And we have a very big family that you'll meet someday soon." She imagined finding an older woman in Gaza with her eyes; being surrounded by her big family; finding the place where she belonged.

The day arrived months later when she crossed the Egypt-Rafah border for the first time. Jamal was there, waiting for her at the border in Gaza. He had trimmed his hair and somehow looked tidier here than he had at the fund-raiser in the United States.

"Welcome, Nur. Gaza is brigher with your presence," he said, taking her luggage.

"It's great to see you and be here."

"You're not still debating whether or not to call me Jamal, are you?" he smiled, and they laughed together.

"You look different," she remarked.

"Ah. Well, yes. My wife doesn't tolerate my tendency for shabbiness. When you saw me, I had been on my own for a month while my wife was in Canada visiting her family."

The word *wife* stepped gently into the space that Nur had made from words and letters and longings.

FORTY-FOUR

Along with Nzinga and her family, Nur's tío Santiago attended her college commencement. He had grown older than his years; his skin had paled without sun and his teeth had become tanned by the heroin that paved his arms. He had sold his guitar but had found a discarded harmonica to put to the music inside him. On that day of Nur's graduation, he played for her with impossible tenderness, wounded beyond healing. And months later, when she received that harmonica in the mail along with a letter telling of his passing, her memory created an image of him fading gently into the melancholy of that song he had played for her graduation.

J AMAL'S OFFICE WAS A small room with bare walls of chipping green paint, a metal ceiling fan, and a cracked window. Piles of disorderly papers and files cluttered the floor, and several dirty coffee and tea cups sat on his desk. He looked absentmindedly through a file. "I think I e-mailed you everything I have. Like I said, I met him twice. His family brought him back a second time after I had told them there was nothing I could do." He shook his head. "People still find the will to hope for miracles in this damned place."

Lines of a poem in the rifts of memory came quietly to Nur.

> *Hope is not a topic,*
> *It's not a theory.*
> *It's a talent.*

Nur leafed through the file. It indicated there was nothing physically wrong with Khaled to explain his coma-like condition.

"Does this say he has a family history of schizophrenia?" Nur was pointing to a note partially in English.

"Looks like his great-grandmother spoke with the djinn. In these parts, that usually means schizophrenia," he said, and a singular name rose from her depths, making its way to Nur's consciousness.

"This is going to sound strange, but is the grandmother's name Sulayman?" she asked.

"Even without knowing the woman's first name, I can tell you it's not Sulayman because that's a male name."

Jamal's car stopped in a narrow alley bordered by tall gray concrete walls that bore graffiti and posters of martyrs, their severe, youthful faces looking out from the shitty grandeur of premature graves. Little girls, one with a baby hoisted on her hip, played hopscotch nearby, smaller children watching them, while little boys enacted scenes of soldiers arresting Palestinians in pretend play using sticks for machine guns. Nur emerged from the car, suddenly burdened by the magnitude of her task and the nagging sense of inadequacy that rarely left her.

As if he knew, Jamal said, "There aren't enough psychologists to handle the need here. So, no matter what, your presence is immensely helpful." He had a brief exchange with some of the children, who led them enthusiastically through a maze of alleys. Jamal motioned for Nur to follow, adding, "And you never know. You might be the miracle the family is looking for after all."

The children stopped in front of a pale metal door spray-painted with graffiti that extended onto surrounding anemic concrete walls, livid with mourning and glued-on posters bearing the picture of a fisherman untangling his net by the ocean. His features were not clear, but one could see that he was squinting, and his darkened, rough skin spoke of an intimacy with the sun and sea. "That's Ammou Abu Khaled," one of the children said, pointing at the poster. "Khaled is broken and can't talk anymore."

The metal door opened and Nur recognized Khaled's mother from the documentary. She greeted them with effusive welcoming, equal measures of Arab hospitality, hope, and faith that Allah brings good things to those who patiently keep trying and believing. "May Allah bring joy to you as your presence brings me joy now," the mother said. In her home, she took Nur's hand, kissing each cheek. "I am Um Khaled," she said. "My mother, Hajje Nazmiyeh, Um Mazen, is in the kitchen. She will be out shortly."

Jamal greeted the women, placing his right hand over his heart instead of shaking theirs. He walked over to Khaled, who sat in a wheelchair in the middle of the room, propped up with cushions. His little sister was clutching a stuffed bear, her body curled into her brother, her thumb planted in her mouth, and both were watching a small television, mesmerized by a wordless *Tom and Jerry* cartoon. A small tray of candles by Khaled's side flickered, melting slowly.

"Say hello, Rhet Shel," Um Khaled prompted, and the little girl got up to shake Jamal's hand, then Nur's.

"Welcome, my son. Welcome, daughter." The grandmother walked in from the kitchen. She wore a traditional fallahi black thobe, embroidered in fine patterns with the rose, olive, and lemon colors of the land. A delicate black headscarf framed her smile and, together with her immense bosom and wide hips, gave her a quality of maternal generosity. Though her skin was creased and rumpled by age, she didn't seem much older than her daughter, as if the lines on her face were nooks and crevices where youth had settled.

Hajje Nazmiyeh, who was considerably shorter than Nur, pulled Nur's face closer with both hands, searched her eyes, then kissed each cheek in greeting with what seemed like disappointment. Then she turned to Rhet Shel. "Habibti, come help me bring out the food."

"Oh no, Hajje. You shouldn't have troubled yourself like that," Jamal said.

Hajje Nazmiyeh looked at him disapprovingly. "You know better than that, son. You come to Hajje Nazmiyeh's house, you will not leave with an empty stomach. And don't worry. My son is on his way. You will not be the only man." She disappeared into the kitchen, helping Rhet Shel bring the rest of the food out.

Alwan, Um Khaled, had taken the day off work in hopes that this new American psychologist named Nur might come with answers to unlock her son and restore him to himself. One of her brothers arrived and they all shared a late breakfast of eggs, potatoes, *za'atar*, olive oil, olives, hummus, *fuul*, pickled vegetables, and warm fresh bread. Though Nur was fluent in Arabic, she found it difficult to follow the rapid Gazan accent, and she did not understand the brief tangent exchange when Alwan questioned her mother's inspection of Nur's face. "Did you think it was her?"

"Of course. How many Americans are named Nur?" Hajje Nazmiyeh said. "But our Nur has Mariam's eyes."

Alwan hid her annoyance and ended their mumblings in front of the guests. "There are probably thousands there with that name. It's not the time, Yumma. This is about Khaled."

Hajje Nazmiyeh was amused that the American Nur could speak Arabic, and while Alwan probed her about her son's condition, what could be done for him, Hajje Nazmiyeh corrected Nur's pronounciations of words. Rhet Shel sucked her thumb, staring at Nur with a mixture of delighted curiosity, shyness, and mistrust.

Seeing one of the candles almost spent, Um Khaled turned to Rhet Shel to fetch a new one, explaining to Nur, "I keep candles burning while he is awake. This is how he blinked the first time. I am sure of it. He responded to the candles." She held her breath with closed eyes, and exhaled slowly. "He is somewhere inside himself."

Jamal and Alwan's brother looked away, helpless before this mother's sorrow. Nur touched her palm to Um Khaled's clenched hands and Hajje Nazmiyeh hastened to dispel the sadness forming in the room. "Enough of that, daughter. Say *alhamdulillah* and welcome whatever Allah brings into our lives." She motioned for Rhet Shel to clear the plates with her.

The men stepped out to the local coffeehouse, leaving the women to plan for Nur's sessions with Khaled. Before leaving, Jamal whispered to Nur in English, "Don't promise anything you cannot deliver."

Boys were playing football outside, so Alwan closed the window, smiling hesitantly at Nur. "Can you make my son wake up?"

Nur looked down, searching the floor for words "Um Khaled . . ."

"In our home, just us women, call me Alwan. It's okay. I know Americans use first names," Alwan interrupted. "I am sure my son is not in a coma."

"I think you're right, Alwan, but . . ." Nur hesitated when she saw how those few words made the sun shine in this mother's eyes and spread a smile through her body and into everything in the room. She remembered Jamal's warning and continued. "I think the best I can do is to try to find a way for him to communicate."

"May Allah fill your heart with joy like you just did with mine." Alwan embraced Nur.

Hajje Nazmiyeh had walked back into the room. "I can't understand a word the American says," she said to Alwan, then smiled at Nur. "It's okay, child. You made my killjoy daughter happy and with Allah's help we will teach you to speak Arabic right."

"Maybe you can help me," Nur turned to Rhet Shel, who was hiding in the corner with her stuffed toys.

Rhet Shel smiled for the first time, a shy thing she covered with her stuffed toy. Nur crouched to her eye level and pulled out what looked to be a plastic toy. "I don't know what it's called in Arabic, but in English, this is a harmonica," she said to Rhet Shel, blowing into it.

Rhet Shel didn't dare reach for it.

"Want to try it?"

Rhet Shel nodded.

"This used to belong to a very special musician. I can't give it to you to keep. But you can play on it as long as you like," Nur said. "Do you think you can take care of it for me?"

"Yes!" Rhet Shel promised. "Can I go show my friends?"

"Of course."

Just then, the boys playing outside scored a goal. The raucous sounds of their elation poured into the room, and Rhet Shel ran outside to witness the fun and share her new music.

Khaled

"Our coffee cups, the birds and green trees with blue
shade, and sun leaping from wall toward another wall,
like a gazelle, and water in clouds of endless forms spread
across whatever ration of sky is left for us, and things
whose remembrance is deferred and this morning, strong
and luminous—all beckon we are guests of eternity."

—Mahmoud Darwish

*I scored a goal playing football with Wasim and Tawfiq today. I
could see Yusra watching from her window. I know it is all in my
head. But I could feel the ball bounce off my foot into the net. I felt the
embrace of my friends. I felt Yusra's eyes upon me and my friends' arms
around me.*

*Wasim came to visit. He stood in my line of vision, then moved
his face to where our eyes could not meet. But I saw him long enough
to see hair on his face. The span of his shoulders had also widened.
Not quite like a man, but not a boy like me. I wondered how much
time had passed.*

*I go to Beit Daras often. Always to the river, where Mariam and
I inhabit an endless space of blue. We wrote a song together. Or
maybe we remembered it. Inherited it somehow.*

> *O find me*
> *I'll be in that blue*
> *Between sky and water*
> *Where all time is now*

And we are the forever
Flowing like a river

My jiddo Atiyeh comes here, too, and knows Mariam well, though it is strange to see him without Teta Nazmiyeh. There is love in every space here and I struggle to understand reality, because I remember they are not living. How do I tell Mama of this freedom? That there is a Beit Daras in a Palestine without soldiers where we can all go?

For now, we communicate with candles. When I am sitting by the river of Beit Daras with my ancestors and the old villagers, a candle lights up the sky and I know it is Mama calling me home. I always go back for her. I always blink for her. She whispers to me that she knows I can hear her. My teta does, too. Teta Nazmiyeh said, "I know you're still here, son." She knows I am inside my body. She sings to me and tells me things in her heart. She tells me stories from Beit Daras, then I live them when I go there. The places and people she tells me about appear when I go back to the river, leaving her alone with my body, which feels more and more foreign to me. A shell of a boy to which I return only to stay with candles my mother makes from the stuff of her heart.

Now, Nur is here and I stay tethered to Mama's candles longer. She is no more the little girl by the river with me and Mariam, but an American woman with a purpose. She talks to Rhet Shel, telling her stories of a grandfather from Gaza, and when I return to the river, I see it was my great-khalo Mamdouh. He had been with us all along there. Nur does not know she has come home. When Teta pulled her close, Nur was also searching Teta's face for traces of her jiddo's stories of a sister whose mismatched eyes Nur had inherited. I want to tell all that I know.

Nur asked me to blink if I could hear and understand her. So I did and Mama declared triumphantly, "I told you so."

Rhet Shel is Nur's helper, and when they talk, I hear my little sister's voice blowing away the anxiety from her small shoulders. Together they are making charts with letters and common words for me.

FORTY-FIVE

Nur came every day and stayed longer than she needed to. She thought she was keeping a promise. Doing something good. Helping. She was, of course, but only by coincidence. She came to bathe in the cramped bustle of family and neighbors. She came to watch life up close, to rub her soul raw with the rhythms of our families. The warm mist of our lives condensed on the cold dry surface of Nur and she sopped it all up. That's why she came, for the dew of family caught on her skin.

"HE STAYED FOCUSED FOR nearly half an hour and answered simple questions. One blink for yes, two for no," Nur said excitedly into the phone.

"That's excellent, Nur. It must be gratifying to see improvements so quickly," Jamal replied.

"I don't know how much we can really hope for, but the biggest change has been with Rhet Shel. Most of the questions came from her," Nur continued. "She wanted to know if Khaled liked her hair, if he wanted to watch a film with her."

It had been a miracle day to witness the emergence, however brief, of two children locked in their own minds in different ways. It was Rhet Shel's idea to play Khaled's old music, and she was sure that he was trying to dance when his cheek twitched. That small muscle spasm dropped Alwan to her knees with tears.

Hajje Nazmiyeh was having tea with the neighbors, all of them making bread in the outdoor communal taboon, when Rhet Shel arrived breathlessly, urging her grandmother away from the matriarchal collective to come see. Hajje Nazmiyeh quickened her pace, praising Allah's infinite glory, as her eager granddaughter explained that Khaled was waking up. Behind them, some of Hajje Nazmiyeh's friends followed.

Despite the disappointment of seeing Khaled still immobilized in his body, they had already been inspired by Rhet Shel's elation and let it spread through them, too. The pop music of Nancy Ajram and Amr Diab leavened the air in Hajje Nazmiyeh's home, giving rising form and lyrics to a day transformed by Rhet Shel's charm. She tied her mother's scarf around her narrow child hips and danced. Her young friends were there, having followed as the matriarchs did. They too danced as their elders clapped encouragement. It wasn't long before Hajje Nazmiyeh joined and pulled Alwan into the fray.

They continued in spontaneous cheer, fueled by Khaled's alertness and blinking on cue. Nur played the songs Khaled chose by blinking for the options Rhet Shel presented. Five songs, through which Rhet Shel's happiness restored and repaired them, lifted Israel's siege, ended the military occupation, and returned them to their home in Beit Daras.

The affection Nur felt for her surroundings edged against the walls of their merriment. She smiled silently, watching ordinary love unpack itself, hoping its splash would land on her.

FORTY-SIX

Propriety wouldn't allow Mama to don niqab again after Baba died, but she wanted to. She'd have happily doused herself in a burqa like the women in the Gulf so she could always be alone in darkness and in memory. Only I could see the depth of Mama's loss. She held her pain in her private world behind curtains. Some of it she balled up into small spheres of anger that she hurled at others for no good reason. But mostly, it festered in her body.

Nur's initial success with Khaled was followed by months of frustration in which she failed to elicit a sustained response from him. Hajje Nazmiyeh told her that miracles are prideful. That they only come when faith is strong. But while Khaled continued to look out vacantly to the world, Rhet Shel flourished. Animated by her responsibility as Nur's helper, she became her brother's keeper, talking to him, combing his hair, washing his face, excavating his ears, nose, belly button, and nails of "the dirty." In the evenings, when Nur left, Rhet Shel would pretend to read to Khaled as Nur had done during their sessions, and she took charge of his feeding, too, especially as her mother returned home from work coughing more, with less life in her face each day, and her teta's eyesight was always too fuzzy.

Alwan would return from the women's co-op pale-faced and tired from embroidering thobes all day, which were smuggled through the tunnels to Egypt and sold around the world. Rich Palestinian Americans—all Americans were rich, weren't they?—were the co-op's most important customers. They paid top dollar for anything from the homeland. Alwan had even heard of a family that spent a few thousand dollars for two buckets of dirt from Nablus to sprinkle over their exiled father's grave when Israel would not allow them to fulfill his dying wish to be buried in Palestine.

"How much you think they'll pay for Gaza's dirt?" one of the women quipped.

They laughed. Some expressed sympathy. "*Al ghorba* is hard on the soul. That poor man lived trying to get home and he couldn't, not even in death. May Allah have mercy."

"We're the poor ones. Locked up in Gaza," another said, shifting in her chair to evenly distribute her indignation. "And before you bring it up, they get something valuable that they want for the money they pay us. Simple. Nobody's asking them for charity. When they fight like we do or send us some weapons to fight, then we can call them Palestinians."

Some women sucked through their teeth in agreement, some took offense, reminding the women of family members who had gone abroad to work and send money home. One woman, the youngest in the group but respected for her militancy, cautioned against perpetuating divisions that the enemy created among Palestinians, but she was quieted by another: "I'm tired of hearing your political lectures!" Then she turned to the others. "Seriously, ladies. Do you think we could make money selling dirt from Gaza?" They continued, but Alwan said little.

"What do you think, Um Khaled?" one of the women asked Alwan. "That American Palestinian seems nice enough. What's her name? Nur?"

Alwan thought of the worshipful way that Rhet Shel looked at Nur, and she remembered how Rhet Shel had told her that she wanted to be just like Nur when she grew up. "It's a sin to speak ill of others," Alwan said. Her friends shook their heads and giggled. "You sure don't take after your mother."

But that conversation gave Alwan permission to venture behind closed spaces in her heart. Nur had given her false hope.

Why had this woman left her life in America to come to their wretched Gaza refugee camp? Was she using her son to study or further her career at his expense? Westerners came and went all the time on poverty and war tours just to go back and write books. Alwan imagined the satisfaction of putting an end to Nur's visits. Khaled was lost to her. She wished death's mercy for him. What life did he have now, with just a body that breathed, ate from and shat into bags, to which she attended on borrowed energy? A slow burn simmered from her inability to make a better life for Khaled or Rhet Shel, who would rush to her when she walked in the door to help her poor mother as she struggled to sit, to move. Her Rhet Shel, still so very young, had become her brother's caretaker. The gravity of bitterness pulled Alwan to its center, where Nur was the reason for all that pained her. And when her coughing began to deepen in her chest, she resented Nur all the more, as if her troubled body were Nur's fault. Then she took ill at Nur for the bile of unuttered acrimony accumulating in her own heart; for the sin of it. She tried to shoo it all away. She prayed to Allah for help, and begged forgiveness for the growing desire in her heart to call on Sulayman.

"Sulayman, if it pleases Allah, please help us. Bring my son back to us," she pleaded.

"Mama," Rhet Shel came running to Alwan, "*el doktor* Jamal's wife invited us to a ghada for Nur tomorrow!"

Nur followed behind Rhet Shel. "I have the center's car for two days to visit patients and they said I could use it for personal travel, too."

Alwan thought she recognized a kind of pleading in Nur's face. Or maybe it was a call for an unspoken truce to Alwan's unspoken animosity. "I have to stay here with Khaled." Alwan looked away.

But Rhet Shel would have none of that. "We can put his wheelchair in the car. Allah keep you, Mama, please?!"

Alwan had heard of Jamal's wife, who came from a well-off Gazan family but whose brother had been suspected as a traitor. She considered whether she would be able to confirm the long-standing rumors about the woman's brother or not. What was her house like inside? Was she a good cook? How do people like her live? Alwan was curious.

"Okay, habibti. We can go if your teta also wants to go," Alwan said.

Nazmiyeh's brow raised. "We will have a lot to talk about with the ladies!"

"*You* will," Alwan corrected her mother, for she had stopped going to those gatherings, hoping that a respite from smoking argileh would calm the persistent cough in her chest. But soon she had discovered the sweetness of solitude, and she had begun to look forward to the stillness of being alone for a few hours a week when her mother joined the neighborhood women to smoke, drink tea, eat *bizir*, and gossip while their children and grandchildren played around them.

But tomorrow the women would gather in their absence. Alwan could hear them in her mind, anticipating reports from Hajje Nazmiyeh about the doctor's wife and her ghada.

Rhet Shel went to Khaled. "Blink three times if you love me. Blink, Khaled! Okay. Just blink two times. Why won't you blink? Just blink, Khaled. Okay. Just one time, blink. MAMA, MAMA, NUR! HE BLINKED. HE BLINKED!" Rhet Shel curled herself next to her brother to watch television and Alwan could hear her say something to him about "a fancy ghada at rich people's house" and "I'll bet they eat at a food table."

FORTY-SEVEN

Teta tended to everything while Mama worked all day. She said we were lucky to have her because our mother couldn't cook worth a lick. On Fridays, our space would fill with the concert of my uncles, their feuding wives, and my cousins. Teta conducted the flow of the day, setting rules, quieting what she didn't like to hear, encouraging what she did. She laughed on these days more than others and she put me in the center of everything, which automatically put Rhet Shel in the center, too. Aromas of cinnamon, cardamom, allspice, and nutmeg wove through laughter and bickering. Later, Teta would lead us to the shore, towing me along, to eat bizir seeds, puff on argilehs, drink sweet mint tea, and play in the company of the moon. Teta's friends, matriarchs in the camp, with whom she had once upon a time shared laundry sessions in Beit Daras, joined her there to renew the bonds that spanned lifetimes of gossip, marriage, childbirth, war, scandal, friendship, prayer, and all the beautiful hard living that had made their parts saggy and wrinkly.

THE DOCTOR'S HOME WAS at odds with the humble man who worked with children in the camp. Nazmiyeh sucked through her teeth at the sight and climbed the wide granite steps to a large arched front door. It was grand, though not in the way of the old Gaza homes built centuries before. This home was new, a showy thing in an expensive neighborhood planted in the world's biggest ghetto.

A strikingly attractive woman, dressed in elegant western attire, her hair uncovered and styled, greeted them, and it seemed to Hajje Nazmiyeh that the woman had been expecting Nur to arrive alone. She searched Nur's face for a response to the woman's surprise, but instead watched Nur take in the woman's beauty. Nur managed to eke out a fake smile, but Nazmiyeh could see insecurity and apology creep into Nur's posture. Faced with the doctor's petite wife, Nur was trying to shrink her tall, big woman self.

Nur extended her hand, "It's nice to meet you, Maisa. Jamal has told me so much about you." Hajje Nazmiyeh knew she was lying.

Nur continued, "Meet my Gaza family: Hajje Um Mazen, Um Khaled, Rhet Shel, and this is Khaled." Hajje Nazmiyeh realized that Nur was trying to assuage the wounded pride that clicked its heels on Alwan's face. She, too, had noticed the woman's surprise at seeing them.

"Of course, yes. Welcome, welcome." Maisa shook their hands and kissed their cheeks.

Before shaking Maisa's hand, Alwan moved a small step closer to Nur in a spontaneous alignment of solidarity. In the intuitive, unspoken language of women, it was going to be Alwan and Nur against this pretentious woman should war break out over the ghada. Hajje Nazmiyeh felt lighter on her feet, energized by the unfolding silent drama, especially since she had taken note of Alwan's growing annoyance with Nur over the previous week. Hajje Nazmiyeh, too, closed ranks with a slight step toward Nur when she shook Maisa's hand. "May Allah expand your bounty, Sitt Maisa, and bless you with a son to carry the family name," Nazmiyeh said.

Alwan nudged Rhet Shel to greet their host and she approached shyly.

Maisa took her small hand. "Allah's blessing on her. She's so cute. May He keep her always. She reminds me of our daughters when they were little girls." She added that her daughters were approaching college age now and currently visiting with her family in Canada.

"You must miss them," Alwan said, adjusting Khaled's head in his chair.

"Yes, of course. We both do. But it's nice for me and Jamal to be alone, if you know what I mean." Maisa laughed. "Come, sit. Welcome."

Nur stiffened, and Alwan was visibly scandalized that this woman would hint so freely about intimacy with her husband. Nazmiyeh leaned back in her seat, satisfied by the gossip fodder. From the contours of their words, the changing postures, involuntary glances, nearly imperceptible twitches of the eyes and cheeks, Nazmiyeh began to understand the reason for this invitation, this ghada.

"May Allah keep el doktor Jamal always strong for you," Nazmiyeh said, looking at Nur, whose jaw had tightened on its hinges.

Amid the uncomfortable chatter and delicious appetizers, a young woman, hired domestic help, began setting the table. Alwan tried to assist, as tradition and decorum demanded, but Maisa, herself comfortably seated, explained that the nameless domestic helper was from the Shati refugee camp and needed the work. "We do what we can to help," she said. "They just recently got running water. Very sad." Maisa shook her head.

Nazmiyeh, Nur, and Alwan exchanged looks, communicating a shared impulse to leave.

"My husband just texted me. He is parking the car," Maisa said. "The food is set. Welcome to our ghada."

Rhet Shel began pushing her brother's chair toward the dining table. "See? I told you they had a special food table," she whispered to him.

Nazmiyeh was surprised to learn that Dr. Jamal was coming alone. Surely he would not stay and be the only man with a bunch of women.

Jamal walked through the door carrying bags of fresh bread and fruits, props for a fictional happy family story that immediately fell apart because Nur was the first person his eyes found and pulled him toward before he stopped himself, changed course, and greeted his wife with the bags.

The young domestic helper, Sherine, scooped rice onto plates. Nazmiyeh thanked her, urging her to sit and eat with them.

"May Allah give you long life, Hajje," Sherine replied. She continued serving, then returned to the kitchen.

Unsure which of the many utensils around her plate to use, Nazmiyeh reached for the large spoon on the right for the rice and proceeded to cut the meats with her hands. She pulled chicken and lamb from the bones and distributed the meat to the family around her, as she always did at meals, and kept the bones for herself, to get the clinging bits of meat and suck the marrow juice, the tastiest part. After she filled Rhet Shel's plate, she piled tender chunks on Jamal's plate, and he immediately resisted. But Nazmiyeh insisted, "Son, you know this is how we do things. You work hard and deserve someone to nurture you."

Maisa felt the sting of that comment, shifted uncomfortably in her seat, then turned back to Nur, whom she had been trying to engage in English conversation. But Nur would only respond in Arabic. Finally, in ill-disguised mockery, Nazmiyeh blurted the English words she knew, "Food. Good. Welcome," and continued in Arabic, praising the hands that cooked it and wishing Allah's continued bounty for her hosts.

Jamal kept his gaze on his plate, moving food around with a fork, hardly eating.

"Excuse me, Hajje. With my daughters away, I haven't spoken English with anyone in a long time. We usually only speak English and French at home so we don't lose our language skills," Maisa said, explaining that with Jamal away all the time for work, she was excited to have someone like Nur with whom to practice her English.

Nazmiyeh could not resist whispering into the space between her and Nur. "I can understand why el doktor stays away all day."

Only Nur heard those words, but others felt their energy. A silence settled and all that remained were the oblivious sounds of Rhet Shel eating and speaking to Khaled.

Jamal barely spoke during the meal, and he took leave shortly after, leaving Maisa to trudge through the thickened air of her home, forcing a make-believe narrative for her life. But in the unstable quiet punctuating their conversations, Hajje Nazmiyeh could see that Maisa would cry and fight with her husband after they left. The thought satisfied her.

The delicious meal was followed with fruit, sweets, hot tea, and coffee, most of which was consumed by Hajje Nazmiyeh and Rhet Shel. On the way home, both of them were five years old, delighting in their full bellies, debating which dish was best, and competing over who had eaten the most. "Well, of course it was me since I have a bigger belly that fits more food," Hajje Nazmiyeh said to her granddaughter.

"But tomorrow you'll be fatter and I'll be taller," Rhet Shel crowed, repeating words her teta had said in the past. Hajje Nazmiyeh had to stop to restore her breath from laughing.

"Allah help me, Rhet Shel is turning out a wisecracker like her teta," Alwan said. She was laughing as she and Nur worked to situate Khaled. Then, with both children in the car, Hajje Nazmiyeh motioned for a moment with Nur and Alwan. They came near, pulled by Hajje Nazmiyeh's seriousness.

Hajje Nazmiyeh spoke deliberately, her face frozen and sober, "Do you think Maisa yells in French and English when el doktor fucks her?"

A burst of hilarity rose from them. It fueled their movements as they got into the car. Even Alwan, who would ordinarily decry her mother's impropriety, could not resist laughing.

Wanting to join in the mirth, Rhet Shel offered a joke. "What time is it when an elephant sits on your fence?" She didn't wait to give the answer. "It's time to get a new fence!"

They laughed with her, and roared when Alwan added, "And while the hired help from the camp is putting up the new fence, you go to Canada to practice your English and French." Rhet Shel was pleased to have provoked such a guffaw and snuggled closer to her unmoving brother. "Blink if you're laughing inside."

As Rhet Shel started to doze, Hajje Nazmiyeh began putting words to the unuttered story she had perceived at the ghada. "I'll admit her food was tasty and her house was immaculate, but don't worry, Nur, she has nothing on you."

Nur instinctively tapped the brakes.

"Keep going, Nur. You can't hide things from me. I'm Hajje Nazmiyeh. Nothing gets past me," she said. "That man is in love with you, and it is obvious his wife knows it. That's what this invitation was all about. She wanted to check you out and make sure you saw how happy they are together. Why else would that man stay by himself with a bunch of women unless she made him? He sat there like an uninvited vagina on its menstrual period. For shame he let a woman control him like that."

"Yumma, stop." Alwan had had enough of her mother's indecent talk.

"Don't tell me to stop. I don't like it when you do that. All I'm telling is the truth. And there's nothing wrong with him being in love with Nur. Allah and his Prophet, peace be upon him, made it halal for a man to take another wife. And why not? He can afford it. Nur would be taken care of. There's no shame in that."

"She's right here. So you don't have to assume she is even interested," Alwan protested, but Nur remained quiet, keeping her eyes on the road.

"I don't need to ask her. I already know she loves him. Isn't that right?" Hajje Nazmiyeh was smiling at Nur, whose fingers tightened around the steering wheel. "Maybe that's why you came here in the first place. No shame in that, either." Hajje

Nazmiyeh shifted in her seat and that seemed to change her thoughts. "Also, how the hell can that woman and her daughters travel so freely in and out of Gaza when the sick and dying are being held up from getting treatment outside? You tell me what that means!"

"Astaghfirullah! Yumma, that's enough. This kind of talk about people's honor is sinful."

"No, it's not sinful. Sometimes I think that midwife switched you at birth," Hajje Nazmiyeh said. "What's sinful is that we don't have a medical picture machine so doctors can get a picture of my grandson's head and help him. It's sinful we can't take him on a couple hours' drive to Cairo to see a specialist doctor. It is also sinful that you have lost so much weight and keep me up at night with your coughing. If you don't go to a doctor in the next few days, I'm going to beat you with my slipper like you're a little girl." Seeing Rhet Shel open her eyes in alarm, Nazmiyeh whispered in her ear, "I'm not really going to beat her with a slipper."

Nur turned to Alwan, compassion in her eyes, and something very soft formed in the space between them, where loneliness recognized itself. They saw each other: Alwan exhausted and ill, and Nur desperately alone. It was a moment of vulnerability that passed quickly and left in its wake a kind of sisterhood.

"Why don't you stay over tonight if you like, Nur. The family is coming tomorrow and I'm going to roll grape leaves for ghada. I can teach you how to make them," Alwan said.

Hajje Nazmiyeh assured Nur that she would do the cooking, and Rhet Shel bounced in her seat excitedly. "You can sleep with me and Mama," she said.

The lull of evening's darkness drew them together, three generations of women and two children, one blossoming and the other wilting. Nur never went back to the hostel again, except to retrieve her few belongings.

191

Khaled

"I have walked far enough to know where autumn begins:
there, behind the river, the last pomegranates ripen in an
additional summer and a beauty mark grows in the seed
of the apple."

—Mahmoud Darwish

*Whenever I missed my mother, I simply grabbed on to the candle
flame and it brought me home. Then I could see, hear, and smell
Gaza in the aroma of Teta's food. This side of life, inside the age of
ten, is wonderful, but incomplete and not wholly home. Talking with
Rhet Shel and Nur makes them very happy, but it is too tiring for
my body. I had much to tell, but faced with the ability at last, my
words retreated from the letter board they created. It no longer
matters that they know Mariam still reads by the river, or that there
is another "now" when Beit Daras is restored to her children, or that
Nur is ours, Teta's niece. I would like to tell Mama not to fear. But
lately, I cannot find the candle flame. Sulayman said eventually the
candle will flicker no more.*

*Sometimes, I don't need it. I just go home because Mama pulls
me to her, as she did in humiliation. I could see her, at that woman's
table, tending to the needs of that chair-bound body, my body, though
it no longer feels like me. I become that boy because my sister relies
on me to blink. She measures her world by the frequency of my
blinks. Rhet Shel is fidgety, clinging to Mama, then to my body, then
to Nur. And I feel increasingly distant.*

I understand Mama's anguish and her want to strike back. But there are so many other emotions in that room. Something thick and sticky moves between Nur and Dr. Jamal. Sulayman tells me it is love, and I think of Yusra and the last Kinder Egg I gave to her. But this is not the same. What runs between these two people is immovable. They cannot redeem it nor can they be rid of it and I want to be a part of it. I sense the weight of it, enticing and intriguing. It remains between them even when Nur leaves with my mother, Teta, my body, and my sister. Talk in the car creates a shifting landscape of emotion. I blink for Rhet Shel when they are laughing and their playfulness settles on Teta's persistent love, Mama's bewilderment, and the viscous trail of thoughts lingering between Nur and Dr. Jamal. Then I leave with Sulayman.

FORTY-EIGHT

Nur stopped wearing shorts in eighth grade after a boy told her that her legs looked like tree trunks. In high school, a popular classmate told her that her ass was so big she should kill herself. A year later, that same girl taught Nur how to be beautiful. "Just stick your middle two fingers down your throat after every meal." It was then, too, that she began wearing brown contacts so she didn't look like a "freak." When she finally took them off, her eyes shook our world. Visitors came daily to hear the story and praise Allah's infinite wisdom and mercy. Teta went back to talking with Mariam and rumors of Sulayman the djinni resurfaced. Fate had been cruel to take one of our own, assemble her destiny from pieces of loneliness, exile, rejection, and longing, then bring her home a stranger. People proclaimed Allahu akbar and praised His infinite wisdom for giving her Mariam's eyes to help her see the way home.

T HERE WAS NO MIRROR in the bathroom. Nur and Rhet Shel instead watched each other as they brushed their teeth and washed their faces before bed.

"What are you doing to your eyes?" Rhet Shel asked.

"I'm removing my contacts. I can't sleep in them. See?" Nur balanced the first lens on her fingertip.

"Why?"

"It could hurt my eyes if I keep them in for too long."

"Why?"

Nur smiled. "Want to see a secret?" She removed the other contact.

"You have different colored eyes!" Rhet Shel exclaimed. "How did you do that?"

"I was just born that way. What do you think about that?"

"It's beautiful." Rhet Shel was awestuck. "I wish I had different colors in my eyes."

Before Nur could respond, Rhet Shel was already out of the bathroom, pulling Nur by the arm, yelling, "Mama, Teta, Khaled! Guess what? Guess what!"

"Rhet Shel, lower your voice. It's late," Alwan said from the door, on her way to a neighbor's home to borrow cardamom for the morning coffee.

"Stop shushing her!" Hajje Nazmiyeh admonished her daughter. "Come here, habibti, and tell your teta what." She lifted Rhet Shel into her lap.

"Nur has a green eye!" she said in a hushed voice, obeying her mother. "She has one normal eye and one colored one. It's green. Look!" She pointed up excitedly at a smiling Nur.

Nazmiyeh's arms went limp. The lines on her face reclined into astonished faith, into the harvest of an old hope. Tears fell, curving against gravity under her chin, as if they would climb back behind her eyes and fall again in a loop, like the circles of her thoughts.

Rhet Shel shook her grandmother. "What's wrong, Teta?" she cried.

Nur lowered herself to the floor, her mismatched eyes staring at Hajje Nazmiyeh from another time. In her heart, Nur understood. "My father was Mhammad. My grandfather was Mamdouh Baraka and my grandmother was Yasmine."

A kind of breathless whisper escaped from a well of quiet within Hajje Nazmiyeh. "You're our Nur?"

Unsteady hands stroked Nur's cheeks, then cupped her face. "Allahu akbar! Allahu akbar!"

Nur trembled under Hajje Nazmiyeh's gentle hands. She was where she had begun, where the first parts of her had been made.

Hajje Nazmiyeh turned to Rhet Shel. "Habibti, go get me Mariam's box."

Rhet Shel hurried to the wardrobe cabinets and returned with a battered wooden box.

Nazmiyeh opened it slowly, her tears renewed by a memory of receiving a package from the United States many years ago.

It was several years after that fateful day in the souq, when Mamdouh's old friend had called Nazmiyeh on the spice merchant's red telephone that had delivered a reverberating grief. The man had called once more. Nur had not yet been settled and her case worker worried that the girl's most important possession might be forever lost to her. A book she and Mamdouh had created together. By law, the case worker could not keep it. Nor did she feel confident in Israel's postal integrity to deliver packages to Gaza. So, she asked Mamdouh's friend, who had been successful in delivering the grandfather's personal belongings to his sister in Gaza, if he would also deliver Nur's belongings. Nzinga had explained the situation to Nur, who at that time was more concerned with managing her life as a teenager than holding on to an irretrievable past. The first was a small shoebox with Mamdouh's watch, old photographs, a worn Quran, his and Yasmine's wedding bands, and what remained of their shabka—a braided gold bangle, which had been given to her by Nazmiyeh at her wedding.

Nazmiyeh had surrendered to the misfortune that she might not ever see Nur. As she had when her sister, her mother, her brother, her son, and her husband had been lost to her, she petitioned providence, called in tearful prayer, and left her heart at the doorstep of fate.

"This book sounds like it should always belong to Nur. I don't know how I will ever get it to her," Mamdouh's friend had said to Hajje Nazmiyeh. He feared that he could not live up to the duty of *amana*, a sacred promise to safeguard something for another person. In the end, he gave the book to another friend who was traveling to Gaza and who would find Nazmiyeh and take it to her. This is how things got delivered in Palestine. Travelers entrusted packages to one another, even if strangers, and no one violated the duty of amana.

Nazmiyeh put the wooden lid aside and Nur could see the contents. A familiar watch, a lot of papers with childish writing she could not decipher. Nazmiyeh slowly removed the papers, and there it was. Nur reached for the book, touched its cover, caressing the words written by her so long ago. *Jiddo and Me*. A drawing of her (a smiling little girl with black hair), her arm (a line) stretching her hand (five small lines) to reach the five small lines connected to a straight line drawn to a smiling old man with gray and black hair. Nur lifted the book from the box; its dusty frayed ribbon was still tied in a bow. As she held the tails of the bow, they were transformed to a bright blue hair ribbon held by small outstretched hands. "Jiddo, will you tie this in my pigtails, please?" echoed a little girl's voice in her mind.

A mature hand took the ribbon. "Which one?" he asked. His voice was resonant and kind, and Nur searched that memory to find his face. But she couldn't. Only the ribbon, her hands and his, her voice and his.

She opened her eyes, the book clutched to her chest, and said to Hajje Nazmiyeh, "I can't remember my jiddo's face."

Nazmiyeh's tears were turning into laughter. "Allahu akbar!" She repeated her praise loudly and powerfully and began speaking with her departed sister. "I know you have a hand in this, Mariam. I know you are here. You never left. Oh, Allah is merciful. To Him all there can be of gratitude. Our child is home." Then she looked into those mismatched eyes, held Nur's face in her hands, lifted it closer to her own. "Our Nur is home. I never stopped praying for you. I never stopped asking Allah to bring you home. You've been here all along! Allahu akbar. Look how

Allah is all-knowing. Look how He brought us together. You see, my child? You see how wise is Allah?" Hajje Nazmiyeh kissed Nur's face, rocking their bodies by the force of this grace. "Oh, how the scents of Mamdouh and Yasmine waft in this house now. Oh Allah, my Lord. How You are merciful."

Bewitched by the unfolding mystery, Rhet Shel ran to fetch her mother from the neighbor's house.

"Allahu akbar! I knew there was something about you. You never felt like a stranger. Allahu akbar!" Alwan embraced Nur the moment she walked in, her neighbor friend in tow.

They telephoned the rest of the family and all the sisters-in-law came early the next morning. News traveled through the camp in all directions like rumors in Rome of a Madonna statue crying bloody tears. "Did you hear? That American woman! Turns out she's Hajje Nazmiyeh's niece. Remember that day in the souq? Remember he had a granddaughter and she was trying to bring her here? That American woman is the girl! They just figured it out, praise Allah!"

People came to the house to congratulate Hajje Nazmiyeh for her answered prayers, and rumors of djinn were ignited and fanned once again. In the noise of miracles, prayers, and innuendo of djinn, Nur retreated inward until evening dimmed the skies and peeled away everyone but those orbiting her heart—her great-aunt Nazmiyeh, Alwan, Rhet Shel, and Khaled. Life had collected her pieces and returned her to love's source. There had been no coincidences. The world was stunning and it occurred to her that not once during her time in Gaza had she felt that old impulse to empty her stomach. Then, at night, she held the remains of love and read its pages to Rhet Shel until sleep came with the lullaby of Hajje Nazmiyeh's snoring, Alwan's coughing, and Khaled's immense silence. Her thoughts wandered in and out of memories and longing. Always, they returned to Jamal. To the details and parts and the whole of him.

VI

Words and stories washed ashore on that ancient
way of the sea, and we made of them new songs.
The sun came again, casting shadows that we peeled
off the street to make of them new clothes

FORTY-NINE

When Mama was a little girl, she unknowingly swam into a school of jellyfish and got stung very badly. After that, she wouldn't let the ocean touch more than her legs, but her distance only magnified the sea's presence inside her, and the sound of crashing ocean waves felt like her own heartbeat when she stood on the shore. There, she looked out at Allah's blue immensity and felt Baba, as if waiting for him to float back to shore, his nets full of bounty.

ALWAN TOOK HER TIME getting dressed, hoping Nur would get frustrated and leave for work. They were already late for the appointment because Alwan was late returning from the co-op. In a last effort to frustrate Nur into giving up on the appointment, Alwan tried to pick a fight.

"I'm so sick of coming home to all this noise," she huffed, silencing the pop music, bringing the dancing of Rhet Shel and her friends to a halt. Nur winked at Alwan in collusion and whispered relief that Alwan had shut that awful music off because she hadn't had the heart to do it herself. Alwan grumbled at seeing her plan backfire and reached down to hug Rhet Shel, who rushed to greet her mother. "It's to make Khaled blink, Mama!" Rhet Shel protested.

Alwan kissed Khaled's forehead. Her daily question to Nur, "Did he respond at all today?" was perfunctory and she didn't wait for an answer.

"I already called the doctor and told him that we will be a few hours late," Nur said. "We have plenty of time and you should eat something before we leave." Alwan grumbled and huffed louder.

Nur called to her again, "Alwan, there's a football match on the south dirt field. I'm taking the kids to go watch; so take your time."

"He used to love to play with those boys," Alwan said, startling Nur as she came up behind her on the sidelines of the dirt field.

"I didn't realize you were here!" Nur said. "Are you ready to go?"

Two of Khaled's friends ran to Alwan, embracing their Amto Um Khaled, begging her to allow her son to remain with them.

"If you think he'll be cared for, it might do him some good to be around his old friends for a change," Nur said, and the boys, encouraged by the American's approval, became more animated in their pleas.

"Okay, Wasim. You and Tawfiq were his best friends. But he cannot care for himself at all; so, you must promise to keep him with you at all times. You must not mess with any of his tubes or else he could get an infection. There's a letter chart by the wall in our house. Get that if you want. Sometimes he will talk to you by blinking yes or no." Alwan paused, peering into the eyes of these young boys to find a measure of comprehension. "Do you understand everything I just said?" she asked.

"Oh, yes! We will take very good care of him," they chimed.

"Here are his eyedrops." Alwan handed them a tube from her purse. "Just put a drop in each eye if he's not blinking on his own. I will be back in an hour or two. Make sure he's home no later than that and make sure you remain with him at all times. Do you think you can do that?"

They erupted with assurances and gratitude, whisking their invalid friend away in his wheelchair. They could be heard saying, as they moved away, "I'll bet we can get him to wake up. It'll be like old times."

Rhet Shel reached up to grab her mother's hand, then Nur's, and she started to cry for her brother not to leave as the three of them walked to the car.

Khaled

"I don't want to die."

—Fifteen-year-old Omsiyat

It seems another life since Wasim, Tawfiq, and I were always together. I was two years their junior, the mediator when they fought, and the object of their teasing when they got along. They were double cousins, their mothers sisters and fathers brothers. We stole a dirty magazine once from Wasim's married cousin, and buried it in a secret hideout. No one ever knew. We loved each other like brothers, and that's what we were. Brothers.

Wasim and Tawfiq pushed me along that day when Mama went to the doctor, maneuvering my wheelchair around and over rocks. We spent time by the old cemetery, an old hangout spot. They smoked cigarettes and talked to me, talked about me, unsure whether I could hear them. Sometimes I could blink. Then I couldn't. My eyes remained open and they applied eyedrops obsessively. I imagined how we looked revisiting our old spots, especially when we arrived at Paradise Lookout, a small peephole, one of several carved out by bullets in a wall. Heaven was on the other side.

Yusra was six when I fell in love with her. I was seven. She had six sisters, no brothers. The town called her father Abu al Banat, which just means "father of the girls." They were all so beautiful that their father used to say he would die of a heart attack worrying about them. It turned out that he died from drowning.

"God forgive me for saying this," Wasim began, "but since Abu al Banat was martyred, Allah rest his soul, it's not as dangerous to

come here to watch our future wives, even though we still have to worry about their mother and the neighbors."

They lifted me to put my unblinking eyes up to the hole.

"They're not in the courtyard, so you have to look up at the second window on the right."

I couldn't see anything, but I envisioned Yusra from times gone by—brushing her hair, fighting with her sisters. Helping her mother wash dishes.

"We have to get more from Tarmal Hill for tomorrow. I didn't get nearly enough today," Wasim said. I couldn't hear everything because they were facing the wall, each with his nose pushed against the concrete to watch through the holes. But I knew they were talking about scrap metal, which is how they helped support their families since Tawfiq had stopped working in the tunnels. Then they were arguing. "Be a man. It's the best place for scrap. It's the Sabbath anyway. Soldiers aren't allowed to kill anyone on their holy day, stupid. I'll bet Khaled isn't scared to go. If he could get out of his chair, he'd be running there by now."

"You're the stupid one. Think about the bombing last year. I'm pretty sure they didn't stop on their fucking Sabbath," Tawfiq said.

"Bombs are different."

"I'm going home and you better come too," Tawfiq said. "We have to get Khaled back anyway."

Wasim's voice deepened. "Come on, brother. Mama's counting on me."

FIFTY

I began to remember more in the hush of my body. Like the day Rhet Shel was born and Baba's eyes trembled with love as he held her. And on my birthday, when the earth shook and buildings crumbled and Baba ... he screamed at Rhet Shel to run. She was clinging to his leg and he kicked her away before the weight of concrete walls pressing on his back conquered and crushed him. Rhet Shel ran away crying and latched on to my leg. Then she lived curled into herself, sucking her thumbs raw, until Nur showed up with music and books and light from another place.

R HET SHEL SAT WITH Nur while the doctor examined her mother behind the curtain. She did not trust doctors, nor anyone else waiting to stick needles into the arms and buttocks of little girls. On her upper arm was a perfectly round scar where a doctor had once jabbed her with a needle and a lie that it wouldn't hurt. Now, rubbing her arm in that spot, Rhet Shel left her chair to sit on Nur's lap as they both waited.

The doctor did not speak much behind the curtain and Rhet Shel was prepared to hear her mother cry out from the shot. But no crying came. Her mother emerged tired, followed by the doctor, who pulled out a small sack of candied almonds from his white coat and handed it to Rhet Shel. She thanked him and changed her mind about doctors.

The adults spoke and Rhet Shel did not fully comprehend, but bits of their conversation would sit dormant in memory until, years later, she would retrieve them to connect pieces of her life. The siege she had heard so much about, the one that the Israelis had made, was hard, they said. As she sucked on the almonds and licked her fingers, the doctor said they had "run out" and opened a cabinet with nearly empty shelves to show them. "We don't even have . . ." Rhet Shel didn't know the word the doctor said, but it contorted his face and she understood that it—whatever it was—was important to have. He said it was best to "remove them" and her mother should think of them as "simply lumps of meat"; that it could give them a full year.

Rhet Shel considered lumps of meat, imagining cooked pieces of tender lamb, and she pulled herself up to whisper in Nur's ear, "Can we get lamb shawerma sandwiches on the way back?"

Without understanding the look on her mother's face, Rhet Shel instinctively knew to climb to her mother's lap and whisper in her ear, too. "Mama, can we get shawerma sandwiches on the way home?"

"Of course."

The taxi took them to Abu Rahman's cart by the shore, and the three of them shared a few quiet moments, eating a small meal, listening to the ocean breathe before heading back to the camp.

When their taxi neared, they could see the camp was heaving. The energy of fear, rage, and outrage shot out from its center. People were running nowhere, as if in circles. Alwan put her hand to her heart. "Your mercy, Allah. Your mercy. It's probably another martyr." She beseeched Allah to give the mother, whoever she was, the strength to bear this terrible fate. "It seems all we ever do is go to funerals of martyrs."

As they got out of the taxi, it became apparent that the crowd was running toward them. "Um Khaled!" someone yelled for Alwan and she hurried, leaving her heart and Rhet Shel on the ground for Nur to pick up.

"Amto Um Khaled! We have been looking for you," said a young boy. "Alwan, your son!" cried one of her sisters-in-law, instantly terrifying Alwan. She began to run, following the young boy's lead. Some tried to stop her but then joined running behind her, shouting, "Allahu akbar!" Just to do something in this time when nothing could be done. They still begged her to stop.

She ran. She ran out of breath. The lumps of meat on her chest, full of tumors, killing her slowly, the doctor had said, were panting in her flimsy brassiere. Tears rolled down her face. Then she heard the bitterness of a woman's voice behind her. "Why is everyone giving so much attention to that boy. He's been dead. He just breathes in that chair between the living and the dead. That family is cursed. He's the reason Tawfiq was martyred. It's his fault. He slowed them down!"

Tawfiq was martyred. Alwan kept going, each leg dragging the one behind it by the force of breath and fear. *Khaled was the reason.* Alwan kept moving. *He just breathes between the living and the dead.*

"Allahu akbar!" The crowd's adrenaline chanted out of sync with the labor of her breath and shuffle of her stride. *That family is cursed.*

There he was, in the distance. It was starting to get dark. "Um Khaled, they will shoot you and make your daughter an orphan. By Allah's Prophet, wait, woman. Those sons of Satan are playing a game. They change shifts in half an hour. We will get him then. Now is too dangerous."

She could see him in the distance. He looked tranquil. If it had been anywhere else, he'd have just looked like a boy in a wheelchair watching the sunset. Hajje Nazmiyeh was sprawled on the ground, slapping herself, screaming to Mariam to tell her why her legs were paralyzed again.

"Why is everyone so upset over this boy who has been dead for a long time?"

Alwan turned toward the woman, who repeated her venom: "It's his fault that Tawfiq is martyred!"

Tawfiq is dead. A man slapped the woman. It was her husband, who then angrily recited a verse from the Quran. "O you who believe! Avoid much suspicion, in deeds some suspicions are sins. And spy not, neither backbite one another. Would one of you like to eat the flesh of his dead brother? You would hate it (so hate backbiting)."

How? Why? Was Tawfiq really dead?

Alwan shook off the shock and pushed through the crowd toward her son, and everyone was grateful that she fainted before she could get to him.

Rhet Shel was mostly shielded in Nur's arms, but she was a child of this violent world and understood enough to make her body into a ball and numb the world by gnawing on her thumb.

Khaled

"But I have never before watched soldiers entice children like mice into a trap and murder them for sport."

—Chris Hedges

Then we were moving. They stopped repeatedly to blink my eyes with their fingers or to put drops in them, until we got to the forbidden dunes, which had once been a neighborhood, home to thousands. But Israel bulldozed it years ago to expand the Buffer Zone. And there was much scrap metal left.

Wasim was right, I was not scared, but my eyes began to burn after a while. In their rush to collect as much metal as they could, they forgot about my eyedrops.

I concentrated on moving my eyelids and tried to summon Sulayman to help me. The world felt empty around me, with only pieces of sound from Wasim's and Tawfiq's hurried movements littering a vast silence. It was the silence of the Buffer Zone. Of the dunes. Then there was a small plop, like a pebble hitting still waters. My eyes had already begun to blur, but I could still see in my peripheral vision when Wasim fell. Another small sound came from him, like a sneeze. I think I shall never forget it. I heard Tawfiq running; the sound of his breath and uncoordinated leaps dissipated the silence and I began to feel the creep of fear. Death lived in the dunes, and we had woken it up.

Blink, blink, dammit, blink. Help me, Sulayman!

Another pebble hit still waters.

Blink, dammit!

"I'll come back with help!" Wasim screamed.

Blink!

The dimness of dusk came and wrapped my body in a blanket of ice. I blinked at last and found myself in a desert, the waves of its sand stretching before me in a familiar path. I got up from my chair. I knew exactly where I was and where I needed to go. I began to walk that familiar road, from the small wrinkles on Teta's left ear, up along the broken paths to her forehead, then the long trek across to the other side of her head. I walked and walked the sandy surface of this desert that was Teta's weathered face until I reached the corner of her right eye and sat on the ink spot to wait. My father, my jiddo Atiyeh, and my great-khalo Mamdouh came, as I knew they would, and together we walked to Beit Daras. We sat by the river there and talked. Three horsemen approached from the distance, and as they neared, I could see that Tawfiq was one of them. I leapt toward him. "Khaled! You wouldn't believe this! This is my great jiddo and the horses my family owned in Beit Daras." My jiddo and great-khalo Mamdouh knew them all and together we went to visit their home in Beit Daras, leaving the women by the river. I looked back once more. Mariam still wasn't there, but as we passed the water well of Beit Daras, I heard someone whisper my name. I looked and saw Mariam curled in a small shelf inside. She seemed frightened, and without moving her lips, she whispered to me across the distance, "Tell my sister Nazmiyeh to come find me."

FIFTY-ONE

Once, when Mama still wore niqab, a western woman approached her very politely in the souq, and her male translator explained that she was a feminist writer working on an article about niqab. The translator explained feminism as a fight for women's rights. The woman smiled beatifically, touched Mama's arm in the way of a savior, and said, "I see very beautiful, exotic eyes and I long to see the gorgeous face I know goes with those eyes." Mama walked away without answering. She understood deeper truths about people. So I was not surprised one day when she whispered to my immobile body, "Son, you don't have to hang on for us if the angels are calling you. We will be okay." And when terror spread through her body that I might be killed in the sand dunes, I understood that when I left, she wanted it to be on my own terms. Maybe donning niqab, then taking it off, had been a way to live on her own terms.

B Y T H E T I M E A L W A N came to, the townspeople had already retrieved Khaled and people near and far were awaiting news of the boy trapped in his own body, alone in one of Gaza's killing zones. Wasim and Tawfiq had limped away for help, but only Wasim had survived to make it out of the dunes, and the soldiers had let Khaled be. But he had sat alone for two hours before it was safe to approach his wheelchair and pull him back to safety. Earlier, two paramedics had tried to brave the distance but shots had been fired at the ambulance until they had turned back. People were helpless to do anything more than watch, but they felt some reassurance that Khaled would be spared because snipers had not already shot him. They didn't consider his eyes were drying.

The voice of that uncharitable woman hung over the town after that. Many thought death would be merciful for the boy, particularly when it seemed he was now going to be blind, too. But things changed after that day, because no one could understand how Khaled had survived. Tubes and bags fed him and collected his waste. He could not speak or move. Now he might be blind and it was uncertain if he had been able to see before. The townspeople contemplated that Allah was keeping Khaled on this earth for a grand purpose. But some thought the mother or grandmother had made a deal with the devil. And the legend of Sulayman was retold.

Hajje Nazmiyeh had to be carried home by her sons, who could recall an earlier time when their mother's legs had stopped working. That night, after the sisters-in-law and neighbors left, Hajje Nazmiyeh, Alwan, Nur, Rhet Shel, and Khaled sat together on floor cushions, letting stillness fall around them. Khaled's eyes were bandaged and Alwan held his head at her chest, stroking his hair. Rhet Shel, who hadn't left Nur's arms, stayed that way and fell asleep in Nur's lap, leaning against the wall. Hajje Nazmiyeh rocked slowly, her numb legs stretched before her, whispering on each *Misbaha* prayer bead passing through her fingers.

"Habibi, Khaled. Can you hear me? My love, my son," Alwan sighed. Nazmiyeh's eyes took her in and caressed them both. Then Alwan told her. There would never be a right time to tell her mother that she was dying, and this was as good as any. "Yumma . . . I have to cut off my breasts to live longer. But I could also die during the operation." She paused to wipe tears, "Either way, it is for sure that I will die."

Nazmiyeh stopped rocking, a rigid protest against the enduring molestation of their future. A fire ignited in her, a burning intransigence against destiny. Against Allah and the dung hole of perpetual death. "Nonsense. I am not letting anything take you from me. I will not, daughter."

"Astaghfirullah, Yumma. You bring sin in our house when you speak against Allah's will like that," Alwan sighed.

"We are believers, and today our son was saved. Tomorrow is another day and, enshallah, everything will be well. *Allah bifrigha*. Rest now and let us all dwell on His mercy, my daughter." There was no capacity in Hajje Nazmiyeh that could hear or take in such news. She did not even let it permeate her, as if she had not heard it at all.

Thus, life and love and death and will were packed close in the small space of their home, and they wore them to sleep together on the floor that night. They awoke the next morning renewed and determined and everyone was pleased to see that Hajje Nazmiyeh's legs had awoken with her. "Allah never gives us more despair than we can handle," she said.

FIFTY-TWO

It took some effort for Nur to unlearn the American assumptions she came with. The first time she took a shower in our home, Teta had to storm into the bathroom and shut the tap off before she used our entire water supply for the month. Then Mama taught her how to bathe by scooping water from a wash bucket and to recycle as much of the used water as she could. The dirty water had to be captured in another bucket that we used for flushing the toilet. Rhet Shel helped her learn to navigate life without electricity during the long power cuts. And Teta taught her the best curse words, when to use them, and how to confront harassment from men in the street. "If you tell them to get lost and they don't, pick up the biggest rock you can lift and go at them with every intention to bash it on their heads. Look crazy. Trust me, they won't bother you anymore." My uncle's wives taught her how to remove the hair on her body with caramelized sugar. "Men shave. You're not a man," they had admonished her. Her most intractable

215

assumption, perhaps, was that fate could be controlled with a host of myths ranging from hard work to winning a lottery; or that ill fate could somehow be redeemed by objections or lawsuits. The day following the violence at the dunes, without intending to, Mama and Teta showed Nur how to carry on without corrosive bitterness that comes from helpless rage.

JAMAL HAD BEEN WORKING in Rafah and didn't get the news about Khaled until Nur texted him two days later, explaining what had happened and requesting another day off from work. "Nur, would it be okay if I came to visit today?"

Hajje Nazmiyeh didn't call any of her sons to be there when the doctor visited. "You're the man of the house," she said to her grandson. She kissed his forehead over the eye bandages and wheeled him into the kitchen, where she began preparing a meal for their guest, even though he had insisted that he would come only for a short while to see Khaled.

Nur was out with Rhet Shel, and Alwan joined her mother and son in the kitchen. "It doesn't matter anyway. His wife will probably come with him," Alwan said.

"First of all, I don't think she likes to get dirty coming to the camps. If she does come, it's because she wants to keep a close eye on him around Nur. If she doesn't, then it's either because he didn't tell her or because they got into a fight over Nur and he stormed out and came anyway," Hajje Nazmiyeh said, pleased with her analysis.

Hajje Nazmiyeh welcomed Jamal that afternoon, "Tfadal, my son. Have a seat. Is your lovely wife coming?"

The good doctor apologized on her behalf, making up a story—she was sick—which they all knew was a lie. Nur saw a look pass between Alwan and Hajje Nazmiyeh and changed the subject to the talk of the town. She struggled to comprehend how the unhingeing events of the previous days could have passed so quickly. Only faint traces of the devastation they had all felt could still be seen in Hajje Nazmiyeh and Alwan. Rhet Shel, too, perhaps taking cues from her mother and grandmother, had unplugged her thumb and uncurled herself. The bitterness of Tawfiq's funeral was still present in what they ate and breathed, but they stopped talking about it. Was it resilience? Denial? Nur searched for psychology terms: Was it *compartmentalizing? Detaching?*

Nur started to recount what had happened. Talking about it was essential to making sense of it. "What happened is done. Let us put our fate in Allah's hands and focus on praying for Khaled's sight," Hajje Nazmiyeh said, cutting her off.

Nur obeyed, kept up with the polite conversation around her, but she slipped into the subterranean parts of herself. Into the lonely places of old shoes and unraveled necklaces.

Jamal had come late intentionally to ensure they would have already eaten, but the hajje insisted and he couldn't refuse when she told him that they had been waiting and hadn't eaten. Nur watched him without looking, feeling what he said, how he moved. He ate with a hearty appetite and she found herself putting more food on his plate, the way she had seen women everywhere in Gaza do for their guests, their children, and their husbands. She didn't notice the silent communication between Alwan and Hajje Nazmiyeh. And after he left, though she could not remember much of what had been said, his presence lingered, and it turned the hours into a compulsion that weighed on Nur. They passed with perfunctory tasks after the meal; changing, wiping, draining Khaled's bags and checking for infection; kneeling, prostrating in prayer; Alwan embroidering, trying to get caught up on lagging work; Nur helping Rhet Shel with homework; Hajje Nazmiyeh gathering with her friends in their homes for tea and sweets and argileh.

The electricity came on at the perfect time, just as it was getting dark and Rhet Shel had to come in from playing with her friends outside. Nur and Alwan, like nearly every person in the camp at that moment, reflexively put their phones on the chargers. The battery pack of Khaled's respirator was already plugged in, waiting. A soap opera series was coming on and Hajje Nazmiyeh hurried back to watch it. On days when the electricity was out, she would go to watch it in a home where someone had a generator. "I prefer watching it in my own house," she said and carried on about the characters, lamenting this one's fate, cursing that one, wishing for some event to happen to yet another. She would yell at the screen sometimes, laugh or cry, and she used it as a teaching tool for Rhet Shel. "See that? That's how you get what you need in life," or "That's the kind of man you want to marry when you grow up." Nur followed along until a text from Jamal pulled her heart wide open.

Can you talk? I am going to the water to clear my head. I could use a friend.

Nur thought he had messaged her by mistake. He hadn't. He said he was leaving his wife. His life had been devoid of love for so long. What was he saying? Why to Nur? The sudden intimacy of his words terrified and thrilled her.

"I'd be afraid. Leave the son of a bitch. He's cheating on you with every harlot in town!" Hajje Nazmiyeh dispensed advice to the television characters.

Then he said it, in a text.

She knows I'm in love with you.

Nur stared at her phone, light from the television dancing on the darkened walls around them, unaware that Alwan was watching her. She did not text back, and Jamal quickly apologized. He said he had thought she felt the same. That she had made him feel alive for the first time in years.

With trembling hands, she wrote and erased that she felt as he did. She wrote and erased how desperately she wanted to see him. Another text came.

Please say something.

Aware of Alwan's attention, Nur went to the toilet and wrote back.

I can meet you by the sea, near Tal Umm el Amr in three hours.

She remembered the first time he took her to those ancient ruins of Saint Hilarion monastery that spanned centuries from the Roman Empire to the Umayyad period in the seventh century. They had stopped to eat lunch after visiting patients and Jamal had talked through five thousand years of history.

The television soap opera had been over for some time and they were already well into watching an Egyptian film when the electricity went out. It was just as well because Rhet Shel had already fallen asleep and both Alwan and Hajje Nazmiyeh were dozing off.

Another hour passed in waking dreams that thickened the darkness with unbearable want. Nur removed the covers slowly and as she got up from the bed, she was startled by Alwan's grasp.

"My love, the sea can wait," Alwan whispered from the depths of sleep.

Nur waited until quiet settled again, and crept out of the bedroom past Hajje Nazmiyeh, who snored on her cot in the family room. The door creaked slightly on its hinges and she paused until the rhythms of the night were restored, then she stepped into a black outdoors. Nur had never known such uncorrupted darkness as Gaza's nights. In places where light appears with the flick of a switch at any moment, the streets are always illuminated. Light would pour from the bedrooms of insomniacs. From the call of twenty-four-hour stores. Street and highway lights. True darkness such as this was unattainable, for it was not merely the absence of light, but the presence of something unseeable filling every crevice of life. Not even the moon nor the brightest stars could light more than their own periphery in this blackness. Nur walked through it, the remains of the day, loneliness and desire clinging to the walls of this darkness to guide her. The sonorous rolls of the ocean, the calls of crickets, occasional scurries of wild cats and rats, and the small intonations of her steps made for the music of that night. She kept walking until she knew where she was. Not far away, amid this beautiful black, Jamal was waiting. She went to the place where they had once shared a lunch. The moon danced on the surface of the ocean, on some of the ruins' edges. She walked until she heard steps not her own. She moved, then heard them again, until Jamal was behind her. "Nur," he said. "I was afraid you wouldn't come."

But words felt like intruders, so they said little else. The darkness panted and Nur was breathless. The taste of his skin, the moisture of his lips moving down her neck. Their breathing grew jagged and hungry. She felt her bare breasts pressing against him and inhaled the air off his skin as deeply as her lungs would allow. And when he slipped into her eager body, a small gasp marked the moment she felt home.

Khaled

"So the darkness shall be the light, and the stillness the dancing."

—T. S. Eliot

They closed my eyes that day, and darkness wrapped around me like a blanket in winter. I thought it was over. That I could not return to the still body in a chair again. But I could hear Mama speak of her sickness and fear, and of love. I think she is not long for here either. Because she sits on the floor and plays for hours with Rhet Shel now. Because of her new unhurried way. Because if she were not dying, she'd have slapped Nur when Nur told her about that married man and what they had done on the shore. Mama had woken up at night and found the door unlocked. But she didn't yell at Nur. She didn't tell Teta or call Nur a homewrecker or a whore. She told Nur she was selfish and reckless with the lives of others, like all Americans were. Then she stopped speaking to Nur for days, except in dry tones when it could not be avoided.

Nur begged her forgiveness. But Mama would have none of it. She had stayed up waiting and Nur had returned barely before the sun. I could feel despondency grow inside Nur, just like cancer was growing inside Mama, and they both confided in me. I was the unintended repository of secrets and quiet fear. A living, breathing depot of understanding that didn't judge or talk back. Nur said, "No one has ever loved or wanted me like Jamal does." And Mama said, "Americans are taught to think only about themselves." They could lay bare their hearts at the same time they changed bags and cleaned tubes and wiped drool and shit and tended to bedsores.

Mama did not think Nur immoral. Whether she would admit it or not, Mama was her mother's daughter and could not have avoided the lesson that cheating husbands, not their lovers, wreck their own homes. Mama thought Nur selfish, because she hadn't stopped to think of the repercussions her actions could have on the rest of the family. On Rhet Shel. Their home would be dubbed a house of whores and her brothers, though they lived their own lives nearby, would be blamed, stigmatized, and pressured to correct the offense against the honor of the women under their masculine purview. "Everyone could be hurt, my son," she said to me. "And for what?" She sighed. She coughed. She went quiet. Then she said, "May Allah have mercy. May He protect my children, for the sake of the Prophet and the heavens." That's where Mama was. In the sensible place of planning and praying and worrying, and she busied herself with the demands and minutiae of fear.

But Nur was planted nowhere. She was raw and utterly lost. I had never witnessed such devastating loneliness. She infected me with it and I would have to leave her there, speaking to an empty body. The doctor had started to avoid her and would not write or return her calls. The earth dropped out from beneath her feet and I could feel the irregular heartbeat inside of her, the endless tears she could not cry amassing into a vortex sucking her deeper into herself. Mama's shunning pushed Nur farther beyond reach. Who in Gaza could understand how this woman who had everything— freedom to travel and live where she wanted, freedom to be safe, to get whatever education she wanted, to work and earn a living, to be blessed with a healthy body and promising future—could suffer so incomprehensibly?

Rhet Shel confided in me, too. "Nur is sad because Mama is mad at her." And finally, Teta grabbed them both by the arms and demanded, "Sit here and tell me every detail of what the hell is going on or so help me I will take off my slipper and beat you both on your heads with it."

I left. Sulayman came and we went again to the river. Mariam had moved from the shelf in the water well to the space behind the wall in our old home in Beit Daras, and I waited for my eyes to open to deliver her message to Teta Nazmiyeh.

The bandages and the tape were removed unceremoniously. A nurse in the clinic. Only Mama and me. That's how she wanted it. My eyes had not died, the nurse said, but she didn't know if I could see or not. They asked me to blink. I blinked. The nurse covered one eye then the other, asking me to blink if I could see her hand.

"Thanks be to Allah, he can still see with the right eye," the nurse said.

"What about the left one?" Mama asked. The nurse didn't think so. She told Mama to trust in Allah, but then she asked what difference did it make.

Mama said nothing more and left. The light of day assaulted me despite the sunglasses when she wheeled me outside, and I returned to the comfort of darkness behind my eyes.

FIFTY-THREE

We all had brown skin and curly black hair, but my sister's tight coils and dark skin hinted of our African ancestry more than the rest of us. Some people called her "abda," even as a term of endearment. "Beautiful abda," they would say, and rarely did anyone question it, until Nur came and took a stand so forceful against that word that even Teta's unbending will melted. It was one of those times when Nur's American logic made sense and changed us, made us better. To hear Teta later threaten people over that word, one would have thought she had never used it herself. Nur showed Rhet Shel pictures on her computer of African queens and goddesses from places like Egypt and Zanzibar and Gabon, and Rhet Shel began to dream of those faraway places, where everyone looked like her.

F RIDAY WAS THE DAY of no school, extra house cleaning, prayer at the mosque, and the best *musalsal* television series. But this Friday was different. It was slow and gentle. Rhet Shel was the first to awake. She made coffee, black without sugar for her mother and Nur, and with extra sugar for her teta. Though Rhet Shel couldn't bear its bitter taste, she loved the aroma of ground and freshly brewed coffee.

She put the tray with two demitasse cups on the floor between her mother and Nur, who slept on floor mats near each other while her teta snored at the other corner of the room.

She shook her mother first, then Nur. "Wake up."

Rhet Shel had awoken wanting to make her mother and Nur happy because they had seemed so sad the previous night. Though Rhet Shel had tried to disentangle their words from faint whispers in the next room, all she could gather was that her teta was not happy with either of them and she wasn't going to live in a house where people didn't talk to each other.

"Oh my little Rhet Shel. What would I ever do without you. No one has ever woken me to coffee like this before," Nur said.

There might have been no sweeter words, until Mama pulled Rhet Shel close, kissed her round cheeks, and declared, "I love this girl more than any girl on the planet."

"*Allah yostur* with all this love!" Hajje Nazmiyeh quipped with a smile. "Where are my kisses?" She feigned outrage and Rhet Shel leapt to smother her teta with them.

"I'm going to get Khaled so he can be with us while we drink coffee," Alwan said, laboring to pull herself up. Rhet Shel noticed that the whistle of her mother's breath had become louder.

Seeing a shadow pass over her granddaughter's eyes, Nazmiyeh said, "Rhet Shel, why don't you get yourself some milk so you can drink with us, too."

The three of them talked, sitting on floor cushions, Rhet Shel in her teta's lap, Nur next to them sipping coffee, while Alwan changed and readied Khaled. And when they were all in one room, Rhet Shel announced, "I've been waiting to show you something." She positioned Khaled's head to be in his line of vision. "Can you see my whole body, Khaled? Blink." And Khaled blinked once. She hesitated. "Khaled, blink twice so I know you weren't just blinking a regular blink." He blinked twice with his remaining good eye. It pleased Rhet Shel, who crouched and began to tumble head over heels on the floor. Then she did a perfect cartwheel.

"Do you like it? I've been practicing all week. My friend taught me!"

There was applause all around and Rhet Shel climbed into Khaled's lap first and left a kiss there on his lips. "Did you like that, Khaled?" He blinked many times, sustaining the momentum of Rhet Shel's smile. Then she crawled into the space between Alwan and Nur to drink from her cup of milk, which she pretended was coffee, satisfied that she had made them not sad anymore.

FIFTY-FOUR

Once, one of Teta's old friends from Beit Daras who didn't have daughters fell ill and needed to be helped with daily living, but she refused to go live with either of her sons because their wives were, in her words, "evil bitches." When the woman's sons tried to force her to move, Teta shamed them, and they left nearly in tears, returning later to kiss their mother's feet. Teta moved in with her friend to care for her. She cooked for her, bathed her, and washed her privates when she went to the toilet. They both knew her days were numbered on this earth and Teta stayed with her until the end. Some of the other women who had been girls in Beit Daras washing their clothes by the river and who were now grandmothers and great-grandmothers came almost daily to sit together around their friend's deathbed, remembering better times—"Those were the days"—and lamenting fate: "Who knew we'd die refugees?" And when they were out of their friend's earshot, they gossiped about the evil bitches and their husbands who were willing to "sell their mother for a wife's pussy." Of course, those were Teta's words and they all laughed, delighting in their friend's audacity as they always had.

THE MERRIMENT OF THAT ordinary Friday morning skipped along to the same tune with which it had started. After Rhet Shel's tumbling show, they peeled, chopped, and soaked ingredients for the family ghada later on, then went to the mosque for jomaa prayers. On their way back to the house, which would soon be filling with the rest of the family, Alwan wanted to stroll by the ocean.

Rhet Shel's spirit seemed to expand and she ran back and forth on the beach, giving repeat performances of her tumbles and cartwheels as the three women watched her, water lapping at their feet. Hajje Nazmiyeh settled down, stretching her legs on the sand, and Alwan and Nur joined her. Every few minutes, Rhet Shel would run to Khaled to adjust his head so she could remain in his view while she played.

"My brother, Allah rest his soul—your jiddo, Nur—used to bring our family here when we lived in Beit Daras," Nazmiyeh began, her eyes searching the horizon. "We thought the ocean would be different after we became refugees. I don't know why. Maybe we thought it would be a refugee, too. It was just me and my sweet brother Mamdouh. We came here and walked right along there, holding hands like we were lovers or something. He was embarrassed at first," she laughed, motioning toward the distance with age-spotted hands. "That was the day we discovered that only one of his legs was growing." And Nur recalled the song of an old man's wobbly walk.

Nur and Alwan listened quietly, eavesdropping on Hajje Nazmiyeh's memories. "He was a good man. He was a provider and a protector. He took care of everyone around him. A good brother and son and husband. He was a good father and a good grandfather." Hajje Nazmiyeh turned to Nur with moist, gentle eyes. "He loved you as big as these outdoors. You were too young to remember, but he gave your mother every penny he had so he could keep you. The two of you were on your way back here when he fell sick. He waited a little because he wanted to sell his car so he could have some cash." Tears glistened on Hajje Nazmiyeh's wrinkled brown face. "Damn money! You should have been raised here with your family, Nur. I'm sorry I wasn't able to get you back. I've been scared to ask you about your life. It should have been spent here with your family. I would have been your mama."

Nur felt her own tears, but they got stuck in her throat and she choked when she tried to speak. She burrowed her hands in the sand and closed them around the warm grains, feeling them slide between her fingers. Hajje Nazmiyeh continued, "And let me say this to you, daughter. You need to think hard about that doctor. We don't do these kinds of things here, and you have to learn that very fast. You might love him and he might love you, but he will break your life. Worse, when people find out, and they always find out, no one will want to marry you. Do you think about that while you're texting him back and forth all day?" Hajje Nazmiyeh looked directly into Nur's mismatched eyes. "I'm no fool, daughter," she said, then smiled briefly. "Not when it comes to love. So now that he is texting you again, what is he saying?"

Nur hesitated, lowered her eyes. "He said he loves me and wants to leave his wife."

"Well, that's a change from last week. Where will his mind be next week?" Hajje Nazmiyeh clicked her tongue.

Nur looked down and took a breath as if to answer, but Hajje Nazmiyeh went on. "Don't say anything. There's nothing to say. I've lived long enough to know how this will turn out. That wife of his will cut off his dick before she'd let him leave her or take another wife. Those people aren't like us."

Alwan furrowed her brow. "Yumma, why do you have to be so crass? Khaled can hear you!"

Hajje Nazmiyeh ignored her daughter, "Nur, I can't hold your American ways against you because I should have tried harder to bring you back. But you are here now and you mustn't take this sinful path. That man better not come to our home unless it's with honor to ask for your hand. Am I making myself clear?"

Alwan reached for Nur's hand and the two women looked on, breathing the winds of the Mediterranean, watching two miracle children and trying to shoo away thoughts of the days ahead.

Watching her grandchildren—Rhet Shel playing with other children and Khaled immobile in his chair under the shade— Hajje Nazmiyeh reached for her daughter's hand and squeezed it. "Tell me, daughter," she said, sensing unuttered words in her child. "Did you make the appointment yet for the surgery?"

And there, the three women sat in a row facing the blue expanse, holding hands, awed by the close proximity of such contentment and imminent pain as Rhet Shel played at the core of all their thoughts.

No one dared say it, but they all understood that Khaled was slowly fading away. His breathing had become increasingly labored, depending more on the respirator, and the doctors said there was nothing more they could do for him in Gaza. His fate was in Allah's hands, they had said, and Alwan assured, "Everyone's fate is in His hands."

FIFTY-FIVE

My sister pretended to read one of my messages from the letter chart to Mama, but most of them got tucked away with her old school papers and drawings. Perhaps she was embarrassed not to read yet. Or didn't want to share my words with anyone else. Perhaps one day when she's older, she will find them and read of my inner world that escapes time and death and sits with Baba, Mariam, and great-khalo Mamdouh, and swims in the oceans and feels people without seeing or hearing them. Perhaps she will think it all a creation of imagination and memory. But she will also read how I loved her and know it was all real.

THE MECHANICS OF THIS day happened as they usually did. Rhet Shel ran home from first grade and was greeted by her mother, who kissed her on the forehead before struggling out the door to her job at the co-op. After seeing her mother off, peeking in on Khaled was her next stop. She climbed up into his lap to kiss him, saying, "I'll be right back, Khaled." Then she hurried to finally go pee. Teta Nazmiyeh was cooking in the kitchen. Nur was still at work.

"Habibti, it's just me and you and Khaled today. Nur is working in the south with a group of children and might stay at a hostel with some of her co-workers," Hajje Nazmiyeh said to her granddaughter. "Your mama will be back around dinner. The center sold double the number of thobes and I'll bet she comes home with some sweets!"

Rhet Shel squealed, jumping up and down. "Did you perform your *thuhr* prayers?" her teta reminded her, and Rhet Shel rushed to do so. A few moments later, she was climbing onto her brother's chair. "I'm back, Khaled," she said, pulling his face toward her. "Nur isn't coming home today."

Khaled didn't blink. "Blink, Khaled!" Rhet Shel demanded. Her brother blinked. Twice. "Let's do the letter thing." She leapt to retrieve the poster-board chart.

She could read some words now, but most of what she copied eluded her, and she grew distressed about hiding another message. "Is this a letter for me?" Khaled did not react. "Is it for Mama?" Nothing. "Is it for Nur?" Still nothing. "Is it for Teta?" He blinked. "Blink two times if this letter is for Teta," Rhet Shel said, and Khaled blinked twice.

Proud to be the bearer of Khaled's message, Rhet Shel tried her best to decipher it. It was only a few words, but it made no sense so she gave up, handing the paper to her teta.

"Go grab the first person you see who can read and bring them here," her teta ordered.

Rhet Shel returned moments later with a fifth grader. Hajje Nazmiyeh showed the little boy a shekel, reward for his trouble. The boy made his own scribbles, his face contorting in thought.

He looked up a few times at Hajje Nazmiyeh unassuredly until she lost patience. "Don't you know how to read, boy?" she barked. "Yes, Hajje," he replied in a shaky voice. Then he lied. "It says, Mariam would like you to have a party. She . . . she, she said she never left and she . . . she is in Beit Daras."

The boy and Rhet Shel watched the ash of shock suffuse Hajje Nazmiyeh's skin. He snatched his shekel and ran out as quickly as he could.

Rhet Shel tried to comfort her teta, who was now sobbing. Hajje Nazmiyeh cried until it was laughter pouring from her face. Then she leaned to kiss away her granddaughter's alarm and said, "We're going to have another party."

She got up and walked to Khaled's chair. "Habibti, get your old teta a chair," she said to Rhet Shel, and she proceeded to whisper words into Khaled's ears, into his eyes, his forehead, his hair, his cheeks, laying so many kisses where her words went. Rhet Shel heard her teta say, "I knew it. I always knew it," then speak endlessly to someone unseen. "I'm ready, my sister. I'll save you this time."

"Rhet Shel, habibti. You and Khaled and I are going to go to the souq to get food for tomorrow," Hajje Nazmiyeh said. "Bring some of your friends so they can help us carry the bags. Bring five friends. All the helpers get candy."

FIFTY-SIX

Nur tried to stop, but the torment of her inflamed heart pulled her deeper into the affair. Far from giving her relief, the texts, calls, and secret meetings only incited her heart until it conquered her will. Their communications were heavy with desire. She lied to Mama and Teta. Told them she was seeing patients in the south. That she was staying in a hostel to avoid nighttime travel alone. But she spent that night with him in a secret apartment he had arranged. He said he wanted to wake up next to her, but they never slept and he left while the moon still reigned over a dark sky.

NUR TRIED TO ENTER the house quietly. A panoply of voices rose and fell around the central command of Hajje Nazmiyeh's banter and laughter. She hesitated before entering, listening. Words of excitement and expectation flowered and hung in the air like decorations. As she turned the corner, she heard a small scream. "Khalto Nur! Teta, Khalto Nur is here!" Rhet Shel yelled and ran into Nur's arms. All the daughters-in-law were there and a few women from the neighborhood with their kids. Some were sipping coffee, others sat around Hajje Nazmiyeh, preparing food. Dicing and chopping, crying over onions. Stuffing this or that vegetable, rolling dough, mixing rice with olive oil and spices. They looked up and cheerily greeted Nur, making space for her to sit in the crowded room.

"We're having a party tomorrow for no reason at all!" Rhet Shel reported excitedly, mindful not to divulge the secret message from Khaled.

Nur walked to the center of all things, bent to her knees, and kissed Hajje Nazmiyeh's hand. "Sit, beautiful daughter," Hajje

Nazmiyeh said. "I'm so happy you're home. You work too much. May Allah look upon my daughters with His favor and goodness always, Amen."

No one understood, but none refused the impromptu celebration. It was a random merriment, but perhaps not so unusual given that its source was Hajje Nazmiyeh. Rows of food trays lined borrowed tables. Steaming spiced rice with browned pine nuts, tender chicken, stuffed potatoes, zucchini, and grape leaves. Women all over the neighborhood pitched in, but the best and largest contribution came from the widow of the old beekeeper of Beit Daras.

"No one can throw a surprise hafla like Hajje Nazmiyeh," people said.

They danced. The old matriarchs and patriarchs looked on at the young and clapped for them. They reminisced over a time and a place long gone. They swayed to the music and to the wind. Young couples with children came, and for one day and one night, troubles and fears lifted away. When the skies dimmed and there was no electricity, candles appeared on every ledge, on mounds of rubble, in windows. Men linked their arms, shoulder-to-shoulder, and danced *dabke* after dabke. Women joined them, or formed their own dabke line. Everyone asked what was the occasion, and they accepted Hajje Nazmiyeh's answer, however puzzling: "Because life is magical and gives us second chances that should be celebrated." Many agreed, adding that a good hafla was the best traditional medicine in their seaside prison. "We find our own ways to freedom. Zionist sons of Satan cannot imprison our joy, can they?" Nazmiyeh agreed, wheeling her grandchild wherever she moved, speaking to him in whispers. Some heard her say, "I always knew you were Mariam's Khaled. I knew it was you," and they assumed dementia was settling into the old matriarch.

Although Nur had met the beekeeper's widow before, she learned that afternoon for the first time that the beekeeper had been her great-grandfather. This woman was her teta Yasmine's stepmother. "But she doesn't look much older than you," Nur said to Hajje Nazmiyeh.

"She's not. The old beekeeper liked them young and got himself a new wife after he wore the other ones out," Hajje Nazmiyeh laughed. "This one was damaged goods. She couldn't make babies and that was just as well. She loved your teta Yasmine and took care of her even though she was only a few years older than her. People like her, but she keeps to herself and doesn't get out much. She has lived alone ever since your grandparents left. People buy herbs and such from her for colds and virility. And nobody cooks like she does. Not even me. But look at her, strong and fat and simple as a mule."

Nur wished Jamal were there. She wanted to tell him about this new revelation. Another piece of her life discovered. She tried calling him to no avail, and created fantasies of a life with him where they would dance together at such haflas. She dialed and dialed, until finally he sent her a text saying that he would call the next day. "My wife is leaving me. Don't contact me until I reach out," the text said.

In time, cheeks were kissed good night and sleeping children were carried home. Despite a herculean effort to remain awake, Rhet Shel fell prey to sleep early in the night. Alwan followed her, spent, as soon as the guests had left. It was never easy to discern if Khaled was awake or sleeping, for his eyes were often shut when he was awake or open when he was somewhere else. Exhaustion was no match for the things stirring inside Nur, for which she had no labels. No words.

At the insistence of her old friend Hajje Nazmiyeh, the old beekeeper's widow stayed, and she opened the stores of her memory for Nur to wander. Tales of her husband, the beekeeper, and his young apprentice, Mamdouh. How Mamdouh would sneak glances at Yasmine, thinking she did not see him. Stories of plants and trees in Beit Daras. Of Yasmine, who at first had not liked her, but who had become her best friend and daughter when they had no one else after the Naqba. Of Mamdouh, the grown man with a limp, who had worked in Cairo to save money to marry Yasmine. Of how they first had gone to Kuwait, then to America, and had only been able to return for visits. Of the love in Yasmine's voice when she had called to tell the widow about their granddaughter, Nur.

Soon, the flickering of Gaza's candles slowly melted and ceased, one by one, as if the night, too, were closing its eyes as the festive bustle went home. A silence so pure yawned across Gaza's skies and Nur remained awake until sleep at last subdued the clamor of her thoughts and the constant checking of her phone.

FIFTY-SEVEN

I stayed for Rhet Shel. It pained me that I could not animate my body for her, and it was all the more wounding because she was content with the blink of my eye. But then it was time. I was by the River Suqreir with Jiddo Atiyeh when Mariam came by with Mamdouh, holding a candle. I knew it was time to extinguish the flame. I took in a deep breath, and blew.

ALWAN AWOKE FIRST, TO what she thought would be a lazy Friday after the hafla. Nur was asleep at the other side of the bed and Rhet Shel was sprawled between them, her little body taking up most of the bed. Alwan smiled, pulling the covers over them as she got out of bed. She shuffled to the kitchen and put a pot of water to boil for coffee, then went to tend to Khaled. She checked his urine bag first, then bent to kiss his forehead. As her lips touched the cold surface of his skin, her hand felt the stiffness of his arm. She didn't move, lingering in the awkward posture of a routine moment. Her heart shook in her chest and she cried, her tears and snot landing on his forehead, lubricating the point of contact between her lips and his skin. Her eyes trembled, then her whole body. She was afraid to straighten up, afraid to move her lips, her hand. She mumbled prayers, unsure what to do now. If she stood up, she would have to face her son's death and her daughter's broken heart.

Strong, kind arms wrapped around her and helped her to a chair. It was the beekeeper's widow. As Alwan moved away from her son, she gave out a mournful howl. Hajje Nazmiyeh sprang up from her bed cushions and needed only to see her daughter to know what had happened. "Allahu akbar ... la ellah illa Allah," she began to whimper and pray, though she could not get up. Her legs were failing her again. The pot of water was boiling in the kitchen and the beekeeper's widow began tending to the women of the house. She brought them both water and went back to make the coffee. She burned sage from the kitchen, suffusing the shock and sadness with the aroma of healing. Hajje Nazmiyeh pulled out the piece of paper on which Rhet Shel had written Khaled's message. "I thought it was going to be me. I thought he wanted me to have a hafla because my time was up," Hajje Nazmiyeh mumbled. "La ellah illa Allah."

"Yumma, what are you talking about?" Alwan squinted through the fog of her mind.

Nur walked in just as Hajje Nazmiyeh was handing her daughter the piece of paper. "Look. You see? Khaled dictated this to Rhet Shel from that poster chart and I did what he asked. I thought it was my time to go and Mariam wanted me to have a party." Hajje Nazmiyeh continued to moan. "Allahu akbar . . . La ellah illa Allah."

Alwan unfolded the paper, trying to decipher the gibberish. She could see the scribbles of the neighbor boy who likewise had tried to make sense of the random letters. But there was no sense in it. It was all gibberish as all of their attempts to communicate with Khaled had been. Her son had been gone for a long time, and Alwan began to feel some strength in knowing her son had now found peace, at last. La ellah illa Allah.

"You see? My daughter, you see? Khaled sent that message to me," Hajje Nazmiyeh repeated through her tears.

"Yes, Yumma. That's what his message said. You gave him the farewell hafla he wanted." Alwan tucked the paper in her pocket and knelt to sit by her mother as Nur dialed the brothers to come.

Just then they heard Rhet Shel, climbing onto Khaled's lap. "Blink, Khaled."

Nur dropped the phone and ran to scoop her up and the whole world was suddenly awash in Rhet Shel's cry. They all concentrated on calming her, but at every moment when her crying would begin to subside, the sight of her brother would spur renewed sobs, until the brothers came and took Khaled's body, and their house was once more crowded, first with family, sleep still in everyone's eyes, then with neighbors and others who came to pay respects.

Khaled

"And even in our sleep, pain that cannot forget falls
drop by drop upon the heart, and in our own despair,
against our will, comes wisdom to us by the awful grace
of God."

—Aeschylus

*The morning when I left, our neighbors awoke to the somber cadence
of Quran readings. People walked out in their nightclothes to discern
the direction of mourning. Word spread quickly that something had
happened in our home. Some could see that my uncles and cousins,
who had left the celebration only hours earlier, were returning with
dark rings under their eyes. Ya Sater, they all prayed in one way or
another for the best.*

"It's the boy," one neighbor said. "May Allah rest his soul."

*"That poor family. Is this what happens when someone dares to
just have a party for no reason? Can't we just be joyful without
punishment following?" said another.*

*"Bite your tongue, woman. You'll go to hell for questioning Allah's
will like that."*

*For hours, people filed in and out. My uncles washed my body,
prayed over it, wrapped it in a white shroud, and blessed it for
burial. Mama and Teta and Nur draped themselves in black. Nur
tended to Rhet Shel, who was mercifully distracted by our cousins
and went to play outside.*

*Many of the women who came to pay their respects were curious
about Nur. They said it was a miracle how she had found her way*

to her family after a lifetime with Americans. Some of them looked both ways and shrank their voices to whisper about "her and the doctor."

"El doktor Jamal?"

"Allah keep the devil's tongue away! Astaghfirullah! Don't make that kind of talk about a woman's honor! And while they are grieving? Astaghfirullah."

But those were only a few. Most women came to help. There was enough food left from the hafla to feed visitors paying their respects, and more food arrived in the following days of mourning, while recitations from the Quran reverberated through the walls of our house. Out of respect, none of the neighbors played music, and they kept their televisions turned low. People came and went on the song notes of Allah's words, entering with bowed heads, drinking bitter coffee. The men and women gathered in separate quarters. There were no adornments, no makeup or polished nails. No colors. Such is the order of grief.

The old beekeeper's widow stayed and helped, especially since Teta's legs were still not working. She took charge of the kitchen, ensuring the constant flow of food and clean dishes.

A woman no one recognized arrived. Everyone noticed her because she did not cover her hair, and though she dressed modestly in black, her gait was buoyed with money and social status. There were whispers: "She's el doktor Jamal's wife."

They heard her express condolences to Teta and Mama. Nur finally came out of the bedroom and Maisa seemed startled by Nur's shocking eyes. But she quickly regained poise, expressing condolences on behalf of herself and her dear husband. She said Jamal was away and it was too bad that Nur's position with the center would be coming to a close soon. "How time flies," she said, and added that her husband had enjoyed Nur's enthusiasm. "He said you were fun," Maisa said pointedly, and left.

FIFTY-EIGHT

At Mills Home, the institution where Nur spent her adolescence, residents were required to attend church services three times per week. Nur was the only Muslim on campus, and when she was caught smoking pot in the church basement with a friend, she was punished equally for the offense of her religion. The administrators and houseparents looked at her with revulsion. Her chores were doubled and she was banned, indefinitely, from everything but school and church. She saw only one way out of this imprisonment. So, one Wednesday at Chapel Service, she walked down the aisle to accept Jesus. She was baptized that Sunday and they all rejoiced. "You're saved now," they said. She was forgiven and her punishment was lifted, but in private, Nur worried for her soul and prayed to Allah.

KHALED'S PASSING ALTERED THE energy and routine of the house. They had not appreciated how large Khaled's silent presence had been. How much of their lives had revolved around filling and emptying the bags that had delivered nourishment and received his body's waste. Or the amount of time that Rhet Shel had spent with his letter chart. Nur realized that Rhet Shel had learned to read and write far beyond her years by trying to decipher these sessions with Khaled. For a while his chair sat in its place, like a stem without its flower. But the family soon sold it and Khaled's place slowly shrunk as Rhet Shel made new friends and began spending more time playing in the neighborhood. Nur took time off from her job. Hajje Nazmiyeh insisted on it.

"I have allowed many things from you with regard to that man, but no more," Hajje Nazmiyeh scolded Nur for the first time. "You are like a reckless teenager. Despite your age and education, your emotions are like those of a neglected child finding love for the first time. He is a cheating husband and an opportunist who has disrespected your love and violated your honor. And if I ever see him, by Allah and His Prophet, I will cut his dick off." Hajje Nazmiyeh paused, corralling more of her outrage. "This is not America where everyone fucks whoever they want whenever they want because it's fun. This is Gaza. This is an Islamic place. I should have been more foreceful in preventing what has happened between the two of you."

Nur cowered, hung her head, lowered her eyes. Her mobile phone testified to more unanswered texts and calls than she cared to count.

Then, Hajje Nazmiyeh softened, and she pulled Nur close. "Please just trust me. I will not allow you to be the fool. Do you think that wife of his came here to pay respects? Of course not. She doesn't care if we live or die. She came here to show you that she had won. It was a declaration of victory." Nazmiyeh repositioned herself, as if she didn't know what to do with her own body. "I wanted to slap the hell out of her. But how could I at such a time? I was so angry, even though you're the one who did wrong. But I would have done it because you're my flesh and blood and because that kind of terribleness should not be laid on the doorstep of a grieving family."

Electrified by her own words, Nazmiyeh could not stop. It felt good to feel angry indignation. She rocked her weight from one side to the other and went on. "I've watched you check that phone every few seconds for days. He isn't going to call or write back. Lick your wounds all you want in private, but in public, your head better stay high." Hajje Nazmiyeh shifted again, charged with her own convictions. "This is one thing I will teach you. The other thing is that here, in your birthright land, culture, and heritage, what you do affects your entire family. And protecting the family must come before your individual fancy."

In the wake of Hajje Nazmiyeh's words, the loosely knit root of Nur's being was both unraveled and restored. Was this a choice between the woman she had been and the one she wanted to be? The untethered one who lived by her whims and an unhingeing freedom? Or the one descended from a family grounded in an ancient earth who was accountable to and fortified by the love and loyalty of family?

As Nur stood there, Nazmiyeh's lecture fading in the noise of her inner turmoil and anxiousness to see Jamal, a text appeared on her phone and made the world stop for the time it took her to read it.

"Please do not text. Things are very bad at home. I am trying to hold on to my family and I am being forced to write you a letter that you will receive later today. Please know that I do not mean a word of it."

FIFTY-NINE

The old beekeeper's widow had been married before she wed the beekeeper but had been divorced because she couldn't bear children. The beekeeper was nearly sixty when he married her. She was twenty, five years older than Yasmine, her new stepdaughter for whom she cared after the Naqba of 1948. She was a simple woman of amiable character, distinguished by an impenetrable intimacy with dirt and food. Her days were spent digging, planting, harvesting, and cooking. And when she slept, she took the earth with her, under her nails and between her toes.

OVER THE DAYS OF mourning, when the old beekeeper's widow stayed with the family, she observed Alwan's frail physical condition and probed her for information. "Child, I am half blind, but I can feel sickness coming through your ribs.

Tell me what the doctor said," she inquired, her massive body pouring over itself in sensuous maternity.

"It's the evil disease. I will go soon to have my breasts cut off," Alwan answered, not believing her own words.

"Have faith in Allah, Um Khaled, and let me help you. We have our own Arab medicine. For centuries we've healed ourselves," she explained. "Let me help you, child. We are family and old friends."

"May Allah grant you long life, Hajje. I have put my fate in Allah's hands and will do whatever He puts in my path. Tell me what do do."

The old beekeeper's widow gave instructions to her Yasmine's granddaughter, Nur. She drew pictures of the plants and where to find them in her garden. "Abu Shanab, the gardener, might be there. Just show him these pictures and tell him I sent you. He will help," she said. "Take Rhet Shel with you, habibti, and make sure no one knows about this garden!"

As Nur turned to leave, the beekeeper's widow continued. "And then we are going to talk about what is making you sad, okay?"

Hajje Nazmiyeh heard her and chimed in. "Good, sister. The more of us talking sense into our child, the better."

Nur liked the sound of *our child* and managed a small smile as she took the picture instructions in one hand and Rhet Shel in the other.

On their way, walking through narrow alleys and the tightly woven lives of lifelong refugees, Nur contemplated the pictures of what looked like cannabis plants. Her smile broadened and she quickened her steps. The garden was located near the western edge of Gaza that was somewhat dangerous to till due to landmines and proximity to Israeli posts, but the beekeeper's widow had done so for years. Nur opened the gate and was stunned to find rows and rows of various plants, manicured and nurtured. Among the various herbs and vegetables grew marijuana plants the likes of which she had seen only in images of drug busts. They were separated in an arid section of the garden, all of them coated with sticky resin. Nur and Rhet Shel began to cut and collect as many as they could. Nur reminded Rhet Shel not to tell anyone about their secret garden, which compounded Rhet Shel's excitement; and with thrilling collusion, they filled their bags. Abu Shanab came just as they were nearly done. He seemed put out by the intruders and repeated the warning not to tell anyone about the garden.

"I won't tell," Rhet Shel promised, looking up at his surly face. "I'm a good secret keeper."

Nur knelt down, searching Rhet Shel's face. She kissed her and held her for a moment before they headed back. "But don't keep secrets from us," Nur said.

They returned hours later, as the muezzin's call to evening prayer spread from so many minarets propping up the sky. "Good timing," said the beekeeper's widow. "Let's go through what you got."

Nur and Rhet Shel unloaded their bags. "Is this enough, Hajje?" Rhel Shel asked proudly.

"It's perfect, habibti. Enshallah, this will help your mama. First thing we need to do is dry these out. I already made sure the roof was clean and lined with blankets. We just need to lay them all out to dry in the sun tomorrow. Then we will start working on the medicine," said the beekeeper's widow.

The next afternoon, Nur and Rhet Shel worked closely with her as she repeated cycles of soaking the dried leaves in solvent obtained from a local welder, extracting the oil, washing, and filtering. The beekeeper's widow worked with the same enchantment she brought to cooking food. She never measured anything, and she knew by smell, color, or texture when to add another ingredient or start a new step.

Hajje Nazmiyeh's legs were functioning again and she left to visit neighbors. The beekeeper's widow suspected that her paralysis had been much more temporary than she had let on.

By evening, they were ready to evaporate residual water from the last wash and siphon off the medicinal oil. Rhet Shel had grown bored and had gone off to play with her friends. Alwan, too, had left in the early afternoon for the co-op. Only Nur and the beekeeper's widow were at the house. "Nur, habibti, I don't live so near and at my size, it's hard to move around. I would like it if you came to visit me more," the beekeeper's widow said, pouring a bucket of solvent into another through a funnel lined with filter cloth.

"I will. My contract at work is almost up and I . . ." Nur didn't know how to finish her thought.

"Yes, about your work. Tell me there's nothing between you and that doctor," the large matriarch said, her words gentle but firm.

Nur looked down at her phone. "I don't know," Nur began, but she hesitated when she met the astonished eyes looking back at her. "I mean . . ."

The old widow stopped what she was doing and searched the face of her Yasmine's American granddaughter. Nur looked as if she could have been the daughter of Mamdouh and Yasmine instead of their granddaughter. "My child, you are beautiful and educated. You come from a good family. Any woman in Gaza wishes she had your height or your strength and independence. You will meet someone who is not married and who deserves your love. El doktor has a family and he is not leaving them. Unless you're willing to be a second wife—"

"No," Nur interrupted her.

"Yes, and that is exactly what his wife will say. I don't doubt that he truly loves you, but even if he wanted to divorce, his elders would not allow it. It would shame Nazmiyeh's sons, too.

There is no room in Gaza for such things. It would hurt everyone, you most of all. You must heed your elders, my child," she said, stroking Nur's face. "Now hand me that pipe and suction bulb."

SIXTY

In high school, Nur fell in love with a boy named Clay Jared, who loved her, too. Mrs. Whitter, her foster parent, forbade her from seeing him. But Nur could not defy the commands of her heart and got caught sneaking a call with Clay Jared. Mrs Whitter snatched the phone, imprisoned Nur once again, and said she was a "nigger-loving truant even Jesus can't save."

NUR LISTENED TO THE beekeeper's widow, helping as instructed with the medicinal recipe, which made the house smell bad. Nur looked again at her phone, hoping for a new text from Jamal. She hoped the electricity would come on soon so she could see if there was an e-mail from him. She knew it wouldn't be good. But he had told her he was being forced to write it.

Nur watched as the black oil climbed into the tube every time the beekeeper's widow pinched the suction bulb. "Alwan needs to take six doses of this every day. It tastes like manure," the widow said, and Nur recalled her pot-smoking college days. She wished she had put one of those plants aside for her own use.

Electricity lit the room and Nur rose quickly to see if she could get a connection on her laptop. Within minutes, she was reading the awaited letter from Jamal.

Dear Nur,

What we did was a mistake. It was wrong and I am sorry that I have not been direct in saying that. I am married to the only woman I have ever truly loved and am committing myself to rebuilding my relationship with her in the wake of my betrayal of her love and the family we created together. As the official ending date of your temporary employment has been moved up due to the death in your family, I would be grateful if you could gather your things from the office when I am not there during the hours between noon and two, when I will be home with my wife.

Kind Regards,

Dr. Jamal Musmar

Nur read the letter, then read it again. And again. She ran to a local Internet café to print it out before the electricity went off. She needed to stab herself with every word, for as long as she could. She needed to bleed to stop from calling or writing to him.

She folded the letter in her hand, then unfolded and refolded it as she made her way alone to the shore, where families lounged on blankets or in plastic chairs, swam in the moonlit ocean, and huddled around bonfires. She walked through evening's shadow, looking for the blur of Jamal's form, waiting for her. But she knew he would not be there. Slowly, her body dissipated into a haze, until there was nothing there where she stood except a tattered old shoe clutching a letter, crying. At last, crying. Alone in the fog of night and heartbreak on a shoreline glittering with moonlight, Nur cried, the whole of her dismantled into three parts: an old shoe, a crumpled letter, and a missed menstrual period.

SIXTY-ONE

Teta wouldn't admit it, but she needed the beekeeper's widow, and she believed that it was Allah's infinite wisdom that had brought her into their midst.

DAYS PASSED IN A surreal tedium. The widow's malodorous laboratory of solvents, buckets, filters, funnels, strainers, boiling pots, and suction bulbs filled and emptied until the flask of black oil was made for the next day's installments of the foul medicine, which Alwan consumed obediently, trusting in Allah's will. Nazmiyeh, too, came to accept the beekeeper's widow as the new sovereign of her kitchen, ruler of all she could survey of dishes, pots, and ladles. And the two old women, who had lived their lives through the same pains of war and loss, and who were themselves family by marriage, became the closest of friends. Although Hajje Nazmiyeh's pride would not allow her to be anything less than hospitable, her true self did not soften toward the coup in her kitchen until life once again inhabited Alwan's eyes.

At first the two hajjes talked of meaningless pleasantries, of which Hajje Nazmiyeh would quickly tire. But then memories and old stories crawled from the sediments in their bones. Ghosts of Mamdouh and Yasmine and others they loved breezed through their words. The beekeeper's widow remembered the days of Um Mamdouh and Sulayman. They laughed, the beekeeper's widow recalling the town gossip during the years when Nazmiyeh was paralyzed but kept making babies. Sometimes tears fell. They both regretted the day Mamdouh and Yasmine had left Gaza.

"Well, you sure are the best cook I've ever known. No one could deny that," Hajje Nazmiyeh admitted. "But wasn't I the prettiest girl in Beit Daras?"

The old widow laughed. "You sure drove a few boys crazy, Nazmiyeh, and more than a few hearts were broken when you married Atiyeh."

Satisfied by that validation, Nazmiyeh wholeheartedly abdicated her kitchen to its new queen, who was happy to teach her how to make medicines and remedies.

"I'll tell you another secret, Nazmiyeh," said the old widow, and her student perked up. "The plants that I make the medicine from are hashish leaves."

"Allah keep the devil away!" Hajje Nazmiyeh said, shifting in her seat, unsure what to say to the beekeeper's widow, someone she had always looked upon as a pious woman who would never veer into the moral ambiguity of hashish.

The beekeeper's widow laughed. "The young Nazmiyeh of Beit Daras would be tantalized by such a revelation. She would ask to try it," she said. Hajje Nazmiyeh stared at her, surprised and tantalized, indeed. She squinted with eyes that were suddenly half her age, cocked her lips in a sly smile, and erupted with laughter that even the neighbors could hear. And when the two of them had laughed enough to empty their bodies of all misery, Hajje Nazmiyeh collapsed it all into scheming whispers. "Do you mean that all these years that I have known you, you smoked hashish? How could I not know such a thing?"

"Um Mazen, I'm still a god-fearing woman. Allah made this plant for all who inhabit His earth. He did not forbid us to use it," she said, and Nazmiyeh agreed.

Although they were nearly the same age, the widow established a kind of maternal affection toward Nazmiyeh and a new order was forged in this home of women where an alliance of matriarchs brewed and got high and plotted and prayed for the restoration of life in their home. For Alwan's healing, Nur's recovery, and Rhet Shel's blossoming.

SIXTY-TWO

Mama was true to her faith, and she judged those who weren't. But the creep of death in her breasts changed her. It loosened her grip on social rules, and she held on to Nur instead. Mama and Nur found in each other a shared fear of loss, loneliness, and longing for love, and it made sisterhood form there.

AFTER SIX WEEKS OF the beekeeper's widow's awful concoction and the general sense of healing it infused in her body, Alwan set out very early in the morning for another physician appointment. She and Nur rode the brown taxi van in intertwined solitude. At the clinic, the nurse drew blood from Alwan's arm as they both looked on. "We test for markers of the wicked disease and this will tell us if they are higher or lower. But, unfortunately, Um Khaled, we can't trust these tests completely anymore because the kits come through the tunnels without any refrigeration or regulations. So, we don't know if they've gone bad in the sun or from any other exposure. We will do the best we can with what we have for you and leave the rest in Allah's hands," the nurse said. "We can get you an X-ray now. But there are many patients ahead of you. It will probably be three hours and then the doctor will see you."

"Alhamdulillah." Alwan thanked Him for all things.

As they waited for the doctor and Alwan clasped and unclasped her hands, fidgeting her fingers and knuckles, Nur squeezed Alwan's hand, slipping out of her own solitude and into Alwan's. And the two of them sat thus, with the same quiet longing for life, more and more of it, no matter how tortured.

In the examination space behind a curtain, Alwan insisted that her sister, Nur, be allowed in as the doctor palpated her naked body, under a loosely draped flowered sheet. The two women kept their hands interwoven.

"Okay. Put your clothes on and we will talk," the doctor said.

Alwan dressed hastily with Nur's help and the two women emerged from behind the curtain to find the doctor holding two X-ray films to the light, comparing them. They had both seen the one in his left hand that showed two tumors the size of peanuts in her breast.

"Alwan, I'm not sure what is happening," his lips said, but his eyes spoke another language. They told Alwan that the film in his right hand, the one without the peanuts, showed that the tumors were barely visible.

Nur's hand still in hers, Alwan said, "I feel that I am getting much better."

"Well, as you know, X-ray is the only imaging we can do and it's not reliable, but compared to the first films a couple of months ago, it seems that the tumors have shrunk. It happens sometimes that people go into remission and tumors don't grow further, but I rarely see tumors shrink to this extent. They're still there, but they are much smaller," he said.

Alwan and Nur looked at one another. They squeezed their hands. "Thanks be to Allah. Only He knows the unknown," Alwan said, careful not to tempt fate.

While they waited for the taxi van, Alwan found a small clearing and knelt in grateful prayer. In the van, Nur carried on excitedly about the widow's medicine. About sharing the good news with the rest of the family. She said how wonderful the next jomaa ghada was going to be with all the brothers, sisters-in-law, and children.

"Stop talking like that, Nur. It is bad luck to go on about Allah's blessing. It invites the evil eye," Alwan said. "Besides, there's something else I want to talk with you about."

Alwan lowered her voice, steadied it with compassion. "Nur, I noticed that you have not used sanitary napkins lately, and . . ."

Nur's face fell. She hadn't seen this coming. "What?"

"Nur, you must know that I am on your side." Alwan moved closer as Nur began to sob. Since that evening on the shore with the letter, tears lived close to her surface.

Some time passed in silence. Then Nur said, "I've never been grateful to be fat until I realized. I thought it would allow me to hide it for a while."

Nur looked out at the street, and Alwan could see the barren, lonely desert in her eyes. She confessed that she had written to Jamal about her situation, but he had not responded. She said she had first thought he needed time to think, but a week had gone by without response. She thought maybe he hadn't received the e-mail so she resent it. And as Nur spoke, Alwan could see the fog of depression in her eyes.

"Son of a dog. I would have never imagined him so lowly," Alwan interrupted her. Then she stated the obvious. "You cannot have a child out of wedlock here. We have to figure something out and we must tell our mother."

Something in the way she said *our*—our mother—made Nur sob harder.

"Okay. Cry it all out, but too much crying is also not allowed in Gaza," Alwan joked, even if truth tinged her words.

As they entered the house, Alwan thought something was burning, but Nur recognized the smell. Hajje Nazmiyeh and the old widow were red-eyed and didn't seem to notice anyone else was there.

"Mama, what's that smell? What's going on? Where is Rhet Shel?" Alwan asked, panic rising with each successive question.

"Habibti!" Hajje Nazmiyeh raised her arm in a loving invitation for her daughter to come closer. "Rhet Shel is with her cousins. It's just us tonight. Sit and tell us what the doctor said. Whatever it is, we will bear it together."

Still confused but reassured and now intrigued, Alwan gave the news casually. Looking at the old beekeeper's widow, her face curled into a smile, "Your nasty medicine is working," she said, and Nazmiyeh began yelling, singing incomprehensibly. She erupted in ululations. The widow laughed, shaking rolls of fat, and admonished Hajje Nazmiyeh. "Quiet, woman! The neighbors will hear. Do you want them coming to stick their noses in our business?"

"Oh, no," Nazmiyeh said, laboring to contain herself.

"What is that you're smoking?" Alwan pointed accusingly to a rolled cigarette.

Nur put her hand on Alwan's shoulder. "Habibti," she said. "Haven't you figured this out?"

Alwan still didn't understand. Then she did.

Hajje Nazmiyeh laughed harder and soon, Alwan was trying it. She coughed hard enough to gag but two hits were enough to make her head spin. "Allah forgive me! This is crazy," she said.

"What are you talking about, child?" the old widow retorted. "Nothing to forgive. He created this stuff just like He created you. And He put it in your life to heal your body."

Nur refused to smoke, instinctively moving her hand over her belly. That gesture, combined with the awkward way Alwan looked away, caught Hajje Nazmiyeh's attention.

"There's something the two of you are hiding and I want to know what it is," she said, not laughing anymore.

Nur began to cry.

The old widow smacked her lips. "I can help. I can make a medicine that will help where you put your hand."

SIXTY-THREE

Nur's nature was unguarded. She moved in the world with a quality of defenselessness, which invited both protectors and predators. She was the most educated among us. The most privileged. The one with the most opportunities, greater promise, and a more assured future. But her pain was the most palpable, and her strength came from being needed. So we learned to protect Nur by needing her.

D AYS ACCUMULATED IN NUR'S belly. The women of her home grew worried and Nur did her best to avoid conversation, which was no more than the same incessant question: "What are you going to do?"

Nur went daily to the Internet café, where she would sit with her secret shame, hoping to find a message from Jamal, or to catch Nzinga on Skype. She would type letters to Jamal. He never answered. She tried pleading, then she cursed him, hoping to provoke some response—anything to mitigate the sprawling wasteland of her heart. What a fool she was. How could she expect a man to love her when her own mother could not? She could not blame him. There was nothing to love. A fat home-wrecker with tree-trunk legs even Jesus couldn't save. She went to the bathroom, knelt in front of the toilet, and stuck her fingers down her throat, but she stopped herself, hugged her belly, and got up.

Twice, she went by the office and waited, but Jamal neither entered nor exited the building. She was running out of time. Running out of money and out of ideas. She went to al-Rimal, the neighborhood where he lived, but did not see him walk in or out of his building. Nor his wife.

She walked to the Mediterranean, along the coast where so many conquerers had marched since history was born. Gaza had always been a place of warriors and survivors. Nur plucked what remnants of courage lay in the sand and walked back to al-Rimal, climbed the stairs of Jamal's building, and knocked on his door. No one answered. She knocked again.

The neighbor's door opened and a young woman in her twenties emerged with books in hand, clearly off to class. "Hello," she said. "Are you looking for my brother's wife?"

"Are you Dr. Jamal's sister?"

"Oh, no. They don't live here anymore. My family is renting their apartment for my brother who just got married."

Something inside of Nur fell from its place, perhaps her heart, and she caught it before it would crash and break on the floor of her life. "Where did they go?"

"They moved to Canada. There was a big party and everything. Their immigration papers finally came through! They're so lucky," she said. "Sister, you don't look well. Can I offer you a glass of water?"

"Oh, no, thank you. I'm an old friend. I've been away and didn't realize they had already left. Thank you. May Allah bless you with success in school, sister. Salaam."

A discarded old shoe, bewildered and pregnant, sat once again by the water. Thank God for the water. Nur thought she might cry, but she didn't. A song washed upon the shore and danced out of her.

> *O find me*
> *I'll be in that blue*
> *Between sky and water*
> *Where all time is now*
> *And we are the forever*
> *Flowing like a river*
> *O find me*
> *Where it's always day*

And always night
There are no hours here
In the blue
Between sky and water
There are no countries here
No soldiers
No anguish or joy
Just blue between sky and water

As the sky grew dim, she headed back and stopped by the Internet café. Finally, the icon next to Nzinga's name on Skype was lit green. Nur hurriedly began typing.

"Nzinga! I'm so happy you're online. I miss you so much."

"Hey, boo! I miss you, too. You still in Gaza?"

"Yes. Can you talk? I can borrow a headset. No picture, though. The camera uses too much bandwidth. The electricity might cut off at any minute and there's something I need to tell you."

"Of course, child. Slow down. Are you okay?"

Nur inhaled and tears leaked from her eyes as she scrambled to connect the headset. "Nzinga, I am desperate to talk to you. I am in trouble and I—"

"Is this about the grant?"

Nur had set up a small office in Nusseirat to hold individual and group therapy sessions for women and children and had been seeking funding. A small grant was forthcoming from the European Union but she did not want to accept American or European money. So she had corresponded with Nzinga about seeking funding sources in African nations.

"No, I mean. Yes, but no . . . it's . . ." Nur was suddenly without words.

"Okay. Calm down and tell me everything. If we get cut off, find a way to e-mail me. I have been meaning to write to you because I am attending a pan-African conference in Egypt next week and was hoping I might be able to see you since we will be so close," Nzinga said. "But tell me, darling, what is troubling you."

"It's Jamal."

Nzinga made a sound that Nur knew was formed from pursed judging lips and raised eyebrows holding back curses she wanted to let loose around that man's name. Nur had told her that it was over and had lied that she had moved on.

"He has left Gaza for good . . . with his family," Nur began.

"Good riddance, Nur. I know you might be heartbroken, but I told you this would not end well. Thankfully it didn't last long and now you can heal and get on with your life. I have news on the grant and now . . ." Nzinga stopped speaking. "Nur?"

The place inside Nzinga where she was a young social worker who met a little brown girl with curly black hair clinging to her dying grandfather had become populated over the years with the ornaments of memories, learning, and loving between them. Words formed in that space that Nzinga did not notice until she heard them emerge from her own mouth. "Are you pregnant, Nur?"

SIXTY-FOUR

My sister spoke to me in the private moments before she slept. Then we visited in her dreams and she knew I would always be with her, even if she couldn't remember those dreams upon waking.

THE STEM OF A lollipop dangled from Rhet Shel's lips. She made sucking sounds as she watched folded clothes stack one item over the other.

"Khalto Nur, can I go with you to Egypt?" Rhet Shel asked.

Nur paused and smiled apologetically. "Not this time, habibti."

"Why are you going to Egypt?"

"I want to visit an old friend who used to take care of me when I was little. And I'm also going to see about a grant for our new office that you and I are going to paint when I get back."

Rhet Shel smiled. "Can I pick the color?"

"Yes! In fact, I think we should have an entire wall just for kids to write on."

"Whoa!" Rhet Shel's eyes widened. "You're going to let kids write on the wall?"

The look of astonishment at such a concept amused Nur. "Yep! And you can pick out the color to paint the wall."

"When?"

"As soon as I'm back from Egypt."

"When?"

"Just a few days."

"What if the Egyptians or Israelis lock you out?"

"Then I'll just wait until the border opens" Nur stopped what she was doing and kissed Rhet Shel's face. "But you can bet that I'm going to come back."

"Promise?"

Nur hesitated, then smiled. "I will also bring you gifts."

SIXTY-FIVE

The beekeeper's widow moved in permanently. No one remembered when or how, but it was natural that her place was in our home. Her enormous body helped close the gap I had left. She suggested a remedy for Nur's predicament. But everyone could see that it horrified Nur. It horrified them, too. But they thought Nur was still too American to fully comprehend what it meant to deliver sin. It was Mama who surprised them by saying, "The sin has already been committed. What she'd deliver would be, enshallah, a child of our flesh and blood." The beekeeper's widow spoke nonsense by suggesting that maybe people wouldn't care since Nur had been raised in America and people there do that sort of thing. Teta looked at her sideways and said, "First of all, for once, my daughter is right and I am wrong. Aborting our flesh is also a sin. Even if people don't know about it, Allah will know." Then they began to scheme. Nur could deliver the baby abroad and come back as if she'd adopted a child. She could leave and pretend to have married and return with a ring. They could say her husband wasn't allowed to cross the border. Or, they could just say she had already been married when she had first arrived in Gaza. A visit with her husband in Egypt, then a divorce, would explain the delivery. How the hell would anyone know differently? My teta and the beekeeper's widow, even Mama, started to secretly fantasize about having a baby in the house.

A LWAN WATCHED NUR WALK into the family room with a large suitcase. A kind of confession bent her posture into a plea. She was planning to leave very early the next morning. "I think I'm packed. The suitcase is nearly empty and, enshallah, I will fill it up on the way back. But you haven't told me yet what you'd like me to bring back from Cairo," Nur said.

"We don't want anything," Alwan began. "Just go and come back home safely."

Hajje Nazmiyeh protested, "Speak for yourself! Um Zhaq passed away last month, Allah rest her soul, and Abu Zhaq might be looking for a new wife. I need to prepare myself." She was already laughing. "Get me some sexy bed clothes. Just in case Allah sends me a husband." Both Hajje Nazmiyeh and the old widow shook with laughter, more so because Alwan was predictably scandalized; and when Hajje Nazmiyeh could take a breath, she said to Alwan, "Habibti, I was only kidding. My thing down there hasn't been used in so long it's probably rusted out." Now the two women were laughing so hard the old widow peed herself. "Look what you made me do, you dirty girl! Calling yourself Hajje."

Nur and Alwan couldn't help but join them as they helped the old widow to her feet to get cleaned up. Hajje Nazmiyeh added, "If it wasn't for peeing we might forget it was even there!"

The old woman hurried to the bathroom, yelling at Hajje Nazmiyeh between gasps of laughter, "Curse you, woman! You made me pee even more!"

"You know it's true. I haven't been a widow half as long as you and mine fell off a long time ago." Hajje Nazmiyeh could hardly contain her silliness.

"Thank God no one else can hear her!" Alwan whispered.

The beekeeper's widow returned, lighting frankincense in a small bowl. They stayed that way into the evening, in this world of women, of mirth and myrrh. They made dinner and Rhet Shel came home, tired from hours of play. They all ate together, Rhet Shel laughing whenever the adults did, even if she didn't know what they were laughing about. She told them jokes, most of which made no sense, but they all laughed to include her in the tight circle. Alwan bathed Rhet Shel after the food was put away and, though Rhet Shel was too tired to stay awake, she refused to go to bed, feeling that the adults would have fun without her. Her tired eyes would fall then flutter at any change in the volume of conversation until at last sleep wrapped itself around her, snuggling close with her mother. Nur bade them good night early and went to bed.

As the quiet of night suffused their home, the old widow turned to Alwan, who leaned against the wall cradling a sleeping Rhet Shel. "When are you going to cut them off?"

Alwan was startled, but gathered her wits and memory. "I marked it on the calendar. The doctors said that they will have space for me in two weeks, enshallah, unless Israel attacks us between now and then and the hospitals fill up again."

"Don't look so down. It's the best thing," the old widow said. "Now that the tumors are so small, once you cut them off you might be cured!"

"What good are they anyway after the kids are too old to feed from them and there's no man to suck on them anymore!" Hajje Nazmiyeh began, but Alwan had had enough. "Yumma, stop it!" she snapped.

"Okay, habibti." Hajje Nazmiyeh was apologetic and tired. "Just don't be sad about it. I was trying to make you laugh."

"Forgive me, Yumma. I'm tired," Alwan said. "Good night."

"Yes. Okay. Well … yes. Okay. Good night, habibti," Hajje Nazmiyeh said and tried to get comfortable on her mat. Then she grabbed a small pillow and threw it at the old widow to interrupt her snoring. "I hate it when she falls asleep before me. Her snoring is ridiculous!"

"Yumma, why don't you sleep with us in the bed? Besides, your snoring isn't exactly a symphony," Alwan said, carrying Rhet Shel to the bedroom.

"I like it out here. Go to bed. I'll be fine. Just leave me some things to throw at her when I need to," Hajje Nazmiyeh said, reaching for more pillows.

Alwan laid Rhet Shel in bed next to Nur. A sweet sense of night washed over her and she walked into the outdoors. The alleyways were speckled with moonlight. She wanted to keep walking toward the ocean, but the sound of her footsteps dislocated the quiet. So she sat on the stoop of their home and leaned against the metal door. In the stillness there, she became aware of a hum of crawling, fluttering, and creaking little lives moving in the crevices of the peaceful darkness. She welcomed it all into her body, thanked Allah for the widow's medicine, and asked Him to keep her on this earth a while longer.

SIXTY-SIX

Nzinga was married with three children by the time Nur completed her master's degree. She attended the graduation ceremony (Nur's third) with her entire family and they created a noisy island in the audience. Nzinga's children waved signs with Nur's name, and they all whistled and clapped when her name was called to receive her diploma. Nur smiled broadly and blew them a kiss from the stage.

GETTING TO CAIRO WAS a long and exhausting journey, though much easier than Nur had expected. The Rafah border was open, and crossing it was relatively uneventful. Getting through Hamas security took only a few minutes, which was typical, and the Egyptians made her wait only a couple of hours. Then she was on her way, bouncing in the back of a taxi van heading to Cairo with other passengers. She rested her hand on her belly, rubbing a lullaby to the secret beneath her navel. She wasn't the only woman in Gaza to ever be in such a predicament. However few or many, they all went to Egypt if they could, and returned with emptied wombs and hollowed eyes.

Nur looked at the time on her phone, eager to get to the hotel where Nzinga was staying. She still had at least two hours. The immense, ancient silence of the Sinai desert enveloped her, its rolling sand hills speeding past her window. She closed her eyes and watched her thoughts assemble into dreams.

There, Khaled picked up words off the ground, small beads scattered about, and strung them together, making a necklace. Is that for me? she asked. *Of course,* he answered. Was it always you in my dreams? Again, *Of course.* What should I do, Khaled? *Help me pick these all up.* Nur looked at the word beads. "Nice," "Light of Jiddo's Life," "Smart." She reached down to gather them, but fell forward. The taxi had slammed on the brakes. Nur's head hit the seat in front of her. She was the only remaining passenger. "Golden Tulip hotel!" the driver yelled back.

Nur waited, impatient to see Nzinga, who was in a workshop until seven o'clock. It was six now. She walked out and roamed the streets of the Zamaalek neighborhood. Evening was casting its shadows and soon darkness walked the streets with her. In Gaza, she loved the thickness of black nights. They were kind and comforting. But here, the night was nervous and the darkness vibrated with threats she couldn't see, despite a few street lights. Were they real or was it true that pregnancy made women more alert and protective of their bodies? She hurried back toward the lights of the Golden Tulip.

Nzinga was in the lobby, asking for her at the reception desk. "Zingie!"

They embraced excitedly and tearfully. Whatever emotions had accumulated in Nur fell away. Everything washed out until there was nothing but a little girl with a baby in her belly holding tightly onto Nzinga's hand.

*

They talked endlessly, and later, at a late dinner, there was still so much to talk about. Their conversation jumped between relationships and drifted across continents, and eventually ended up in the past. Nur said, "You know, foster care was adequate. I never faced or witnessed the horror stories you sometimes hear about. There was enough food, shelter, all the basics were there. No one abused me there. And yet, it was somehow intensely wounding."

Nzinga listened with attentive, maternal eyes as Nur continued. "On the ride through the Sinai, it occurred to me why that is. And it's the same reason why you are the one person in the whole world that I needed to see most at this hour." Nur paused, moving her food around on her plate. "It's all about having a thread that links your years. To have another living person who just knows you. Someone who has seen you from childhood. That's the missing piece in Gaza. They love me there. I know they do. It's almost instinctive. But I wonder how much they know me. They don't see me as you do, Zingie. Flawed and scared and—"

"Wait a minute. That's not how I see you," Nzinga protested.

"I mean . . . I don't know. I just don't know what to do. I can't have this baby in Gaza and I can't abort it, either. And there's nothing for me in the States. My only connections there are institutions and a handful of friends that I'm not close to anymore."

"Well, first things first. I don't see flaws and fear when I look at you. I see strength, determination, smarts, sass, kindness, love. I can go on, but I bet that's what your family sees, too. Second, I know you're scared and this seems like an impossible situation. But it's not. You've always lived your life the way you wanted. That's the thing you got from not having family. You got a chance to own your decisions, make up your rules and live by them. But now you have the family you always wanted and you think it's a choice between being true to the person you are, the person you made on your own, or living by new social rules to protect and love the family that also protects and loves you," Nzinga said. "How am I doing so far?"

"You make it sound so simple, but it's still an impossible choice," Nur said.

"Am I right to say that, one, you want to remain in Gaza? And two, you want to keep and raise your baby?" Nzinga continued her distillation of Nur's inner chaos.

"Yes."

"We know you can't deliver the baby in Gaza without being married. But how about raising an adopted baby in Gaza?"

Alwan had hinted to her of that possibility and of others, which Nzinga had also apparently considered. They talked through scenarios until the world did not seem so grim.

Because Nzinga's family had been active in the anti-apartheid struggle and she herself had risen to prominence in her field of social work and community organizing, she had been able to arrange a fellowship grant for Nur through government offices. This was the news that Nzinga shared with her now. "You know, Nur, the African National Congress has always been supportive of the Palestinian struggle. So, many international government programs are open to Palestinians in particular," Nzinga said.

Nur touched her belly and said, "This is probably the only time in my life when I've been happy to be fat. I can go back and stay for another month to figure things out. I can't thank you enough for helping me get a grant to continue the counseling project. It feels good to do something meaningful. The fellowship could give me the time away that I need and I won't have to go back to the US."

"What about the other thing? You know you can't be doing that now." Nzinga's words landed heavily on Nur. "Oh, Nur, don't look at me like a question mark. You know how I always ask you to show me your nails when we Skype?"

Nur was more puzzled. "Yes."

"I was never looking at your nails, darling. I was looking for the two marks over your knuckles that are made by your teeth."

She stretched her hand in front of her, seeing calloused old brown marks that had once been raw and red, however small. She didn't think anyone had ever noticed them, the place where her two front teeth would press down on her hand when she made herself vomit.

Nzinga took her hand lovingly. "That's how I knew you were home when you went to Gaza. You didn't have those red marks anymore."

"No, I don't do that anymore," she said, tearing up.

"Maybe you don't see this now, but I think that man had something to do with that. Just feeling truly loved by a man, even if it was only for a while, is something I don't think you've ever really felt since your jiddo passed away," Nzinga said.

"Maybe. And maybe it's one of the reasons I always looked for Tío Santiago," Nur said. And as the hours yawned, Nzinga asked about the last meeting she had had with her mother. "I don't want to rehash that again now," Nur said.

"Actually, Nur, you've never spoken about it. Every time the subject came up, you'd say you didn't want to rehash it, just like now. You're about to be a mother and maybe you should go there with me now, so you can hear, out loud, about the kind of mother you don't want to be," Nzinga said. "I have all night. Let's get some coffee first, though."

SIXTY-SEVEN

Nur's Tío Santiago had been a source of love for her, however brief and intermittent his presence was. Sometimes, Santiago would call Nzinga to ask about Nur when she was still in school. Then he would disappear for long stretches of time, and Nzinga knew he was either in rehab or prison, or using heavily. When they met in Cairo, Nur showed her the old harmonica. "He was a kindhearted, haunted man," Nzinga said.

T HE WAITER POURED TWO small cups of Arabic coffee for the women.

"Arabs sure know how to make coffee," Nzinga said, flirting with the young waiter, who smiled good-naturedly and replied, "Arabs invented coffee, Madam."

"Is that right?" she asked, holding him in place with her vast brown eyes. "Let me ask you something, son." She scanned his dark skin and wooly hair. "Do you consider yourself Arab or African?"

"I am Egyptian, Madam."

"Is Egyptian African or Arab?"

"It is both, Madam," he said, and he continued when he saw that she clearly had more questions. "And as an Egyptian, I am proudly African and Arab. They are not mutually exclusive."

"Are you saying that because I'm black?" She went back to flirting.

"Do you consider yourself black or African?" The waiter gave it back. "Isn't black a pigment category that white slavers invented to reduce the inhabitants and diverse cultures of our continent?"

By now, an immense smile had unfurled on Nzinga's face, the gap in her front teeth like an accessory to her benevolence.

"Ooooo. Handsome, and damn smart! If I were younger, you'd better watch out. What you say is true, but you know, now we own the word *black* and we put our unity in it and get power back, you see." Nzinga laughed, raising a Black Power fist. "Did you meet my young friend, Nur?"

At that, Nur and the waiter both blushed as they nodded politely to each other. Then Nur spoke to him in Arabic. "Thank you, brother, for this excellent coffee."

"You are welcome, sister," he answered, and walked away.

As soon as he was out of earshot, Nzinga whispered, "You should go for that fine brother, Nur!"

"Nzinga, you remind me so much of my aunt Nazmiyeh. I never made the connection before, but you're so similar."

"She sounds magnificent," Nzinga said. "You should learn to flirt a little. No harm in it."

"That's the last thing on my mind right now," Nur sighed.

"It's gonna be okay. The first decision you need to make is whether you're going to keep this baby. You know how I feel about it, but this is your life and your body."

"I think you know what I want, Zingie."

"Say it."

Nur hesitated, lowered her voice. "I want it."

"Want what?"

"To keep it," Nur said; but Nzinga's expression demanded more. "I want to be a mother." A tear formed and fell from Nur's eye. It ushered more silent tears and then more words. "I want someone to love who will love me back. Someone who is mine. Not in the owning way, but in the spiritual way. I want to know what that feels like."

"Love is the best reason to have a child, my child," Nzinga said. "And this baby has already changed you. I've known you for most of your life and tonight is the first time I've ever seen you cry since you were a baby. That's a good thing. Everything is going to be all right, Nur. That's where you start. Even if it's hard. It's gonna be fine. You're gonna be just fine, beautiful girl." That made Nur cry all the more, but she did so without sound, with some happiness, too, and relief.

"Is there something else on your mind?" Nzinga asked. She waited long for an answer.

"What if I'm a bad mother . . ." Nur finally managed, then gulped those words back into her throat with a sob.

Nzinga took her hand. "There is nothing in you that remotely resembles your mother, Nur." Nur said nothing, and Nzinga continued. "Let me ask you this: Do you love Rhet Shel? I mean, do you look at her and want for her the best that life can possibly give her?"

"Of course."

"That is your proof that you are not your mother and never will be. I'm sure you've figured out along the way that she is a classic textbook narcissist."

"I'll tell you about the last time I saw her." Nur looked away, then back at her coffee. She took a sip, placed the cup back gently. It was two A.M. now. The night stretched over Cairo as Nur inhabited a trauma of memory.

SIXTY-EIGHT

We were locked up in Gaza. Of one and a half million people, five or six could trickle in or out each day through Egypt. Misery leaked into the streets and fermented under the sun for years. But seeing Nur helped me understand the freedom we did have. We wanted to consume the world outside our borders, to take in the sun of another shore, open our eyes to a moon of another sky, walk the ground of another earth. We wanted to live, to move and travel, to work, produce, and export. Our prison was not being allowed to see or do, and our escape was to find ways to taste the rest of the world. Nur was allowed to move as we couldn't. But rather than taking in all there was, she went everywhere trying to empty herself, because her prison lived within her, and the escape she longed for meant disrobing herself of her skin. Until love was planted in her belly and began to grow there.

I T WAS EASY FOR Nur to find her mother's address. She and Sam had moved to San Diego and had their twins, Eduardo and Tomás, who were in middle school when Nur decided to visit when she was still in college.

Across the street from her mother's home in the Clairemont neighborhood, Nur waited in a rental car. A mist of light began to illuminate the street. The red of the front door emerged from the shadows, and a decaying, once-white picket fence was revealed around the small ramshackle property. Nur recalled that her mother had always wanted to live in a house with a white picket fence; and she heard words rise up from a burial ground of memory. *Why can't we use the trust for a house? Why can't one fucking thing in my life go my way?*

An old man walking an old dog peered into her car suspiciously as he passed on the sidewalk. The small sound of a cat rummaging in someone's trash moved Nur's attention. When she turned back, she saw a tragic version of Sam walking out of the house, closing the door behind him. His yellow hair was dusted with gray. He wore old jeans and a black T-shirt that seemed to be made entirely of sadness. It was hard to see the details of his face from afar, but there was no mistaking the weight of gloom pulling his skin. Life sagged and dragged in him, as if it couldn't wait to leave him, and he walked with heavy steps and a vacant expression. Nur watched him until he disappeared down the street, around the corner. Strangely, she felt no anger. Not even when she tried. Only pity.

The doors of other homes opened and closed with men, women, and children leaving to start their days at work or school. Soon, two boys came out. Eduardo and Tomás, surely. They were skinny, with disheveled stringy brown hair, and had book packs hanging from their backs. Nur was squinting to make out their features when she saw a slight woman in tight jeans and a nice peach blouse walk out behind them. The woman turned immediately to lock the door and, in an apparent act of habit, the boys kissed her cheeks before running off at full speed down the street, disappearing around the corner where other students were also heading. They were already out of sight when the woman turned around from locking the front door. From her car, Nur saw the face of her mother, her hair pulled tightly at the back of her head. The years had not made her older and Nur was surprised how beautiful she looked. A rush of warmth flushed Nur's chest and she felt weak with a sense of forgiveness. She fumbled with the car door handle until she was finally out, standing by the side of the car, in full view of her mother. The woman craned her neck to make out the person staring at her from across the street. Then, she froze. Even from a distance, Nur could discern the stone of her character and the contours of suddenly iced-up thoughts. Nur's initial impulse to run into the imaginary outstretched arms of this woman was doused in the cool morning air and trampled by the old shoe growing larger inside of her. She stood motionless, her motherless fate holding its breath.

Her mother turned on her heels back toward the red door, reversing her motions of a moment earlier. Nur watched her, still unable to move, and noticed the smallness of her mother's waist—and a memory intruded.

You sure don't get this shit from me, Nubia, her mother had once said, pinching the flesh of Nur's belly. *Look how small my waist is,* she had continued, and Nur had sucked her abdomen in to hide as much of herself as she could.

The red door finally opened and Nur's mother disappeared back inside. Nur exhaled. She felt her knees buckling and quickly got back into the car, where she gripped the steering wheel to steady her shaking. She stayed that way for what seemed like an eternity, and by the time she had mustered the strength to move her limbs, either to start the car and leave or to open the door and get out again—she didn't know which she wanted to do—someone was knocking on her window. Startled, she looked up to find a police officer. He questioned her briefly and suggested she move along.

As Nur started her car, she looked up at her mother's house and saw the corner of a curtain in an upstairs window lifted, a figure standing in the room. Then the curtain closed. Nur looked back at the officer, then drove away.

"There is something extraordinary about being rejected by one's mother," she told Nzinga. "It impoverishes the soul. It leaves holes everywhere and you spend your life trying to fill them up. With whatever you can find. With food. With drugs and alcohol. With all the wrong men you know will leave you, so maybe they will replicate the original hurt you felt. You do it to feel abandonment over and over because that's the only thing you know of your mother. And it's all you know to do to bring her close."

"Oh, Nur, my child." Nzinga, for once, did not know what to say.

"It's okay, Zingie. I've made whatever peace I can with it. The biggest part is a commitment to being the kind of mother I always wanted to have myself. I have no choice but to have and love this baby, no matter what it means."

"Ever since you were a little girl, Nur, you have had some kind of self-awareness. People live and die without ever knowing themselves the way you do," Nzinga said. "Tell me, is this also why you insist on returning to Gaza?"

"Maybe so. I keep thinking about Rhet Shel. I don't know how long Alwan will be around and Aunt Nazmiyeh is too old to take care of her. She has a big extended family. Uncles, aunts, cousins. But Rhet Shel will just get lost in the shuffle. They all have so many kids. I had trouble in the beginning remembering names and who was whose kid. There isn't room for Rhet Shel to get the same love and attention. And she deserves that."

The next shift began filing into the hotel. It was nearly five A.M. when both women succumbed to the trample of exhaustion. Nur lay in her bed looking up until a dream began to dance on the white ceiling.

There was a river, and the little boy of her dreams appeared for their Arabic lesson. "Khaled!" Nur cried. "It was you all along!"

"Of course," he said.

"But where is Mariam?"

"She is waiting for my sister Nazmiyeh in the water well," said a man's voice.

"Jiddo!"

And Nur awoke to the sound of the noontime adan.

VII

In the abandon of that solitude, we could see how tiny we were, how small and defenseless our earth. And from that terrible dignity, we heard the susurrus of a long-ago old woman's words: *This land will rise again*

SIXTY-NINE

Nur was always on the way. Maybe it was the impermanence of foster care. The idea of aging in or out of home; of not having the option to return once you leave. She had no real anchors in the world, and so she was always on her way. On her way to herself. On her way to redemption. On her way to language. To something heavy enough to weigh her against the wind.

GETTING BACK INTO GAZA was difficult, fraught with the trifles of officialdom and the inquiries of oppression. The Egyptians closed, then opened, then closed the border. Nur's papers were missing a dot or a dash. Her answers were insufficient. They told her to wait. She talked to people. Sang into her womb. Then she found a way to the tunnels with other travelers. Young men with the grime of subterranean work on their skin and on their spirits led Nur and a group of travelers through, pulling their luggage in a trolley on a wooden track. She held on to a rail with one hand and her belly with the other as she descended steps into the cold, damp underworld. At the base of the tunnel, her eyes adjusted to the darkness. Small lanterns a few meters apart hung on a wire running the length of the tunnel, effervescent pearls shimmering in a black void that whispered of rats, snakes, and crawling, biting creatures. She kept walking. For twenty minutes. Then there was light and she was on the other side, back in Gaza.

She went to the nearest empty taxi at the border. "Can you take me to Nusseirat?" she asked. As they moved away, she saw a large group of people run to greet a woman and her children who had traversed the tunnels with her. They hugged and kissed in the habits of family and the tempers of love. Nur imagined

Alwan, Rhet Shel, all the cousins and sisters-in-law surrounding her. She hadn't called ahead to let anyone know that she had made it through the border. *They will be surprised*, she thought. Her heart pounded, anxious to arrive.

"Turn here," she told the driver. As the taxi moved slowly down the narrow street, honking for children to get out of the way, a young boy threw his football at the car and yelled at the driver to stop honking.

"Let me out here. It's a short walk and cars can't get through much farther."

Several children ran to help her with her bags. One of them tried to speak what few words he knew in English and Nur heard a young man yell, "Idiot! She's not a foreigner! That's Hajje Nazmiyeh's kin." Nur recognized him and waved. "Salaam, Wasim." He nodded and ran to help carry her bags. The sun was still in the sky and life was bobbing along. Nur quickened her pace.

A child's voice screamed, "Khalto Nur! Khalto!" and Rhet Shel sprinted out of a crowd of children. Nur whisked her up in an embrace. They hugged and kissed until Rhet Shel wiggled herself away, running ahead to announce the news. When Nur finally caught up, the women of her life had poured from their home and were waiting for her. Even the old widow who could not move well had come out.

In the warm midst of her aunt Nazmiyeh, Alwan, the sisters-in-law, a couple of the brothers, Rhet Shel, neighbors, and more children than she could count, Nur touched her belly. Laughter and conversations swirled around her. Tea and coffee and various sweets and snacks were passed around. It was the first homecoming she had ever had. The first time she had returned to a place that embraced her. She had always been compelled to move away. To leave and hope the next place would be better.

Her hand still on the center of her world, Nur watched the room around her with joyful eyes. But for one interminable moment, all she heard was the heartbeat of certainty. Hajje Nazmiyeh looked at Nur's hand, then at her face, and she pulled her near. She leaned into Nur's face and whispered in her ear. "We will figure this out. People will touch their heads when they mention your name or your baby's name. That's my flesh and blood. But for now, take your hand off your belly so people don't start thinking too much." Nur pulled back to look into Hajje Nazmiyeh's weathered face. Mischievous eyes that loved life looked back at her.

Nur had brought gifts from Cairo, but nothing made such an impression as the magical chocolate eggs. "This is a Kinder Egg," Nur said, handing one to Rhet Shel, who could hardly believe her good fortune. She was afraid to open it, or eat it, or discover the toy inside, lest it be gone. But when she realized there was an entire box of them in Nur's luggage, she invited her cousins. They peeled away the thin foil, gently, and experienced a moment of chocolate so sweet that everyone around them felt it. They stayed in the charm of that day until the house slowly emptied of guests and night slipped in. Rhet Shel fell asleep in her mother's lap, and the old widow began to snore.

"Let's have another gathering on the beach tomorrow in honor of Nur's return," Hajje Nazmiyeh announced, throwing a pillow at the old widow to wake her up. "But we're not inviting *her*."

Without opening her eyes, the old widow said, "I heard you. Nobody's gonna come if they know I'm not the one doing the cooking."

"*Fasharti!*" Hajje Nazmiyeh laughed. "Abu Zhaq will come."

"Little girl," the old woman wagged her finger at Hajje Nazmiyeh, trying not to laugh, "why are you always bringing up

Abu Zhaq? Either you've had a little taste of that stuff or you've thought about it."

Alwan and Nur both looked at Rhet Shel to be sure she was sleeping.

Hajje Nazmiyeh laughed. "I hear there's nothing *little* about that man!"

Alwan threw a pillow at her mother. "Yumma! I'll kiss your hands and feet and do whatever you want if you will stop talking like that!"

Hajje Nazmiyeh and the old widow laughed conspiratorially. "Okay, daughter. But you don't have to worry. The only snake I've ever seen was your daddy's," Nazmiyeh said.

"Allah help this woman to find the righteous path." Alwan threw her hands up in surrender and carried herself and Rhet Shel to bed.

"That's what I keep saying," the old widow said.

"You're just as bad as she is," Alwan huffed over her shoulder at the beekeeper's widow.

Nur finally got up to join Alwan and Rhet Shel. "I love you both," she said to the elderly women.

Hajje Nazmiyeh looked back at the beekeeper's widow. "And how about this one? She doesn't mind us talking about Abu Zhaq, but she won't stop it with that American *I love you* stuff."

The debris of the day's merriment settled, and the percussion of the two hajjes snoring filled the rooms, lulling the house into dreams.

SEVENTY

When I was younger, Hamas fighters captured an Israeli soldier named Gilad Shalit. Israel broke the ground open looking for him, but they couldn't find him. They killed so many of us to get their soldier, but they couldn't. Like a spoiled child having a tantrum, Israel hurled objects of death and destruction at us from land and sky and sea that mutilated, ruined, wrecked, and shattered us. But again, they came up empty-handed. Hamas was beyond their violence.

T HE BANTER BETWEEN HAJJE Nazmiyeh and the old widow picked up again in the morning, alternating between lewd and silly, as they rolled grape leaves to make *waraq dawali*, cleaned chickens to make *msakhan*, and soaked rice and carved zucchini for koosa.

When Alwan woke up for work, Hajje Nazmiyeh had breakfast with hot tea waiting for her. "Don't be mad at your old mama, habibti," she said.

"That depends on how good the breakfast is." Alwan smiled.

"You're definitely my daughter! Nobody switched you at birth," Hajje Nazmiyeh said.

Alwan made appreciative sounds as she ate the fried eggs, sunny-side up the way she liked, *zeit* and za'atar with warmed bread. The tea was sweet and flavored with a lot of mint.

"Yumma, this is perfect," she said. "Don't forget Rhet Shel has a music class at ten. I'm letting her sleep in with Nur," Alwan said, heading out the door to deliver two caftans she had embroidered. But the old widow stopped her.

"You still have to drink this every day," she said, holding the vial of marijuana oil.

Alwan gulped it down. "Tastes like a son of a whore!" she said, shaking her head to dislodge the aftertaste.

Rhet Shel was grudgingly leaving for the music lesson when her mother returned, and she begged to stay home so she wouldn't miss the party.

"Habibti, it's not a party. We're just having ghada at the shore. I promise that nothing will start before you're home."

"But I won't be able to help set up," Rhet Shel protested.

"That's too bad. Now go!" Alwan said and Rhet Shel went off in a huff.

Moments later, she returned, alarm swimming in her eyes, pursued by car horns and the noise of shouts in the street. The women of the house stepped out onto their stoop and found their neighbors doing the same. Some were jolted by curiosity and others were reticent, so some ran out into the camp while other crept. Cars packed with young men honked as they drove through. People soon began to pour into the streets and alleys, and streams of bodies emerged dancing. Through the chaos arose the news: Hamas had won. Gilad Shalit, the captured Israeli soldier, would be exchanged for one thousand Palestinian political prisoners.

Hajje Nazmiyeh hastily tied on her scarf and ran out the door, shouting, "Mazen!"

SEVENTY-ONE

I said it before: We were used to being the losers. So the small victories were intoxicating, and all paused their lives to celebrate together. My khalo Mazen's name was on the list and Teta hurried through the streets, her face and arms reaching to the heavens, shouting Allahu akbar. The whole of Gaza did the same. The same jubilation. The same relief and triumph. The same sense that Allah was merciful. That the dignity of patience and the humors of family were our wells of strength. Rhet Shel didn't understand, but it was enough to know that school had been cancelled for a massive celebration.

A S THE EUPHORIA SUBSIDED, details of the prisoner exchange emerged. They would be released in stages, the actual transfer of one Israeli prisoner happening in Egypt after five hundred Palestinians were returned home. In seven days, Mazen would be returned home.

"Today is Tuesday, is that right?" Hajje Nazmiyeh asked.

"Yes, Yumma," Alwan answered. "They said Mazen will be home, enshallah, on Monday."

Hajje Nazmiyeh counted on her fingers. "That's seven days." She counted again to be sure.

"Enshallah, my brother will be home with us for the next family jomaa ghada." Alwan kissed her mother's forehead.

"Everybody and their cousin is at the beach today. But we should still gather there. I like praying by the ocean. It makes me feel closer to Allah." Hajje Nazmiyeh's chin quivered and she began to cry. "My son," she whimpered. "Mazen is coming home. I didn't think I'd live to see the day." *You hear that, Mariam?*

*

The beekeeper's widow cooked without respite, invigorated by the recent score: Israel 1, Hamas 1,000. As the sovereign of the kitchen, she instructed her subjects, Nur and Rhet Shel, to pick vegetables and leaves from her garden, to hand her this or that, peel and chop this and that, boil, sauté, salt, and spice. "Allah is merciful. La ellah illa Allah. He gives us gifts when we don't expect them," she said to Hajje Nazmiyeh, who went off to the mosque. By the time she returned, the food was prepared and covered, waiting to be carted toward the ocean. Rhet Shel could hardly wait. The news of the morning had soaked through the day, and the elation hung like mist. She missed her brother, Khaled, and wished he were still there as she and Nur sat on the wooden planks of Abu Marzooq's donkey cart with trays of food, bouncing on rutted roads and beach sand as other children ran alongside. When they got to the beach, they saw that the sisters-in-law had already laid blankets and the brothers were starting a firepit that would burn into the night.

After ghada, other families walked over and joined them. Hajje Nazmiyeh and the old beekeeper's widow sat together, joined by other matriarchs of the camp; and the place where they sat became the head of the table, the focal point and command center of the shore. The ocean sprayed them and propelled the wind to caress their faces. These women sat in a circle of plastic chairs. They wore caftans stitched with a thousand years of embroidery and headscarves as old as Islam. They smoked argilehs even though Hamas had banned women from smoking in public. No one could get away with questioning these grand-mothers and great-grandmothers, and their defiance was a public insistence on the dignity and authority of mothers. At the helm of this impertinence was Hajje Nazmiyeh, the eternal ringleader, who now basked in the grace of the ocean's breath, anticipating redemption in just seven days. They spoke of a

thousand Palestinian sons and daughters who would be returning home soon, praise be to Allah. All the women had captive
kin in Israel, and each imagined and prayed for reunion.
"Enshallah, Mazen and all of his comrades, all of our captive
kin, will be with us the next time we gather like this," said Hajje
Nazmiyeh, and all the women raised their pleas to the heavens
to bolster that prayer.

An idea occurred to Hajje Nazmiyeh and she whispered to
the old widow. "Maybe Mazen and Nur will marry! He will
need a wife and she needs a husband. This is the perfect solution
if they agree, enshallah."

"Americans don't marry their kin like we do, and do you think
Mazen will agree to be the father of another man's child?" the
beekeeper's widow replied. "But Allah is great. His will shall
be done."

"She's not American anymore, and my son is a kind, gentle
soul," Hajje Nazymiyeh responded with annoyance. "Allah is
great. His will shall be done."

Someone pulled out a *tabla* drum and the men formed a
dabke line and danced. People sang. Rhet Shel and all the children played and fought and cried and laughed and danced and
tattled on one another. Alwan was happy, in a way she had not
been for many years. It was an inexplicable joy, perhaps the kind
that comes from having been kissed so many times by death and
then finally being spared. So she danced with other women
around the bonfire. It was a rare thing for her generation to link
arms with men like that in a dabke. But the crowd gave cover to
the offense against rectitude.

Nur danced, too, and the celebration continued until the sun
tired and the day faded. Then they fell silent as the sky shone
with streaks of gold and rust and fiery red. Nur saw a tear run
down Hajje Nazmiyeh's face as the yellow sun fell toward the
edge of the ocean, pouring itself over Gaza's waters. It dipped to

a half circle, then only a crest as it tucked itself under the water, and the people watched in the silence of humility. Then it was gone.

To no one in particular, Hajje Nazmiyeh mumbled, "My mother once said this land will rise again."

The bonfire was revived and it rose like a defiant fist. The moon arrived full, a welcome guest that they all greeted with awe. It was the same moon looking down on the world beyond their seaside cage and it made them feel free.

Everything seemed possible in those moments. The uncertainties and precariousness of old age, a disease in remission inside a mother's body, fathers and brothers without work, a son returning after a life behind bars, a baby in an unmarried womb, and a little girl's potential—bounded by an ocean and warships to the west, electrified fences and snipers to the east, and formidable armies at the northern and southern tips—could be redeemed.

It grew late, and as they packed up to retire home, a familiar song danced in the marrow of their bones, then hummed in their throats. Hajje Nazmiyeh sang it first, and the others joined in.

> *O find me*
> *I'll be in that blue*
> *Between sky and water*
> *Where all time is now*
> *And we are the forever*
> *Flowing like a river*

Khaled

"In the primal sympathy which having been must ever
be."

—William Wordsworth

*I was there with the women of my life. I was in the colors. In the
mulberries, magentas, and corals of a tired sun. In the blue between
sky and water.*

*I was there, watching. Their conversations and laughter anchored
the ground in place, tucked the shore under the water, hung the sky
and decorated it with stars and moon and sun. All of this happened
in Gaza. It happened in Palestine. And I stayed as long as I could.*

Shortly after I completed and submitted this novel for publication, Israel attacked Gaza with particular savagery in the summer of 2014. For seven weeks, they pounded the tiny enclave, already imprisoned and under their siege. In the cold prose of statistics, 2,191 Palestinians were killed, the overwhelming majority (approximately 80 percent) civilians, 527 of them children; 71 Israelis were killed, 93 percent of them combat soldiers; 11,239 Palestinians were injured, 61,800 Palestinian homes were bombed along with 220 schools, 278 mosques, 62 hospitals, and the last remaining electric plant in Gaza. Through it all, Palestinian resistance fighters, holed up in tunnels with little more than bread, salt, and water, refused to surrender, and continued to fight a vastly superior military force. Despite the horrors and terror they suffered, Palestinians in Gaza supported the resistance because, in the words of one man, "We'd rather die fighting than continue living on our knees as nothing more than worthless lives Israel can use to test their weapons."

I'd like to salute those Palestinian fighters. They willingly stepped into a realm where death was all but assured, for nothing less than the cause of freedom. Their courage was the stuff of legends.

ACKNOWLEDGMENTS

I'd like to thank the following people for their contributions to this novel. Mame Lambeth was the first to read and comment on the full draft, then again on another draft. Before that, Martha Hughes, my primary editor, read the initial stream-of-consciousness ramble that was the beginning of this novel. She stayed with me, encouraging and cheering for me through my self-doubt until the story finally took form. Special thanks to Anton Mueller and Alexandra Pringle for believing in this novel, and to everyone at Bloomsbury who helped turn this manuscript into a book; to the team at Pontas Literary Agency for their excellent representation. Thank you to all my foreign publishers, in particular: Gunn Reinertsen Næss, Synnøve Helene Tresselt, and Asbjørn Øverås at Aschehoug; Gunilla Sondell at Norstedts; Fabio Muzi Falconi at Feltrinelli; and Britta Claus at Diana Verlag. I'm grateful to my friend Sameeha Elwan, who took time from her hectic schedule to read this story, particularly for cultural and geographic competency of descriptions of Gaza, her home. Likewise, my friends Amal Abdullah, Hanan Urick, Jacqueline Berry, Rana Baker, Aya El-Zinati, and Professor Richard Falk, who read the manusript and offered valuable input. Ramzy Baroud's book *My Father Was a Freedom Fighter* provided the basis for place (Beit Daras and Gaza) in this narrative. I am eternally grateful for the wisdom, knowledge, and friendship of these individuals.

Page 1: From Conal Urquhart, "Gaza on Brink of Implosion as Aid Cut-off Starts to Bite," *Observer*, April 15, 2006.

Page 149: From Breaking the Silence, *Breaking the Silence: Soldiers' Testimonies from Operation Cast Lead, Gaza 2009* (Jerusalem: Shovrim Shtika, 2009): www.breakingthesilence.org.il.

Page 157: From Dr. Mads Gilbert and Dr. Erik Fosse, *Eyes in Gaza* (Charlottesville, VA: Quartet Books Ltd, 2010).

Page 177: From Mahmoud Darwish, "State of Siege," trans. Sabry Hafez and Sarah Maguire, in *Modern Poetry in Translation* 3, no. 1 (2004), ed. Helen Constantine and David Constantine. From *Halat Hisar* [State of Siege] (Beirut: Riad El Rayyes Books, 2009). Used by permission of Syracuse University Press.

Page 193: From Mahmoud Darwish, "A Traveler," trans. by Sinan Antoon, in *Jadaliyya* (August 2011). From *La Uridu Li-Hadhi 'l-Qasidati An Tantahi* [I Don't Want this Poem to End] (Beirut: Riyad El-Rayyes Books, 2009).

Page 205: From Nour Samaha, "The Voices of Gaza's Children," *Al Jazeera*, November 23, 2012.

Page 211: From Chris Hedges, "A Gaza Diary," *Harper's*, October 2001.

Page 221: From T. S. Eliot, "East Coker," *Four Quartets* (New York: Harcourt, 1943). Used by permission of Faber & Faber.

Page 239: From Aeschylus, *Agamemnon*, trans. by Edith Hamilton, *Three Greek Plays* (New York: W. W. Norton & Co, 1937).

Page 287: From William Wordsworth, "Ode: Intimations of Immortality from Recollections of Early Childhood," *Poems in Two Volumes* (1807)